THE RESOLUTE

STAR LEGEND BOOK FOUR

J.J. GREEN

INFINITEBOOK

The way of the warrior is resolute acceptance of death.

— Miyamoto Musashi

1

The boy toiled under the hot sun. Exposed skin on his neck, arms, and calves had begun to burn, but the day's work was far from over. The pumpkin crop was ready. The ripe vegetables had to be brought in before the season turned, or mice and rats would gnaw and damage them and make them unfit for storage. The harvest had to last the group until next year. In a few weeks the wet weather would arrive and the pumpkins would rot.

His scrawny arms wrapped around a large pumpkin, the boy walked to the cart, stepping through the rough remains of faded foliage. The vegetation crowded closely in the field, sprawling over and between the rows. Tiny hairs on the vines would scratch him and embed themselves in his skin, leaving sore, itchy welts, so he was careful to avoid brushing up against them, but sometimes he couldn't help it.

Two horses stood at the front of the cart, lazily flicking flies with their long tails, ears twitching and thick haunches moving as they shifted their weight from one foot to another. The horses were the only thing the boy liked about working in the fields. He wanted to rub their soft noses and reach up to stroke behind their ears, but he didn't dare. The supervisor sitting on the cart's box seat seemed able to see everywhere all the time. The minute anyone slowed down or stopped doing what they were supposed to he would notice. If he was feeling lazy, the perpetrator only received a harsh word of warning, but more often than not, the man would be out of his seat in a flash, racing over the field, and laying his stick across his victim's back.

The boy knew the feel of that stick too well. He was careful to never slacken his pace if he could help it, no matter how tired he got.

Straining with effort, he lifted the pumpkin high for the supervisor's assistant to take and stack with the others in the back of the cart. Relieved of his burden, the boy took the long way around the vehicle to return to his row, briefly enjoying relief from the blazing sun as he dipped into the cart's shadow.

The field stretched as far as he could see, and everywhere children were working in it. Carts and horses waited on the dusty red lines of tracks threading through a sea of gray-green, dying plants. A faint odor of decay hung in the air, accompanied by the gentle rustle of quiet labor.

When the pumpkins had been gathered, they would start on the soybeans. That's what Summoner Seba had said at dawn before they left the compound. Next would come the task of shelling the beans and putting them in the big pottery containers to protect them from weevils. Not that the containers worked. The boy had eaten plenty of beans dotted with tiny, dead insects. At first, he'd been disgusted. Now, he didn't bother picking them out.

A crescent of orange peeked out from among the dead leaves. His next pumpkin. He pulled his small knife from his shirt pocket and cut the sinewy vine that attached it to the plant.

"That's a monster," said a voice.

Narrowing his eyes against the sun's glare, the boy spied a girl a little older than him in the next row over. He didn't know her name. She was from a different section of the compound. Children from different sections were not allowed to mix. Talking at work was forbidden, too, but the supervisor was too far away to hear.

"Yeah," the boy agreed, taking care not to pause in what he was doing.

"Gonna be hard carrying it," the girl went on. "Want a hand?"

In rare cases, when a pumpkin was too heavy for one child to carry by themselves, they were permitted to help each other. But it was risky. The supervisor had to agree that help was needed, and that couldn't be decided until the two children had reached the cart. If the supervisor didn't agree—and some of them never agreed, out of pure spite—the kids were punished.

"No thanks," the boy replied. "I'll manage."

The size of the pumpkin daunted him, and he was grateful for his neighbor's offer, but he'd grown strong in the months since his arrival on the farm. He guessed he could probably carry it by himself.

He slipped his knife into his pocket, and then squatted and grabbed the pumpkin. It was so big, his hands didn't meet on the other side. As he straightened his legs, his already tired arms began to ache.

He set off.

The cart appeared impossibly far away. He staggered forward, the great weight forcing him to push through the tangled vegetation rather than step over it, heedless of the tiny cuts scratched on his legs. He began to regret refusing the girl's offer. His destination seemed to come no closer despite his efforts. Now he'd started, he couldn't stop. The supervisor would notice if he put the pumpkin down to catch his breath and rest his arms, and even if he didn't notice, the boy would have to pick it up for a second time, and he wasn't sure he could do it again. He would just have to make it all the way. Maybe the assistant would be kind and jump down from the cart to take the massive vegetable from him.

Trickles of sweat ran like spiders down his neck and legs. He'd been thirsty for a while, but no water would be given out until the short afternoon break. He hoped that was soon. It had to be soon. The sun had begun its journey down the sky.

His ankle caught on something! But his forward motion propelled him onward. He couldn't stop. He overbalanced and fell.

Despair and fear erupted from his lungs in a yell, abruptly cut off. His ribs had impacted the vegetable at the same time it hit the ground and forced the rest of the air soundlessly from his lungs.

Though it had been short, his cry was enough to attract the supervisor's attention.

With a growl, the man leaped from his high seat and stomped across the field.

The boy knew what was coming. He closed his eyes, curled into a ball, and braced himself.

"Lazy, stupid, worthless child!"

Thwack!

Stinging pain burst from the boy's back as the stick cracked against his spine.

"You only have to do one thing! A simple, easy thing, but even that's too hard for you."

Thwack!

The pain redoubled as the stick hit the same spot. The boy whimpered.

"A waste of time, a waste of food, that's what you are."

Thwack!

More pain, from lower down his back. Tears filled his eyes,

but he refused to cry. Mam had said it was okay to cry when you were hurt or sad, but he didn't want to. Crying meant giving in. Crying meant you'd let them get to you. Crying meant forgetting who you were and where you were from.

"I'll teach you to slack off."

Thwack!

"I'll teach you to be clumsy."

Thwack!

Thwack!

Thwack!

THAT NIGHT, the boy was hunched over as he waited outside the compound. His back hurt too much to stand upright. The carts, piled high with pumpkins, stood in a line at the closed gates of the compound. White sweat coated the horses' flanks.

All the children huddled in one group. They had walked the long distance home while the supervisors and their assistants had ridden on the carts. A lot of the kids appeared dead on their feet, especially the younger ones, only just old enough for field work. But they still had a while to wait until they could rest, drink, and eat.

The snap and click of a lock opening broke the evening quiet, quickly followed by the loud rattle of a chain being pulled against metal. One of the double gates swung open. A creak and clunk signaled it was secured. Then the second gate opened.

"Walk on," ordered the supervisor in the lead cart, slapping the reins on the horses' backs.

Wood groaned and wheels rumbled. The line of carts began to slowly move forward. One by one, they disappeared into the gap in the high compound fence.

The last cart went in. Now it was the children's turn to enter, but not before the final check.

A woman walked out of the shadowy interior, a clipboard in hand.

"Lukas," she read from the board.

"Here," a boy answered.

He split from the group and trudged into the compound.

"Ben."

"Here."

A second boy shuffled apart from the others.

"Hannah."

"Here," a girl said.

It was the girl who had offered to help the boy with the big pumpkin that had been his downfall.

She walked through the open gates.

The woman read more names, one by one, and each child answered in a weary tone before they were allowed admittance.

When only a few kids were left standing in the dark, the woman called out,

"Elias."

It was not his name. Not his *real* name. It was the one they'd given him and forced him to use. He remembered his true name and he would never forget it. But, tonight, if he wanted to eat and sleep, he had to answer to the false one.

"Here," he said, though the word grated like sandpaper in his throat.

Grimacing, he hobbled toward the opening that led to food and rest, until tomorrow.

Later, when his belly was full of watery porridge and boiled vegetables, he searched for his sister among the little kids in the barn where the children slept. He found her sitting alone in a corner, her skinny little legs sticking out from the skirt of her grimy dress. She was holding a bunch of grass stalks and he thought she might be about to eat it—hunger had tempted him to eat all kinds of things—but then he saw she was talking to it and bouncing it on her lap.

"Hey," he said, sitting beside her.

"Elias!" she exclaimed. The stalks fell from her grasp as she grabbed him around his neck. He winced but tried not to show his pain.

Had she forgotten his name? She was smart, and when he told her she had to call him something new, she'd caught on right away. He was glad. It had saved her from beatings less clever children had received.

"What's that you're playing with?" he asked.

"Oh!" She noticed the scattered stalks and picked them up again. When she held the bunch again in her small fist, she whispered, "This is Mam."

"*Mam?*" he said softly.

"Uh huh. I'm telling her to come and find us. I want to go home. I don't like this place."

He put an arm around her. He hated the place too, and he was worried about his sister. She was too thin. He could see the bones under her skin. Sometimes, in the morning, one or two of the other kids didn't wake up, and when he came back from working in the fields, they were gone. No one ever mentioned them again.

"Is Mam gonna come and get us?"

"I don't know. I hope so. But don't worry. If she doesn't, I'll look after you."

"I know. But I miss Mam. I want to see her."

"I do too. Maybe one day we will."

His sister put her head on his shoulder and clutched the grass to her chest, crooning over it like a mother soothing a baby. He guessed she'd reversed roles and she was soothing 'Mam' in the way she wanted to be soothed by her.

An ear-piercing crack split the air, making all the children jump and shudder. Echoing reverberations of powerful engines followed, quickly dying down. A second crack followed, and a third. Fighter jets were passing overhead, Alliance planes, off to fight in the war.

2

Taylan adjusted her scarf, pulling it forward over her head so it concealed her face like a hood. Hoping she hadn't missed something vital from her disguise, she pushed the pub door open and stepped inside.

She recalled how, before they were invaded, the British had loved to make fun of Earth Awareness Crusaders, saying they were ignorant fanatics with wild, irrational beliefs. In truth, no one was really sure what they did in their day to day lives because communication with the outside world was banned in every EAC nation state. But rumors of their odd, regressive lifestyles had spread from the continent, along with smuggled images, vidclips, and audio diaries, confirming the stories.

In her short experience of the cultists she had seen plenty of strange things too, but she'd also found that in some ways they were not so different from her own people. For instance, both cultures liked to drink.

A wall of warm air hit her, heavy with exhaled breath, yeasty beer, and weed smoke. At the same time, sounds washed over her: arguments, laughter, the clink of glasses. If the pub patrons had been wearing different clothes and speaking her native tongue, the scene could have been any ordinary weekend night from her youth. She could have been there to meet friends and hear the latest gossip, complain about work, or just to have fun and relax.

But having fun was the last thing on her mind. She was embarking on a path that could lead to her death. It was the only way she might learn what had happened to Patrin and Kayla. She was convinced they weren't in Ireland or in an EAC orphanage. If the latter were the case, Dwyr Orr would have found them. They had to be somewhere else. Perhaps a Crusader family was hiding them or they were in another place beyond the Dwyr's easy reach.

They were not dead. She refused to believe that, but also she was sure if they were she would feel it. They were still alive. She clung to that conviction. But the information she needed to find them wasn't readily available. To uncover it, she had to insert herself into Crusader society. And now that the Britannic Alliance had the Dwyr in custody, the vendetta the woman had been waging against her and her kids was over, she hoped.

She was at the lowest level of the pub facing a large, central bar surrounded by tables and booths. Two sets of dark wooden stairs led to the second and third levels, their seating areas and customers visible through balustrades of the same dark, old wood. She guessed the place had to hold two or three hundred people, perfect for her plan. However, the bartender, a stocky, broad-shouldered man, was already looking at her suspiciously, as if deciding whether to throw her out. If she tried to ply her trade immediately, he probably would.

She went up to him.

His frown eased a fraction. "What can I get you?"

Beyond him, two younger, female bartenders were giggling flirtatiously with the men they were serving, angling for tips. She was relieved the male server had seen her first. He might feel a little sympathy for her.

She reached inside her robes to an inner pocket and took out the card before handing it to him, heart in mouth.

The few simple words she'd written on it were the culmination of weeks of work. Of all the challenges she'd faced in returning to West BI, learning to write by hand had been the hardest. Stealing food, staying hidden, studying the examples of the costume she needed and sourcing the clothes, all these had been difficult, but they paled in comparison with the laborious effort of creating words on paper that didn't look like they'd been written by a four year old.

She'd seen plenty of examples of handwriting on copies of old documents in history lessons. She knew what it was supposed to look like and she'd thought it would be easy enough to do it. What she hadn't properly understood was that what she'd seen was the result of years of practice; hours a day spent writing, writing, writing, for every subject at school, and then, later, writing letters, diaries, notes, reports, and so on, as adults. Stripped of technology by their Dwyr, Crusaders had done the same. They'd grown skilled at the craft, and if she was to fit in her efforts had to match theirs.

Speaking to them was out of the question. Her accent would give her away in a minute. She couldn't mimic it like Marc, Angharad's son. He'd succeeded in fooling the people at the Crusader midsummer festival on Ynys Môn but she couldn't take that chance.

"Hmpf," said the bartender after reading the note. He peered over the bar, his gaze traveling from her embroidered shoes to the decorative scarf overhanging her face. "What do you do? Write? Point?"

It was safer to avoid testing her shaky writing skills unnecessarily. She touched the lever above one of the beer signs and then pointed at a shelf of glasses.

"Pint of Old Black Hen, coming up."

Tension oozed out of her like ice cream melting on a hot summer's day.

While the bartender was pouring her drink, she checked out the pub's clientele again. A few were looking her way. She was already attracting interest. *Good.* She picked up her card from the bar and slipped it back into her pocket. Hopefully, it would come out many more times tonight.

When her beer was ready, she paid for it with a few stolen coins.

"Look," said the bartender, scooping the coins into his other hand, "I know why you're here, and I don't mind. People like a bit of entertainment. But the boss won't approve. If he comes in you can expect to leave soon after."

She nodded her thanks for the warning and picked up her drink.

It wasn't until she reached the second floor of the pub she found an empty table. Round-topped, sticky with spilled drinks, and wobbly, it was clear why the other patrons had avoided it. The table was also situated in a dark corner with only two single bench seats flanking it. For her purposes, it was perfect.

Old Black Hen was not bad at all, and her experience of beer was extensive. When she'd drunk a quarter of her pint, someone approached.

In the half light, Taylan couldn't see her first customer too well, but the woman appeared very young, too young to be in a pub legally in old West Britannic Isles. Maybe the EAC didn't care about such things. She was wearing a long skirt and a blouse, covered by a tabard decorated with symbols.

"Excuse me. I couldn't help notice you sitting here alone. I was wondering, are you working? If not, I'll leave."

Taylan was already taking out her card.

The woman frowned as she took it and turned it toward the light. Her eyebrows rose. "Oh, you can't speak!"

Taylan held out her hand. The woman gave her the card back.

"But if you can't speak, how can you tell me my future?"

Opening her satchel, Taylan took out a sheet of paper and a pen. With a sweep of her hand, she invited the woman to sit down.

It had taken her ages to come up with a way to live among the Crusaders undetected. At first, it had seemed impossible. How could she live among people whose lives were a mystery to her and who were actively seeking her out to hand her over to their mentally unsound leader? Then she'd remembered the fortune tellers at the ceremony to launch the invasion of Ireland.

They'd been dressed in colorful, patterned robes and had gone from person to person, group to group, offering their services. She guessed they were probably itinerant, moving on to new grounds when interest dried up. No one would be surprised by the arrival of a new fortune teller, and it was the kind of job that required no skill or training. It wasn't like she could get anything wrong. It was all nonsense anyway. And adding a vow of silence to the mix would only make her seem more mysterious and interesting.

People told fortune tellers all kinds of things, and what better place to hide than in plain sight?

3

HMS *Resolute* was a grandiose name for a patrol boat, even a new boat of the latest design and top-of-the-range tech. When Colbourn had informed Wright of his new orders, she'd focused on the merits of the vessel, trying to spin the news into something better than it was. She'd emphasized he would be in command of his own ship, a *very special* ship. The fact that the brigadier hadn't been able to look him in the eyes said everything. Basically, it was a demotion. After his damning psych assessment he had retained his rank, but as to his dignity, pride, and reputation…

He'd gone from serving aboard three of the most powerful and vital starships in the BA Space Fleet, the *Valiant*, the *Fearless*, and the *Gallant*, to twiddling his thumbs aboard a tin-pot vessel, patrolling the Australian coastline. Tasked with keeping watch for incursions into Alliance waters, all he could look forward to, probably for the rest of his career, was endless days at sea. Even if the EAC did decide to attack Oceania, his little boat's role in the action would be minimal.

It was a hard pill to swallow, and he had a feeling it would remain stuck in his throat forever.

He leaned on the gunwale and gazed at Sydney Harbor, growing steadily closer as the *Resolute* cut through the water on her approach. He'd spent a brief time in the city before assuming his command, and he had fond memories of it. The buildings of the central district were sunk halfway into the ground and a network of pedestrian walkways and road tunnels connected them, leaving the tree-lined streets on the surface quiet and tranquil. The architectural style had been adopted hundreds of years ago, he'd learned, to cool the buildings and conserve energy as well as to protect from bush fires. It would be a great shame if the EAC got its hands on the place and plunged it into technological darkness.

The sun from a crystal sky beat on his back and glittered on the waves. He was uncomfortably hot in his stiff white uniform jacket, but he had to wear it to greet the Marines who would be joining the ship. He would be glad to get back to sea and informal working attire.

He straightened up and comm'd the helmsman, Warrant Officer Jeong. "How long until we dock?"

"About twenty minutes, sir."

"Thanks. I'll be in my cabin."

"Aye aye, sir."

He descended the ladder to the second deck and walked the narrow passageway to his compartment. Opening the door, he was hit by a smell.

"*Shit.*"

It was, literally.

He'd been house-training the cat Ellis had given him, Boots. His efforts were hit-and-miss, or, rather, the cat's were.

He went to the litter tray in the corner and saw with relief this effort was a hit. As he was dealing with it and wondering whether a cat could be trained to use the head like a regular Marine, Boots came out from under his bunk and rubbed up against his leg. He awkwardly patted her.

He hadn't been allowed pets as a child. His dad had been a clean freak. He wasn't sure what he was supposed to do with Boots, how to care for her, but he seemed to be doing okay. The cat appeared healthy and happy and she hadn't tried to jump overboard yet. The last had been his greatest fear. If he ever saw Ellis again, he wouldn't know how to tell her he'd drowned her cat.

He sat at his desk to go over the ship's manifest. Five crew members would be leaving the ship when they docked and only three would be joining her. On the face of it, the loss of two Marines wasn't significant, but it was a symptom of the difficult times. The Britannic Alliance had clawed back to global dominance by retaking the Caribbean, but its grip was weak.

All four branches of the military were stretched thin and each was finding it harder and harder to meet enlistment targets. Perhaps the younger generation felt the Alliance's time was drawing to an end, or, with Ua Talman's colony ships due to depart in a few years, people felt the future lay in the stars. He wasn't sure. Either way, every military man and woman counted, now more than ever. That was why one particular name on the list of Marines joining the ship puzzled him.

Boots miaowed to be let out of the cabin. He opened the door. After staring at the gap for long seconds as if deciding what to do, the cat finally left.

Pets of any kind were against regulations, but he hadn't even attempted to keep his a secret from the crew. At first, he'd justified his decision by telling himself a cat aboard ship would be good for morale, but finally he'd realized he just didn't care about regulations anymore.

He opened a book on his interface to pass the remaining time until the boat docked.

∼

THE NEW CREW members were standing together on the quay, kit bags at their feet. As soon as they spotted Wright walking down the gang plank followed by his lieutenant, the two men and one woman formed a line, stood to attention, and saluted.

"At ease," he said. "Welcome to the *Resolute*."

The man he was most interested in made eye contact but instantly looked forward again.

"I hope you have many happy days serving aboard her," Wright went on. "Lieutenant Ford will take you to your berths and explain your duties. You can board now."

The men and woman picked up their bags and began to file past him.

"Corporal Abacha," he said. "As soon as you've settled in, come to my cabin."

"Yes, sir," the man replied, not breaking step.

It seemed an odd coincidence the man who had served under him had ended up on his ship. Marines usually aspired to be transferred from the surface to the Space Fleet. Movements in the opposite direction were rare and there was nothing about a transfer request in Abacha's file. Maybe the Marine had done something to piss Colbourn off, and sending him to the *Resolute*, too, had immediately sprung to her mind as a suitable punishment.

There was a knock at his cabin door.

"Come in."

Abacha looked uncertain as he entered, perhaps wondering why he'd been singled out to speak to his new CO.

The corporal was tall, stooping a little to get under the door jamb. Though he wasn't burly, he was muscley, his neck muscles and biceps rounding out the lines of his shirt. If Wright hadn't seen it with his own eyes, he wouldn't have believed Ellis had defeated the man at hand-to-hand combat.

"Sorry," said Wright, realizing Abacha had been waiting patiently for him to say something. "Take a seat."

His look of confusion deepening, the corporal sat on the chair by the side of Wright's desk and rested his hands on his knees.

Wright sat on his bunk. "Congratulations on your promotion."

"Thank you, sir."

"I wanted to speak to you because, to be honest, I'm surprised our paths are crossing again."

"I'm glad to be serving under you again, Major."

After an awkward pause, Wright said, "Can I ask—"

A soft miaow sounded outside in the passageway.

Abacha's eyes widened in surprise as he turned toward the sound.

Wright opened the door. "Uh, I might not be the only one you recognize aboard the *Resolute*."

"Ha!" Abacha grinned with delight as the cat trotted in. "How on Earth did he get here?" Then he gave a slight shake of his head. "Huh, why am I asking? As if I didn't know."

"He?" asked Wright. "I thought Boots was a girl."

"You did? Why would you think that?"

"I, er, I must have just assumed. I didn't check."

"Hey, little fella," said Abacha, leaning down to pat the animal, apparently forgetting he was in the presence of his CO. "How have you been?"

From the way Boots readily leapt onto his lap, he clearly remembered Taylan's friend.

"Gee, I used to hate this cat so much," said Abacha. "Always shitting and pissing everywhere."

"She...he still does that. But he's getting better."

The arrival of Boots had dissolved the awkward atmosphere.

"Do you know where Taylan is now?" Abacha asked, stroking the cat, a look of bemused nostalgia on his face.

Wright leaned backward and propped himself on his arms. "The last time I saw her, she was headed back to West BI."

"Still looking for her kid," Abacha said flatly.

"*Kids*, as I understand it. Two of them, pretty young, I think. That's about as much as I know."

"Ah. She never talked about them, but it wasn't hard to guess what her problem was."

I miss her.

Wright almost blurted his thought out but managed to stop himself just in time. What was wrong with him? He was forgetting his position. He could have made an embarrassing error in front of his subordinate. His terrible experiences in Jamaica, his de facto demotion, the loss of everything he'd worked for and believed in for most of his adult life...it was all getting to him.

He needed to get a grip.

But, then again, did he?

"Would you like a drink?" he asked. "A beer maybe?"

The corporal's mouth fell open, but he wasn't too shocked to refuse. "A beer would be very welcome, sir. It was hot out on the harbor waiting to be picked up."

Wright took two cans from his refrigerator. There were some perks to being in command, no matter how small your boat was.

Handing one over, he said, "Abacha, I think I can be open with you. You seem like a good guy. Let's face it, anyone who could put up with Ellis for any length of time has to be a saint."

Abacha popped his can and took a long drink before replying, "Yeah, she's a pain in the ass, that's for sure. Whatever you want to tell me, it won't leave this cabin, sir."

"Right. Well, I was wondering, do you have any idea why you're here?"

"I'm not sure what you mean."

"Do you know why you were assigned to the *Resolute* in

particular? It isn't the most obvious career advancement after serving on the *Valiant*."

"I don't have any special duties, Major Wright, if that's what you mean. I'm being straight with you."

"I believe you, but, didn't it strike you as strange that you would be transferred here?"

"It did. But I'm not in a position to question anything. I just do what I'm told."

"Maybe the higher ups are holding something back from both of us."

Warrant Officer Jeong comm'd him. Reflexively, he touched the implant behind his ear. "Yes?"

"We're out of sight of land and visual contact with any other vessels, sir."

"Okay, take us down."

The ship's speakers emitted three short, loud bleeps and a section of steel slid over the cabin window, cutting out the light. The cabin lights brightened in response. Boots jumped down from Abacha's lap and went to hide under the bunk.

"Don't worry," Wright said in response to Abacha's expression of alarm. "You're perfectly safe."

Clunks and whirrings sounded all around, and the ship juddered. Above them, the outer hull was extending to enclose the main deck, and the pressure hull was also rising around the bridge, which would become the control room. The *Resolute*'s hydrofoils also were converting into hydroplanes, and water was pouring into the main ballast tanks.

Within a couple of minutes, the transformation was complete. The ship began to submerge.

Wright remarked, "Yeah, the *Resolute* has a few secrets of her own."

4

A line of cards lay face upward on the table. Six in all, they forecast the future of Taylan's customer. On the far left lay the Queen—unmistakably a Dwyr, under a horned headdress. Next to her, the naked Lovers were entwined stylistically in each other's arms. The third card Taylan had drawn was a wheel set among clouds, symbols she didn't know the meaning of around its edge. She didn't know what this one was supposed to be, so she'd written something about a period of time passing. The King followed the Wheel, seated on a throne with a sword held high. The penultimate card was the Sun shining over a green landscape, and the last card Taylan had drawn, inwardly wincing when she saw it, was Death, a black-hooded figure wielding a scythe.

Her customer's eyes had widened in dismay as it had been revealed. Taylan's imagination, already stretched to its limit in conjuring up some rubbish to interpret the cards, struggled to spin Death in a nice way. She'd patted the young woman's arm reassuringly and wrote:

It is only through endings we have new beginnings. You will enter a new phase of your life.

A look of relief came over the woman's face as she read.

"A new phase in my life. I like that. And I loved the bit about getting the attention of someone important. You don't think it could be the new Dwyr, do you?"

Dwyr Perran Orr had taken his oaths three weeks ago. Like the former Dwyr's 'funeral' and as with most public events in the Crusader world, few had actually witnessed it. Taylan had seen the public notices go up and she'd overheard people talking about it, gossiping about what the boy had looked like and how he'd acted. She'd wondered how they could know the reports were true? But factual truth wasn't highly valued in their society.

The only item of news she'd thought was reliable was the fact that Perran's initiation ceremony wouldn't take place for a few years. She guessed the unspoken reason for the delay was they had to wait until he was sexually mature before he could participate.

Gross.

Was that what her customer was thinking about?

She wrote: *It could mean someone important in society like the Dwyr or someone important only to you.*

That was the great thing about telling fortunes—all you had to do was write predictions so vague they could mean anything. The next time the woman attracted the attention of anyone she deemed important in any way—and it was impossible she wouldn't—she would believe the prediction had come true.

Taylan gathered up the cards, signaling the session was over.

"Thanks," said the woman. She scanned the paper again and nodded thoughtfully. "That makes a lot of sense. You're very good. The last fortune teller I saw told me I'd be pregnant and married within a year, and that I'd go on to have ten children and never leave West BI. That isn't the kind of life I want. I want to do something interesting. All my mother did was look after us kids and then her grandkids. I don't want to be like her."

Taylan felt a spark of sympathy for the stranger. The genuine fortune teller's reading was likely to be more accurate than her own. She doubted contraception was promoted in Crusader culture. It would be seen as too technological and interfering in the natural course of things. She'd told a more exciting but far less possible tale, including foreign travel and meeting important people. The pub was mostly full of men. The few women present were young. No doubt the older ones were at home caring for a brood while their partners enjoyed themselves. Crusader ways were anachronistic in the extreme. She couldn't understand the appeal.

"What do I owe you?" the woman asked.

It was a rhetorical question. She was only being polite. From the sessions Taylan had spied upon, the custom was that the client paid whatever they felt the reading was worth.

She spread her hands and smiled. Only her mouth would be visible. She'd been careful to keep most of her face in shadow. She knew from the time a Crusader patrol had attacked her that the people knew her likeness and were on the look out for her.

The young woman pulled a small cloth purse from a pocket in the fold of her skirt and took out two coins. It wasn't much. The beer had cost more. But Taylan didn't betray any disappointment. She wasn't there for business purposes anyway.

"I know it isn't a lot," said the woman as she handed the money over. "But I'll recommend you to my friends. Will you be here tomorrow?"

Taylan nodded and gave her the paper.

Now for the real work.

Before the woman could leave, Taylan wrote on a second sheet of paper, *What do you do?*

"I'm an embroiderer. I made this." She lifted the hem of her tabard to display it. "Do you like it?"

Genuinely impressed, Taylan wrote, *It's beautiful.*

Beaming, her client said, "Thanks. It took me hours."

An embroiderer was unlikely to have any contact with children. There was no point in prolonging the conversation. *Good luck with your work*, she wrote.

"Thank you."

As the woman left, a man rose from his seat and began to walk over. Her clientele was on the increase already. She only hoped she might learn something useful from them.

THERE WAS no defined end to serving hours at the pub. As the evening wore on, things grew rowdier and then quieter as people left or the drunks got too inebriated to cause any more trouble. The servers began wiping down tables and waking up the people who had passed out before forcing them out onto the street.

No one had approached her table in more than an hour. It was time to pack up shop and leave. With a heavy heart, Taylan drained the dregs of her second pint and put away her cards, paper, and pens. Despite gently probing her customers with questions, she hadn't heard anything that might give her an inkling of where her children had gone.

Maybe she was expecting too much. It was only her first try after all. If there were a place the native children had been taken, it could be something only a few people knew about. It might be weeks or months before she heard a whisper of it.

Weeks of spouting drivel for credulous idiots? Ugh.

That was *not* something to look forward to, and as time went on her chances of being recognized increased. But she didn't have any better ideas. Whatever it took, and however long it took, she wouldn't give up her search.

Pushing open the heavy outer door, a blast of cold, humid air hit her face. She stepped out into the night. The scent of approaching rain washed over her as she walked the dark streets to the place where she'd been sleeping for the last few weeks. Autumn was passing quickly. When the winter cold arrived, she would need better accommodation, but that was a bridge to be crossed when she came to it.

The little town was set in a valley, the roads snaking up the hills on each side. She hadn't been here before, in that almost-mystical time before the invasion, but it hadn't taken her long to find a quiet spot to hide away. Half the houses were empty, abandoned by the fleeing townsfolk, or the former habitations of those who hadn't made it out. Still, she hadn't dared take over a house in case the Crusaders had a system of allocating them. She couldn't afford to attract attention by falling foul of it.

Instead, she'd set herself up in a garden shed. In the before-days, it might have been a man cave. The wooden building at the end of the long garden was spacious and dry, and though the large-screen interface no longer worked, the small camp bed was comfortable. There was even a little single-hob stove, though it required batteries and she hadn't been able to find any of the right kind to steal.

After checking up and down the street and seeing no one else about, she turned into the narrow alley between two terraced houses that led to their rear doors and gardens. Behind the houses, nature had taken over. Brambles arched over pathways and the ornamental shrubs were wildly over-grown. She knew the route through the vegetation well, which was lucky as she had to navigate it in pitch darkness. As she reached the black shape of the shed, heavy raindrops began to fall.

Groping down along the crack where the door met the wooden wall, she felt for the stick she'd placed across the entrance earlier when she'd left. The door opened outward. If someone entered the shed, they would move the stick.

It wasn't there.

She took a step backward, but at the same time the door jerked open, hitting her in the face. She vaguely made out a tall, broad figure before a large hand fastened on the front of her jacket.

"Gotcha," a voice growled.

Stunned by the blow to her face, she didn't react immediately. She was dragged into the shed and pushed to the floor.

"Stay quiet and I won't hurt you," said the man looming over her. "No need to be scared."

There was the sound of a belt being removed.

She wasn't scared.

She was *furious*.

It took all her self-control to wait for him to get on his knees. Kicking sharply upward, she was rewarded with the sensation of her shin bone smacking into a soft and vulnerable area of his body. An agonized yell erupted from his mouth, handily allowing her to locate his face in the darkness as he bent toward her. She punched, hard, and then slid to one side as he continued floor-ward.

When he was down, she twisted his arm behind his back and knelt on him to keep him there.

What to do?

It would be easy to take out the knife she carried in a hidden sheath at her belt and slit his throat. The mess wouldn't matter. She couldn't stay in the shed now anyway.

But the last thing she wanted to do was to attract attention, and in a small town like this a murder would be big news. People would be wondering who the killer was and they would be looking askance at strangers. She couldn't take the risk.

Yet she also couldn't allow her would-be attacker to get away scot-free.

He'd begun to recover and was squirming, trying to throw her off. She pushed his arm higher, forcing it upward with all her strength. He hollered and wriggled madly and kicked his legs. Then he screamed. The resistance she was pushing against gave out as his shoulder dislocated.

"Stop, stop," he mumbled, tears of pain in his voice.

Taylan put the tip of her knife below his ear lobe and pressed in until it scraped on his jaw bone.

Leaning down, she hissed in his ear, "Come near me or any other girl again, and I will kill you."

She leapt up, grabbed her small bag of belongings from under the bed where she always kept it filled, ready for a quick getaway, and ran out.

During the short-lived scuffle, the heavens had opened. Rain pelted down, instantly soaking her to her skin.

5

Kala Orr floated in a sea of nothingness. No light reached her eyes, her ears picked up no sound, and she could feel nothing, not even her own body. She had no idea how long she'd been in this state. At first, she'd tried to keep track of time by counting, but she would lose her place and then, frustrated, begin again. She lost track of how many times she'd counted to ten thousand or more. Finally, she accepted there was no point to her efforts, except perhaps to prevent herself from going mad.

If she slept, she was not aware of it. She had no memory of drifting to slumber or waking. All was painful consciousness. In the beginning, she had fretted endlessly about Perran. What was Morgan doing to him? Had he forgotten about her? Was he safe? Then her worries had given way to fury. She'd imagined many varied and excruciating punishments for her usurper, for everything she'd done Kala had released her from the mine. She'd relished thoughts of Morgan's screams of agony and pleadings for death.

While the extreme emotions had coursed through her, another nibbled at the edge of her mind: despair. Unpleasant questions arose, but she hastily pushed them aside. Would she ever be released from her mental prison? Or would she spend the rest of her life cut off from the outside world? What was happening to her body? Was Morgan giving her water and food? Or was she wasting away, soon to die?

Then the hallucinations began. Confused, she'd thought they were signs she was about to be released from her nightmare. Brilliant flashes of colored lights dazzled her and whispered conversations—the words indistinct—teased her with potential meaning. Pins and needles pricked at her nerve endings, their intensity building in waves. It wasn't until the memories began to play she understood nothing she was experiencing was real.

They were not true memories. She was not in control of them, choosing to think back over the scenes of her past. They arose before her, surreal and dream-like, the faces smudging and distorting, voices loud or too quiet to hear, the colors wrong, the events incorrect or transformed into something bizarre.

The Marine she had tortured tottered toward her on broken legs, the working muscles visible, his mouth impossibly wide, red, and raw. The lips opened wider and wider, bending his head back. He swallowed her and she found herself descending the tunnel that would take her to Morgan, flying along, crashing through cobwebs. At the end of the tunnel lay a newborn baby. Its skin glistened and the purple, pulsing umbilicus still protruded from its stomach. The baby mewed like a cat and wriggled. It was Perran. His eyes opened wide and staring.

"Go away!" he yelled. "Go away, Mother!"

Loose, yellow feces streamed from between his buttocks.

She backed away, not looking behind her, and fell into a chasm. Rock faces streamed past her as she tumbled over and over. She caught a glimpse of Jon, swinging by his neck in his nightgown. A monstrous Morgan leaned out from a gap in the stone and tried to grab her. She slipped between the giant, grasping fingers.

Her descent slowed and she stopped spinning. She was looking downward at a town, a small, old-fashioned place with twinkling lights shining from spires and turrets. The town expanded as she neared it, spreading over the bottom of the chasm, roads growing like dry riverbeds filling with water in a flash flood, houses popping up on each side. It wasn't until she reached it she realized she was looking at Berline. Her spread-eagled body became vertical and her feet touched the ground as lightly as a feather coming to rest.

She was walking along one of the old streets. Blocky, blank-faced edifices rose on each side, built windowless hundreds of years ago when interface walls displaying landscapes were all the rage. Crude graffiti defaced the walls at street level. Some things never changed.

Ahead of her, the street heaved with black figures, fuzzy as if seen through an unfocused lens. They were talking in murmurs interspersed with snatches of songs. As she drew closer, they didn't become clearer but remained dark gray, formless shadows. As she passed between, they became wisps of smoke and disintegrated on the breeze.

"I am your Dwyr!" she thundered. "I command you to stay here. You cannot leave. Come back!"

The street was empty. Above, the wraiths glided swiftly upward.

Were they the souls of the people who had died during her rise to power and the expansion of the EAC across the globe? The sight of them bothered her, sparking deep regret and self-hatred. She tried to ignore the feelings but found she could not. In her current state, there were no distractions. She was forced to acknowledge all she'd done. She tried to give the usual excuses, how the blood sacrifice would be worth the outcome, how she had to break stones to lay the path to the future, but her words sounded hollow.

Berline was gone.

She was alone in the dark.

The flashes of light started up along with distant strains of discordant music.

If she didn't do something soon, she would lose her mind. The lack of external stimulation was sending her insane, her brain creating fantasies in compensation for the absence of input. She had to go inward. If her outer world could not supply sensory information, she would create it in her inner world. She would recall memories, go over old conversations, make plans for the future, anticipate difficulties and devise strategies to overcome them.

If Morgan could survive thousands of years trapped without light and avoid descending into madness, so could she. She would grow stronger, and when her time came to return to the world, she would defeat her mortal enemy.

6

For years, the EAC and AP had been suspected of smuggling operations in Australia, but no one had ever caught either organization in the act or figured out exactly what their contraband was. The country's coastline was vast and much of its territory was remote and isolated. The Alliance could watch the skies, but the surrounding seas and oceans were another matter.

That was where the *Resolute* came in.

If it weren't for the weak, organic humans who crewed her, she could run for centuries without surfacing. Not that she required a crew to operate—she could be fully controlled remotely, even at substantial depths. The idea of an unmanned patrol sub had been mooted in the planning stages, but eventually Sea Lord Fox had vetoed the proposal, citing the risk of a hostile power taking control and turning the Alliance's latest sea defense into a weapon to be used against it.

Wright explained the boat's short history and her purpose to the new arrivals the day following his chat with Abacha. He also told them about all her capabilities, including the rim-driven thruster and scanner-deflecting hull that allowed her to travel through the water without detection, and her complement of AUVs for widening her field of surveillance.

As he spoke, he found himself feeling better about his situation. He felt the stirrings of pride and attachment to this vessel under his command. She truly was a remarkable boat. Maybe his depression and resentment over his new appointment were churlish and ungrateful. He'd been awarded a level of autonomy unusual for someone of his rank, and now that the Caribbean had been retaken, Oceania had risen in importance as a potential site for a Crusader invasion.

He finished his talk by saying, "Our remit isn't only to keep watch. The *Resolute* isn't big, but she's deadly. We could be tasked with defensive engagements with enemy vessels encroaching into Australian waters. If we are, we'll be busy. There are only eight of us, and that's the bare minimum required to keep our boat operational. But while we're only patrolling, you'll probably find yourselves struggling to keep busy. Many of the tasks the submariners among you are used to doing are automated here. Lieutenant Ford has given you your duties. In your down time, find something to occupy yourselves —a hobby or something. I've heard Abacha plays a mean game of xiangqi. Unless we receive different orders, we're down here for six months."

Abacha raised his hand.

Wright nodded his permission to speak.

"I'd be happy to arrange a xiangqi tournament. It'll help pass the time."

"That's a great idea."

"What will the prize be?" asked Ford.

"I don't know," said Abacha. "I'll think of what I'd like, as I'll be the one winning it."

∽

ONE SMALL ADVANTAGE of Wright's new posting was the availability of time to sleep. Even during quiet periods of serving aboard the *Gallant*, Colbourn's rigorous approach to leadership had led to regular disturbances of his daily routine. If she wasn't running an emergency drill she would think up another way to keep everyone on their toes, such as changing the entire crew's work schedules at short notice. In her case, her command style probably made sense. A starship like the *Gallant* could be called into battle at any time. But the *Resolute*'s purpose was different. Discovering what the EAC were doing in Australia, if anything, would require long periods of simply watching and waiting.

And during those long periods, Wright would take advantage of the opportunity to indulge one of his few pleasures in life: unconsciousness.

That would all have been fine and dandy if it weren't for Boots. The cat had a special talent for destroying sleep, ranging from walking over his head to miaowing to be let out then quickly miaowing to be let in, to getting the zoomies and running around and around the cabin at top speed.

And yet he couldn't find it in his heart to get annoyed at the animal. He provided a connection to Taylan, who was often on his mind. Caring for Boots gave him an irrational feeling that one day he would see her again and be able to return the cat to her, and she would be pleased he was healthy and happy.

Three weeks after the change of crew, when the *Resolute* was working her way up the Coral Sea, east of the Dead Reef, and Wright was deeply asleep, an annoying noise dragged him awake. Thinking Boots either wanted to come in or go out, with his eyes still shut he groggily mumbled, "Door, open."

He'd fixed the door comm so that the cat's miaows activated it. Otherwise he would never hear him from the passageway through the solid steel. He heard the scrape of the portal opening, but the sound continued. Forcing himself to rise to a higher level of alertness, he concentrated on it.

The noise wasn't coming from Boots. It was coming from inside his head. It was his personal comm giving an 'urgent' signal.

"Wh...?"

His voice was hoarse and his throat dry. He must have been mouth-breathing in his sleep. He swallowed and tried again.

"What is it?"

"Sorry to disturb you, sir." It was Lieutenant Ford, his second-in-command.

"It's all right. What's happened?"

"The long range scanner has picked up something the computer can't identify. I thought you might want to investigate."

"Give me a minute. I'll be right there."

Pushing down his covers and climbing out of his bunk, he was reminded of the time when the *Gallant* had picked up the ancient distress signal coming from a mountain in West BI. What an escapade *that* had turned into. It had resulted in Arthur, Merlin, and the whole shebang. But he was out of all of that now and he was glad. Let others figure out how the ancient king and suspicious alien would fit into plans to defeat the Alliance's enemies.

He hastily pulled on some pants and jogged the short distance to the control room.

Ford was looking at the interface that displayed the scanner data. In the confines of the small room there was no space for a holo display. They had to make do with 2D imagery, though the sensors were sophisticated.

Four shadowy oblong shapes floated on the screen.

"Non-organic?" Wright asked, peering over Ford's shoulder.

"That's what the computer says. Ninety-three percent probability."

He could see why. The shapes were too uniform and evenly spaced to be shoals of fish or whales.

He checked the shipping information he'd been given against the position of the anomalous bodies in the water. "We don't seem to have anything scheduled to be there right now," he mused.

"The range is only accurate to fifty K, but, anyway, they're nowhere near a bay," said Ford.

Wright took the statement on board without questioning it. His lieutenant was a native Australian and no doubt knew what he was talking about.

"How long will it take us to reach them?" he asked.

"At our current speed, about five days. If we travel at maximum knots...three and a half, roughly. I'll have a better idea the closer we get."

"Okay, tell our new engineer to crank up the engine. Let's go take a look."

"Wilco, sir. Another thing. These ships—if that's what they are—we found them through passive sonar, triangulating with sea bed devices. I took the liberty of checking with the surveillance stations on the east coast. None of them are picking anything up in the area. The ships seem invisible to radar."

Wright wasn't sure what to make of that information.

Perhaps reading his confused expression, Ford continued, "It means they could be wooden or fiberglass."

"Ah, I see." Wooden ships would be right up the EAC's street, and apparently made them easier to hide. "Notify me when we're an hour away."

He returned to his cabin to grab another couple of hours of sleep. The *Resolute*'s state-of-the-art scanning tech and massive computing power was already paying off.

As he lay in his bunk, his eyes closed, another idea popped into his head.

He put in a request for satellite data on the region where the non-natural objects had been spotted. If radar wasn't picking them up, perhaps satellites could provide imagery. His request might not be answered before they arrived, but the information would be worth having regardless.

7

Taylan was fairly sure she'd spotted her attacker the next day. It was only a small town. There couldn't be many young men wandering around with one arm in a sling. He was tall and wore a scruffy ginger beard. When they passed on the street, he briefly made eye contact with her. The short encounter had made her blood boil again and she had to resist the urge to dispense some more punishment for his attempted crime, but she had to avoid suspicion. There was already one member of the community who knew she was not as she seemed.

He must have stalked her to find out where she lived, and then waited for her to come home. She was lucky it had been dark. If the man had seen her face, she would have had more than sexual assaults to worry about.

Now, a couple of weeks after the altercation, she decided it was time to move on. She'd picked the place dry in terms of customers and what they could tell her. No one had given any hint they might know something about Alliance children who had disappeared during the invasion, and the meager fees she'd gathered in return for the fantasies she'd spun was barely enough to survive on.

She sat up.

Each night since the attack, she'd found somewhere new to sleep. This morning, she'd woken in a derelict house on a dead end road leading up into the hills. Damp had infiltrated the rooms, probably due to a hole in the roof. The plaster had cracked and was falling off the walls, and the floorboards smelled of mushrooms. The building wasn't much different from the little house she'd bought for her family or the one she'd grown up in. Her heart heavy, she wondered what had happened to the family who lived here.

Basing herself in one spot had been a mistake, though she knew why she'd done it. The notion of a place to call home, however decrepit and awful, brought her some comfort. More than ever, she was lonely. Her time as a Royal Marine had been a trial, but she'd made friends. Now, she couldn't afford the luxury of familiar faces or places. They allowed anyone who was watching her to predict her movements. It made her vulnerable.

She began to pack up her stuff: the fortune-telling deck, scarves, spare clothes, a purse of coins, a small cake of soap, packets of dried food, all the bits and pieces she'd stolen or bought with her tiny income. Life as a fortune teller was hard and, from what she'd seen, other Crusaders didn't have things much better. Why anyone would *choose* to live this way was beyond her.

Her backpack on her back, she peeked into the street. Gray and glistening from last night's rain in the early morning light, it was empty. She stepped out and began the long walk to the train station.

Crusaders had few choices when it came to transportation. Technology of most forms was frowned upon, and that included cars. If a Crusader had to travel somewhere not within walking distance, they would most often take one of the public coaches pulled by teams of horses or try to hitch a ride on a delivery cart. Yet even EAC philosophy had been forced to concede some larger forms of transportation were necessary. Trucks still drove the deteriorating roads and trains ran on poorly maintained tracks. Another option was to travel by barge on the canals or by boat around the coast.

For Taylan's purposes, a train ride was called for. She'd decided to go to Abertawe. In the large city, she might meet people who were more in the know about the inner, secret activities of their cult, and—she hoped—it would be easier to remain invisible.

The station was small. A single track ran through it, bordered by two platforms. The times for that day's trains to Abertawe were chalked on a board. The first one wasn't due for an hour and a half, according to the clock hanging over the platform, so she sat on one of the benches and settled in for the wait.

Another aspect of Crusader life that irritated her was that it was so boring. All everyone appeared to do was work, stay home, or go out to drink. She'd seen some games of football played in the street by young lads, but the adults seemed to have little imagination or will to occupy themselves in interesting ways. Her discovery explained their wild, hedonistic behavior at their festivals. Repressed by their uninteresting, restrictive lifestyles, when the opportunity came to let loose they really went for it.

She occupied herself in the way she usually did, descending into her memories of happier times, before the invasion, when she'd had her kids with her. At the time, she'd thought their lives were not so great. They didn't have much money and she couldn't afford to buy her children the fun toys their friends had. But they never went hungry or wanted for any essentials, and they were happy. What wouldn't she give to have those times again? Or just to simply be together as a family.

Realizing her thoughts were sending her into a black hole of despair that always sat on the edge of her mind, she drove away the memories and returned to the present. Only forty minutes had passed. Sighing, numb with boredom, she took out her pack of cards and began to thumb through them. She would think up some bizarre interpretations to offer her customers and see how far she could go before one of them called her on it.

There were two that always freaked people out: the Hanged Man and Death.

She had no idea what they were supposed to mean, but it was odd there were two cards for what was essentially the same thing. Naturally, she'd never told anyone the cards meant they were going to be hanged—though that was a punishment in the Crusader justice system—or that they were about to die. Predictions like those wouldn't earn her much compensation for her time and trouble. If either of the cards came up, she usually wrote something about the client's problems coming to an abrupt end or the death of something that had been worrying them. Making shit up to please people was so easy.

She held up the Hanged Man.

Someone special will give you a gift, perhaps a necklace or a scarf.

Or...

Your eyes will nearly pop out when you hear some surprising news.

Time dragged by as she tried to entertain herself with her musings until sounds of people arriving on the platform drew her attention. A group of young men were passing through the open barrier. One of them had a short ginger beard, though his arm was no longer in a sling.

Damn.

She looked at the clock. The train was due in five minutes. There was nowhere for her to hide and as the only other person waiting, she stuck out like a sore thumb. She could leave, but there wouldn't be another train for two hours.

She put away her cards.

She'd been spotted. The young thug she'd incapacitated was sauntering toward her, something like arrogance or bravado in every step. As he sat down next to her, she stared ahead.

"Don't I know you?" he asked.

When she didn't answer, he went on, "You're that fortune-teller who's been hanging around here for a few weeks, right?"

One of his buddies had cottoned on that a bullying session was about to begin. The bench creaked as he sat on the other side of her.

Taylan clenched the backpack on the ground between her feet, mentally rehearsing the scenario that would involve her taking them both out. But she couldn't. She couldn't attract attention to herself. News of a soothsayer who was also an expert at unarmed combat would soon spread. She had to stay in character.

"Wait a sec," said the friend, a bulky man whose thigh pressed disgustingly against hers, "if it is her, how's she gonna answer you, Nat? She's dumb, ain't she?"

"Oh, I bet I could make her moan," joked Nat. He stretched out an arm and fastened it around Taylan's shoulders. "Wanna give it a try, darling?" Brave now he had his friends with him and it was broad daylight, he was trying to salvage his pride.

Visions of punching his nose flat raced through Taylan's mind, but she managed to stay in control.

"That's not funny," said another of his companions who had also walked over. "You're being a creep. Leave her alone."

Risking a glance at the newcomer, Taylan saw a boy younger than the others. Like most Crusaders, he was bearded, but his had barely begun to grow. She was touched by his intervention but couldn't do anything to acknowledge it.

"Piss off," said Nat. "Who invited you to the party?"

"She's alone and you're scaring her. She doesn't know you're only messing around."

"You'll mind your own business, if you know what's good for you."

Nat's hand had begun to travel down Taylan's arm. He was heading for a grope of her breast, secure in the fact she would be too embarrassed and intimidated to do anything about it.

The sound of metallic rumbling came down the track. In the distance, the approaching train could be seen.

She abruptly got to her feet, knocking the offending arm away from her.

"Hey," Nat protested, "no need to be unfriendly. Are you going to Abertawe? We can sit together...and chat."

His last comment drew a guffaw from the other guy on the bench. Nat's tall form loomed at her side.

The idea of spending a couple of hours in the company of this goon made her skin crawl.

His hand grasped her shoulders again.

"I'll keep a hold of you," he said, "so we don't get separated in the crush."

That was it.

She swung her pack at him, knocking him down. But in her anger, she swung too hard and the bag flew from her hands.

The train was drawing into the station, its unoiled brakes shrieking.

The other goon picked up her pack. Nat was getting to his feet, shame and fury in his eyes.

"Give it back to her," said the nice youngster.

The train had stopped.

"No," Nat spat. "Give it to me." He held out a hand.

An official had noticed the commotion on the platform and

come out of her office. "What's going on? What are you young men doing? I won't have fighting at my station."

The nice youth marched to the man holding the pack and wrestled it away from him before giving it to Taylan.

"Don't you get on that train!" ordered the station official, approaching the bench. "I want to have a word with you."

Taylan assumed she wasn't included in the order and ran to the train. The guard whistled. Clutching her pack to her chest, she turned to face the young man as the door began to close.

"Have a safe journey," he said.

"Thank you," she replied. Horror at her mistake rose in her throat as the words left her mouth.

The man's eyes stretched wide. The door closed, and his surprised face moved away as the train pulled out of the station.

8

Iolani Hale had become Lorcan's unwelcome sidekick, he realized as she disembarked his shuttle with him on his visit to the Britannic Alliance's flagship, the *Fearless*. Everywhere he went, by hook or by crook she found a way of coming with him. This time, she'd argued that for something as important as a plan of cooperation between the Antarctic Project and the BA, he needed independent advice. Not that she was as independent as she liked to make out. In the months she'd been working with him on the Project, she'd become as enmeshed in its challenges as he was.

At least she'd left her blasted dogs behind. The damned hounds followed her everywhere, and they'd maintained a dislike for him ever since he'd first encountered them with Hale in her jungle hermitage. They accepted pats and strokes from others aboard the *Bres*, but they reacted to his presence with lifted lips and barely audible, rumbling growls.

"Whoa," Hale breathed, gazing up and around at the vast shuttle bay, home to ranks of military craft. "I've never been on an Alliance starship before. Have you?"

"No," he replied shortly, his tone deliberately unimpressed.

Okay, he admitted to himself, the bay was larger than any of the passenger bays on his colony ships, but it wasn't as big as some of his cargo bays. Of that, he was confident. The cargo areas were to be converted to storage facilities as the date of departure drew nearer, and to supply the needs of the million-plus souls who would be traveling with him to the stars, they had to be vast.

"I hope they're better at warfare than they are at receiving visitors," he commented. The only other people in the bay were engineers and technicians working on the dropships and fighter ships. No one had appeared to greet them or take them wherever they were supposed to go. "Do they expect us to figure this out by ourselves?" he asked acidly.

A figure entered the far end of the bay and walked quickly toward them. An older woman, her gray hair cut perilously close to her scalp, she seemed flustered and irritated. She looked familiar, but he couldn't place her.

"I'm sorry for keeping you waiting," she said. "There was a miscommunication. The *Fearless* has only recently returned to operational status and we're still ironing out the wrinkles."

"That's all right," said Hale. "We only just arrived."

"If you would please step this way..."

As they followed her, she added, "I'm Brigadier Colbourn. I'll be present at the meeting."

"You will?" Lorcan replied, not bothering to keep the surprise out of his voice. He wasn't particularly au fait with military ranks, but he hadn't expected to consult with anyone lower than the heads of the branches.

Colbourn didn't react to his implied condescension, only responding, "I will. I have somewhat of a history with two people who will also be attending, so my presence was requested by Admiral Yorkson."

The passageways of the flagship hummed with activity. Autotransporters trundled by bearing their loads, armed troops in full armor marched past on their way to take part in exercises, Lorcan presumed, and skilled laborers of various kinds made their way to and from their work. They even saw someone operating a mech, its heavy footfalls making the deck vibrate. Lorcan's interested gaze followed the mech as it continued down the passageway. It seemed to be a new type. He wondered if it had superior manipulation capabilities than the models he was currently using. Mechs were useful for cargo handling, but only humans could perform certain tasks that required fine motor skills, and human labor was expensive.

Colbourn halted outside a door and spoke into the comm.

Inside the room was a scene that caused Lorcan to pause before entering. The military officials in their uniforms sitting around the table were not the problem. What bothered him was the two civilians. One was a giant of a man with flowing reddish-golden hair and beard. The other was a tall, lean individual who, by his bearing, gave the impression he thought of himself as the most important person in the place. This man's hair was cropped almost as short as Colbourn's and was a similar shade of gray, but, unlike her, his face appeared almost youthful. These had to be the people Colbourn had mentioned in the shuttle bay, but he hadn't expected such an odd pair.

He was trying to fathom who the two additional attendees might be when he noticed the sword.

The ancient weapon stood propped against the bulkhead in the corner of the room.

A sword.

It was a beauty, to be sure, very long with a finely wrought hilt and grooved blade. But it was still a damned sword. Was the BA thinking of reverting to medieval battle tactics? Dwyr Orr would be delighted. It was the kind of thing she would love.

Then he recalled Kala Orr was dead and her son, Perran, had assumed her role. He felt the tiniest twinge of sadness at the recollection. Only the very tiniest.

"Welcome to the *Fearless*, Ua Talman," said a short man, rising to his feet. "I am Admiral Yorkson. I'd like to introduce Chief of Defense Staff John Evans and Sea Lord Stephen Fox."

"Pleased to make your acquaintance. This is my associate, Iolani Hale."

The two men nodded their greetings but remained seated. Middle-aged and non-descript, they were of a type Lorcan knew well. Molded by their privileged upbringings in the higher echelons of Britannic society, their attitudes and prejudices fixed and immutable, he had dealt with many similar men and women as CEOs of multinational companies.

His attention quickly moved on to the civilians, but Yorkson didn't introduce them.

"If you would like to take a seat?" the admiral suggested. "Please help yourself to refreshments. We appreciate your agreeing to come to us rather than the other way around."

Colbourn had already sat down. Lorcan sat in one of the two vacant chairs, not moving his gaze from the strange pair. Hale sat beside him.

Yorkson cleared his throat uncomfortably. "As you can see, we have also invited two people who are significant to the future of the Alliance to this meeting. Their existence and presence here may seem, er," he coughed again in a strangled tone "remarkable. I ask you to suspend your disbelief and accept our assurances that what you're about to hear is absolutely correct and verified. Brigadier Colbourn, if you would please do the honors?"

What followed was the most astounding tale Lorcan had ever heard. The word 'remarkable' didn't come close to doing it justice. As the officer gave her account, he had to consciously close his mouth twice after his jaw dropped. When she'd finished her story, he was dumbstruck.

In truth, if he had to imagine what King Arthur and Merlin had looked like—if they'd ever existed—the two men sitting before him would have fitted his expectation pretty well. The larger man did look like a warrior chief from the BI's Dark Ages, and the one they claimed was a wizard had a distinctly otherworldly air about him. Not that their appearance meant much. If anything, it was evidence they were fakes, that the Alliance had picked them due to their resemblance to the mythical figures.

Hale was silent, apparently as nonplussed as he was.

Eventually, he spluttered, "You can't honestly expect me to believe a single word of that ridiculous narrative."

Sea Lord Fox replied, "None of us believed it at first. Like yourself, we're practical people. We aren't prone to being fooled by mumbo jumbo of the kind the EAC espouses. But now, after the proof we've seen, we all believe it."

"Proof?" Lorcan asked. "I'd like to see that proof myself."

"I'm afraid all the documentation and recordings relating to Arthur and Merlin are highly classified," said Evans, "and if you or Ms Hale mention anything about either of them in public at this time, the Alliance will vehemently deny their existence and do everything in its power to discredit your statements."

"Well!" exclaimed Lorcan, once again at a loss for words.

Yorkson put his elbows on the table and leaned forward. "The way I look at it is, whether or not these two gentlemen are genuinely who they say they are, and we believe them to be, is immaterial. They possess abilities unexplained by science and they have a...shall we say...a certain mystique that, when their return is announced, will hold great sway over the minds of the world's citizens. These are the aspects of their existence that are important to the Alliance, and to you, we hope, as you fulfill your very welcome promise of support."

Lorcan recalled Camilla Lebedev telling him about a rumored 'secret weapon' the BA was using. Were Arthur and Merlin the source of the rumor?

"You're going to reveal them to the world?" asked Hale.

"The timing has to be optimal," said Fox, "but yes, we will, as part of our overall strategy to protect civilization on Earth," adding, "which is where you come in, Ua Talman."

He'd been wondering when they would get around to his reason for being there. He almost replied something along the lines of, *Why do you need me when you have the Once and Future King and his magical friend*? but he kept his sarcasm in control—something he'd been learning to do better since Hale had forced her way into his team. She could match his cutting remarks word for word and it just wasn't worth the bother.

"I have to confess you have my colleague to thank for my presence here," he said. "Iolani has persuaded me the Antarctic Project *may* have an interest helping you in your work. But I'm not completely convinced. I'm interested in hearing your vision for the Project's role, nothing more than that. I'm sure you understand I have many demands on my time and resources. I'm reluctant to add to the load, especially as..." A memory flashed into his mind. Brigadier Colbourn had been in command of the BA starship he'd helped to defend. What had it been called?

He turned to her. "You're in command of the *Valiant*?"

"Yes. She's my vessel."

He returned his attention to the room in general. "My starships have come to the Alliance's aid in the past and I received nothing in return."

"As I recall," said Evans testily, "it was AP forces that helped the Crusaders take the Caribbean from us! I don't know about anyone else but *I* would say you owed us a favor or two."

"Now, now," said Yorkson, raising his hands in a calming gesture, "going over old history won't benefit anyone."

"No," said Fox, "but it would be helpful to have reassurances regarding exactly where Ua Talman's sentiments lie. If we're to combine forces, we need absolute trust in him."

"Absolute trust in me?!" Lorcan exclaimed. "Don't you think I have enough to do without adding your war to my list? What precisely do you think I'm getting out of this, except another plateful of work and expense?"

"To be honest," said Fox, "that's exactly what I'd like to know."

Lorcan was on the verge of storming out. The last thing he'd expected from attending this meeting was to be insulted.

But then an unfamiliar voice spoke. "Could I say something?"

It was the man who claimed to be King Arthur.

"I'm all ears," Lorcan replied, forgetting his earlier resolve to dampen his sarcasm.

"I am not confused by your presence here. I believe I can see into your heart. You're a good man, though you carry a heavy burden that pains you." He addressed the military officers. "I will vouch for this man. He doesn't wish the Alliance any harm."

He spoke with an odd accent Lorcan didn't recognize. Though his first impulse was to make a scornful retort about how he didn't require anyone to vouch for him, his words dried on his lips. There was some quality about the Arthur fellow that would have made his response sound churlish and mean-spirited.

From the corner of his eye, he saw Iolani blink in surprise. The effect on the military leaders was similar. Fox and Evans had been scowling belligerently, but after Arthur's short speech they appeared embarrassed.

A short silence followed, during which 'Merlin' gave a small smirk.

What a curious pair they were.

"I agree with you, Arthur," said Yorkson. He made a fist and coughed into it, avoiding eye contact with Lorcan. "The bit about not wishing us any harm, I mean. Shall we move on?"

9

Disembarking the train at Abertawe had been one of the most nerve-wracking moments of Taylan's life. She'd done her best to change her appearance but she only had a few spare clothes, and as a single woman traveling alone she wouldn't be hard to spot among the newly arrived passengers. Crusaders seemed to mostly travel in pairs or as families. If guards tried to detain her, she wouldn't have any choice about going with them wherever they wanted to take her. She was carrying no weapons except for a couple of knives, for practical and circumspect reasons. Due to the EAC's hatred of technology, places to charge energy guns were scarce, and a fortune-teller toting a beamer would look highly suspicious anyway.

So as she'd walked through Abertawe Station, she been tense and fearful, expecting any moment to be approached and questioned as to why she was pretending to be under a vow of silence. Then the harder questions would come, like who was she, where was she from, and what was she doing here.

She had no answers and no means to fight her way out of the situation.

Only no one had accosted her.

Whether Crusaders' methods of communication were too slow or faulty and no message from the town she'd left had come through, or the boy who had heard her speak hadn't reported her, or she had entirely exaggerated the severity of her mistake, she didn't know, but nobody had shown any interest in her at the station.

She'd slipped into anonymity in the crowds at Abertawe and continued her quest to find her children.

She'd maintained her habit of never staying longer than one night in the same place. It wasn't hard. There were plenty of abandoned houses in the city, and nature hadn't yet had time to make them entirely uninhabitable. Each one she entered, however, made her sad for the people who had lived there. Her own people, driven away or killed, their lives and possessions taken by the invaders. More than once, she was reminded of Meilyr's conversation with her in the Resistance hideout in the Preseli Hills, when he'd said they had to work together to get their country back, implying that acting alone was selfish. But what choice did she have now? She'd betrayed the Resistance and could never work with them again.

She guessed that festivals were where her customers would be most likely to let slip sensitive information. At these events, Crusaders would get wildly drunk. As everyone knew, intoxication loosened lips. But as far as she could make out no festivals were planned until late autumn, when the biggest one of the year would take place.

She'd resolved to bide her time, keep moving around, working in pubs and, if the weather was nice, in parks, making enough money to keep herself fed, maintaining a low profile.

Twice, tantalizing threads of information had been dangled before her. The first time she'd been in an upmarket alehouse on the edge of the city's harbor. At least, it was upmarket in Crusader terms. The floor had been swept, the tables weren't sticky, and more than one type of beer was on offer. Her client had been an older man, in his fifties—an unusual demographic in her market. She felt a special hatred of the older generation of Crusaders. These were the ones who had been around long enough to not have been brainwashed into accepting the ways of the cult. He'd chosen to eschew modernity and progress of his own free will. The younger ones, she mostly pitied.

He'd taken a long drag of a joint and looked down his nose at her before taking a seat at her table.

"You're the one who's vowed silence, right?"

Taylan nodded. Her cards were already out in a stack on the tabletop. She picked them up and started to shuffle them.

The man spread his knees and leaned back, taking up the small space with his physical presence. There was something particularly annoying about him, more so than other middle-aged Crusaders—an arrogance that made her clench her jaw.

In the background, the man's companions were jeering and laughing at him, but he ignored them. His gaze was on Taylan's semi-shadowed face as she placed the first card face upward.

The Lovers.

Ugh.

She'd been hoping for the Hanged Man, just to see his expression.

She took another card from the top of the pack.

"Wait," he said, grabbing her wrist. "What about this one?" He poked the Lovers. "What does this mean?"

Taylan paused. What did he expect her to do? As far as he knew, she couldn't answer him verbally and he could hardly expect her to write down her answer while he was holding her arm. She glared at him, her mouth set. Despite the way her scarf hooded her features, he must have been able to see her face a little bit. He released her arm.

She laid down the second card.

The Cart.

That was what she called it, though it didn't look like a Crusader cart. The driver stood rather than sat and it was drawn by two lions.

This was better. She could spin something nasty out of this, a prediction for a nasty man.

She wrote, *A loved one will soon leave you.*

He frowned as he read, and then folded his arms with a scowl.

She turned over the third card.

It displayed a blindfolded woman in a toga bearing a sword: Justice.

Excellent.

She lifted her pen. *You will be punished for a great wrong you have committed.*

Reading her second pronouncement, his scowl deepened. "This isn't like the usual predictions I get. Are you sure you've got it right?"

Taylan wrote, *I can only tell you what the cards say.*

The fourth card always reminded her of Merlin. It showed a magician performing a trick with cups. She couldn't quickly think up of a way to spin this one into bad news, so she held up a hand, signaling to the man to wait, and turned over the fifth card. This was the Hermit, depicting a lone man in a cave. Her pen poised over the paper, she hastily wracked her brains.

The answer came.

After deceiving someone important, you will be banished from the BI.

Her heart thumped, partly from controlling herself so her hilarity didn't show, and partly from fear. Had she gone too far? Probably. But she was bored, sick of the ridiculous stupidity of her job, and frustrated that her efforts seemed to be getting her nowhere. As an afterthought, she added at the end of the final sentence, *Sorry.*

Her customer's reaction was predictable. Blood suffused his face and he brought a fist down on the table, making it wobble. "This is bullshit! It can't be right. You're useless. No good at all. I don't want to hear any more of your lies." He stood up so fast Taylan grabbed the table, thinking he might knock it over. He jabbed a finger at her. "*You're* the one who should be banished. You should be shipped off to Oceania with the other misfits."

He stalked away, naturally not paying her anything, but what he'd said was more useful than any amount of money. Unless she was even more out of touch than she'd imagined, the EAC hadn't invaded any of the countries of Oceania. Was it really shipping people there? If it was, it had to be under the noses of the Alliance's military.

Was that where her children had gone?

The second tidbit of possibly useful information had come only a day later from a sad old woman. Taylan had felt the familiar prickling of dislike on seeing a member of the older generation approach her table, but it had faded when she saw her face more closely. If ever there had been a visage with guilt and unhappiness written into every wrinkle, it was this one. Did she regret joining the cult? Had her life not turned out as well as she'd expected? It had certainly seemed to Taylan that the women bore the brunt of hardship in Crusader households, the majority of the tasks that were usually automated falling to them.

She had given her a kind, hopeful reading, telling her that her troubles would soon be over and she would find joy in her life. It might be unlikely, but the prediction would bring her happiness for a short while. As she left, after smiling at Taylan's writing and picking up the paper, she'd leaned over the table and squeezed her forearm, saying, "Maybe it's because of the ones we saved. We didn't kill them all. Not the little ones. Maybe I'm being rewarded for that."

Taylan spread her hands in an *I don't know*, gesture, struggling to stop herself from trembling.

The woman straightened up and looked toward the side of the alehouse that faced the quay.

"I still remember putting them on the ship," she mused. "They were all alive then. They were crying. Missing their parents. But they were alive."

Remembrance of where she was returning to her face, she dug in a pocket in her skirt and handed Taylan some coins. "Thanks. You've brightened my day."

And she had Taylan's, though she didn't know it.

The two sets of comments from unrelated customers hadn't only given her hope, they'd given her leads to follow.

But she remained without any clear method to continue her research. In her role in Crusader society she was nobody. She had no access to officials who knew the details she needed if she were to stand a hope of locating Kayla and Patrin. The only information she could glean in her current situation would be basic and not actionable.

She needed to try something new, but she didn't know what.

10

"So they passed through here," said Ford, his fingertip poking a red line on the holo in the *Resolute's* control room, "and carried on sailing toward the coast."

The holo displayed a section of ocean off the coast of Far North Queensland. The jagged topography of the Dead Reef dropped away on the coastal side, then the sea bed rose gradually until it became the shore. As Ford had mentioned when their boat's computer had interpreted the passive sonar readings as 'non-natural', no harbors were visible.

"Sailed?" Wright asked. "You're convinced they're sailboats?"

"I can't think what else they could be. It would explain why coastal surveillance isn't picking them up on radar, and their pattern of movement, well, it would take too long to tell you why, but to me it looks like they're sailing. The area they passed through would accommodate a draft of four, maybe five meters at high tide, and it *was* high tide."

Fairly big sailboats, then.

As Wright frowned, Ford went on, "I know what you're

thinking. No satellite imagery. If they're sailboats, why aren't our satellites seeing them? I can't explain that."

"Could they be subs?"

"Traveling just under the surface? Might be. The ocean's wide, deep, dark, noisy, irregular, and cluttered. Even the *Resolute's* computer must struggle to interpret the data."

"But where are they now?" Wright mused. "That's the real question."

Ford jabbed the holo again, this time at the spot where the red line ended. He asked the computer to give him the distance to land from there. A green line flashed up, bearing the numbers 187.

"A hundred and eighty-seven meters from the shore," he said, "they disappear into thin air. Or water."

"That's how it looks," said Wright. "But they must have gone somewhere. What if the sonar readings just became too low to register at that point?"

"Yeah," agreed Ford. "The sea-bed readers are kilometers away. There's only so much they can do."

It was a frustrating mystery. A day from their target, all signs of what they'd been chasing had vanished. Wright was sure something illegal was going on but what was anyone's guess.

"What *is* there in that part of Australia?" he asked.

"Along the coast, rainforest. Further in, plains and desert. People used to farm there once but it's mostly empty now. It's a beautiful part of the country but not really good for agriculture or industry. It's too far from everywhere else, for one thing."

"What about mines? Any old uranium mines in that area?"

"Good point," replied Ford. "I hadn't thought of that. I'll see if I can find any records."

Uranium mining was banned in Australia, but it was exactly the kind of resource Ua Talman would be interested in for his ships.

While Ford was searching the database, Wright sent a report detailing the latest events and requesting permission to go ashore and look for signs of illegal activity. It would take an hour or so to hear back from Oceania Command, so to kill time he went to the crew lounge, where the xiangqi tournament was heating up.

Abacha had devised a system of matches so complicated no one really understood it. Everyone relied on him to tell them who they had to play next, and who was in the lead—after Abacha, of course—was anyone's guess. But everyone was having fun so it didn't seem to matter.

Wright, Warrant Officer Jeong, Abacha, and the ship's engineer, Krol, were due to play that day. One of the recent arrivals, the engineer was a taciturn woman, grim-faced and laconic. Wright couldn't tell if she was quiet because she was shy or if she was generally uncommunicative. There was nothing on her file to indicate any problems in her background. She'd served aboard three Royal Navy ships and, unusually, had experience in both marine and weapon engineering, which was why she'd been assigned to the *Resolute*. The boat needed a jack-of-all-trades to maintain her range of cutting-edge equipment. As long as she did her job, he wasn't worried about her standoffishness, and she had agreed to join the xiangqi tournament so she wasn't entirely anti-social.

Krol faced Abacha over an interface that displayed a xiangqi board, leaning her folded arms on the tabletop as she glowered at the pieces. Hers were green and Abacha's were red. Her concentrated frown gave the impression she was trying to move her pieces via telekinesis. Wright doubted her engineering skills extended that far. She was no Merlin, though she was an excellent engineer. One day, when Jeong had reported a strange, soft whine coming from the vicinity of the boat's propulsion system—a serious issue as the *Resolute* was designed to slip through the water in near silence—Krol had listened carefully outside the casing for a minute, then tightened a single nut. The whine instantly stopped. Shrugging off expressions of wonder from the assembled crew, she'd left, spanner in hand.

Now, she seemed to be applying the same level of concentration.

The game of xiangqi was new to Wright. Each player controlled an 'army' consisting of a general, advisers, elephants, horses, chariots, cannon, and soldiers. There were rules governing where and how the pieces could move on the board, which was a grid with demarcated sections including a palace, a river, and castles. The pieces sat on the intersecting lines of the grid, and the object of the game was to checkmate the opposing side's general. He enjoyed playing it because it exercised the tactical part of his mind, but he'd quickly learned he was no match for Abacha.

Krol moved her general to a new spot, sliding her finger over the screen.

Abacha flashed a grin, leaned over the board, and took his turn. He relaxed in his seat and watched her reaction with hooded eyes.

The engineer hadn't changed position, absorbing his play, appearing to mentally digest it. Her face didn't betray any reaction to Abacha's move. Her mouth was generally down-turned and she had a permanent crease between her eyebrows, so it was no indication she was feeling discouraged.

"You know," murmured Jeong, who was watching the game along with everyone except Lieutenant Ford, "we should really set a time limit to make a move."

Krol didn't react. Her entire attention was on the board.

"That wouldn't be fair," said Seaman Hadley. "We can't change the rules after the tournament's started. Besides, most of us are playing for the first time."

Abacha's gaze flicked to Hadley and back to Krol, but he

didn't comment. He appeared calm and not at all impatient for his opponent to take her turn. Putting the back of his hand to his mouth, he yawned. "Could someone get me a coffee?"

Hadley went to the machine, poured a cup, and brought it over.

Still, Krol hadn't moved a muscle, let alone one of her pieces.

Then, as Abacha was sipping his drink, her stubby-fingered hand reached out and she slid a green piece across the board. Now it was Abacha's turn to frown. He studied the move, and his frown deepened. For the first time since the beginning of the tournament, he appeared worried. His coffee sat forgotten by his side as his gaze roved the interface. He lifted his hand, hesitated, and put it down without moving a piece.

The silence in the room grew tenser as the audience strained their eyes and ears, waiting to see what would happen. Was it possible Abacha might lose this one? He'd beaten everyone else swiftly with minimal effort. All the times Wright had played him he'd had the impression Abacha could have beaten him blindfolded, simply by predicting his obvious moves.

Abacha rested his chin on his upturned palm and moved a red piece, watching Krol for her reaction. The piece of hers he'd taken disappeared from the screen.

She didn't react.

The audience settled in for another long wait, but the engineer only took a few seconds to decide her next move. One of Abacha's pieces vanished.

He nodded thoughtfully. He reached out. His finger pushed a piece to another square.

Immediately, Krol did the same.

The game sped up.

What had been an agony of waiting turned into a match that moved so fast it was hard to follow. The pieces flashed across the board and disappeared at a breathtaking rate. At first, Abacha seemed to be winning, then the tide turned in Krol's favor. Was it possible the champion might be beaten?

But, gradually, Abacha's wins began to mount up and the board's dominant color shifted to red. Krol's moves slowed. Her grim expression grew grimmer. Abacha moved a piece, and she straightened up, her arms falling to her sides. The game wasn't over, as far as Wright could tell. Krol's general still had some freedom of movement. But she was done. She held out a hand over the interface.

"Good match," said Abacha as they shook.

"Yeah, not bad. It's an interesting game. I like it. I'll look forward to our next one tomorrow."

It was more than she'd uttered at one time since she'd come aboard weeks ago. The crew stared as she got up from the table and walked out. Wright was also impressed that she knew when she would face Abacha again in his complex system of matches.

"Sir," Lieutenant Ford comm'd, "I've found something you'll want to take a look at."

"I'll be right there."

It didn't look like much at first. Just an indentation in the coastline, not very different from any of the other irregularities in the topography at the ocean's edge. Then Ford brought up a satellite image from last year and moved it next to the other.

He said, "I couldn't find any old mines of any kind within a hundred klicks of the coast, but I thought, if someone is smuggling something in or out by sea, they'll be making tracks. There aren't any roads in that part of the country. So I compared the most recent scan of the area with historical ones, and that was when I saw it." He jabbed the indentation.

"Someone's blasted out a section of land?! How did they manage to do it with no one noticing?"

"The area's very remote. Unless we were looking in that

exact place, I reckon it could be done. Hell, it looks like they did it. You could bring a medium-sized ship right in there."

Wright studied the two images.

"Well done, Ford. Well done. Let's go and take a look."

11

The crush at the parade was unbelievable. Taylan was contemplating leaving. She hadn't been able to work at all yet, with few places to sit and everyone intent on what was happening in the street. On the other hand, she had access to a wider range of people than she usually had, people who didn't go to pubs or parks. It seemed like half of Abertawe had turned up to see the new mayor sworn in.

Rope barriers lined the street, separating the crowd from the road, where floats and entertainers were passing by. Giving up on getting any work done until the main event was over, Taylan watched the proceedings. Squashed against a barrier, she had an excellent view, though she was also uncomfortably reminded of Dwyr Orr's launch ceremony. This was a less intense affair, though. A lot of the walkers were clowns, playing comic instruments, pulling faces, bursting balloons, and performing other, supposedly amusing, acts like dropping their pants and mooning the audience.

Taylan had already seen enough asses to last her a lifetime but the onlookers seemed to love it.

The floats depicted stories from fairy tales among other

things. She recognized a few from her own childhood. A young man clung on halfway up a tall vine, swaying precariously as the cart trundled along. Someone was wearing a cat costume with high boots. A small pang of sadness hit her. On another float, a man with a sword fought a dragon.

Predictably, many in the crowd were drunk or off their faces on weed or mushrooms. She'd been groped more than once, but she'd found a vicious backward kick put off subsequent attempts.

How much longer would it go on?

She guessed the final float would carry the mayor to the town hall down the road, where the official ceremony would take place. Once his float had passed the barriers would be taken down, the street food sellers would set up their stalls, and the real party would begin.

She'd been pleased to hear there would be another celebration before the late-autumn one. Every gathering of drunken Crusaders was an opportunity for her to build on the little bits of information she'd already gleaned that might lead her to her kids. It was irritating to be squashed in among the inebriated cultists, but she just had to hang on a little while longer.

A shout went up and the people around her surged forward, pressing her stomach against the rope. She locked her knees and leaned back, sticking her elbows back too for good measure. No one took any notice. The mayor's float had been spotted.

Taylan felt sick. The man's conveyance was like the one Dwyr Orr had used at the launch ceremony. The sight of it sparked a flood of memories: her children—not real, but *looking* very real—the Dwyr holding a knife to Kayla's throat; Arthur, slicing through people who stood in his way; Wilson, horribly tortured and still alive.

She swallowed.

The new mayor was not protected by a transparent screen

as Orr had been, and she had no desire to shoot him, but the similarity to that other time was too great. She had to get away.

She turned and tried to squeeze between the bodies behind her, but it was hopeless. Everyone was jammed in tightly. There was no possibility of escape until the barriers were taken down. Grimacing, she turned to the front.

The mayor's float slowly moved forward. Unlike the others, it wasn't pulled by horses but traveled under the power of an electric engine. Naturally, those in higher social ranks had access to technology others did not, but she had never heard a Crusader remark on the hypocrisy. It was not surprising. They were capable of all kinds of mental gymnastics to explain and justify their backward thinking.

The new mayor stood proudly on the end of a V-shaped platform protruding from the front of the float, waving and smiling at the crowd. He was dressed in a dark robe that fell to his feet and wore a three-cornered hat. As she gazed up at his face, Taylan was surprised to feel a twinge of familiarity about him. It was odd because she'd never seen a Crusader she recognized before. They didn't generally record themselves in vids or stills. They didn't have the means to. So why did she think she might know this man?

The float was almost level with her. She squinted as she peered closely at the face under the stupid hat. He was middle-aged, broad-chested, and clean-shaven. The latter was weird for a Crusader. Was he a former customer but he'd been bearded at the time?

"What's the new guy's name?" she asked a burly woman pressed into her right side.

The woman gave her a look of disbelief. "Why, it's Joseph Fry of course. How could you not know that? Been living under a rock?"

Joseph Fry?

It didn't ring a bell, and it wasn't a typical West BI name

either, so she guessed he wasn't someone from her childhood or the town where she used to live. He had to be a Crusader.

She imagined him with a beard.

Shit!

That man was no Crusader, and his name wasn't Joseph Fry. It was Hans Jonte, former head of SIS for the BA.

The new mayor of Abertawe was Hans Jonte?!

She was so surprised, if she hadn't been held upright by the people jammed in around her, she would have had to sit down.

He was gone. The float had passed by. On its rear end, two women in gossamery costumes threw flowers onto the street and into the crowd. The cheering was dying down. The parade was over and the attendees were growing restless, waiting to be released.

Taylan barely noticed. She was trying to process what she'd seen and what it could mean. She hadn't heard what had happened to the BA Government after the Caribbean fell except for some horrible gossip about two military heads being burned alive. She'd assumed they'd all died, executed under Dwyr Orr's orders. Even if some had survived, the last place she would have expected to see any of them was back in the Britannic Isles. Jonte was taking a terrible risk. Then again, so was she. But she had a good reason.

What the hell was *he* doing here?

His work had involved espionage, so maybe he was here as a spy for the new government. That would make sense. He'd infiltrated the EAC in order to find out information that would help the Alliance defeat it. Though it seemed strange that he would take a high profile role like mayor. It would be hard for him to do anything without scrutiny. Yet being mayor probably gave him access to intel no ordinary Crusader would ever lay eyes on.

She felt a growing respect and admiration for the man.

Here he was, in the lion's mouth, carrying out the Alliance's work to free the BI from its invaders.

The rope barrier dropped, and the crowd pushed forward.

"Hey!" she protested as she was nearly knocked over.

But in another second the pressure was gone and she could move freely, though the throng remained thick.

"Would you read my cards for me?"

A skinny girl had approached her, eyes wide and hopeful.

Distracted by the revelation, Taylan momentarily forgot her disguise and replied, "What are you talking about?"

"Oh, er..." The girl flushed.

"Uh, sorry," said Taylan, remembering. "I'm not working right now."

The girl wandered away.

The germ of an idea was forming in Taylan's mind.

She set off in the direction of the town hall.

12

Lorcan was juggling, trying to think. The meeting with the Alliance officers had been remarkable in many ways. Not only had they claimed the two odd characters present were figures from ancient history, they had also revealed they had Dwyr Orr in custody. Though 'Arthur' and 'Merlin' had put on a convincing show, they had to be fakes. The BA was clearly deluded about them. He could see the appeal. He knew the old story about the king who would return to save the Britannic Isles. Who wouldn't be delighted to discover two beings with superpowers had returned to save the day?

Perhaps it didn't matter that the Alliance was having the wool pulled over its eyes. As long as their people were convinced, the belief could rally them and give them the confidence and strength of will to throw out the invaders. It was the *belief*, rather than the actuality, that was important.

On the subject of the Dwyr, he didn't doubt what he'd been told was true. He hadn't seen her with his own eyes as she was being held in sick bay on another ship, the *Gallant*, but the assertion was too momentous for it to be a lie. Also, the Alliance's military were not generally a deceptive bunch, unlike Kala Orr. But it sounded as if the woman was out of action entirely, deep within a coma induced before the Alliance kidnapped her.

If that was the case, how useful was she now? Maybe only in the same way as Arthur and Merlin—as a name, a figurehead, an idea for which people would give their lives.

"Do you *have* to do that?" asked Iolani.

He caught the ball currently in the air. "What?"

"What do you mean, what? Throwing those balls around all the time, of course. It's very distracting."

The rest of the team in the *Bres's* control center ducked their heads.

Anger welled up in him. Who did she think she was, ordering him around, complaining at him, on his own ship?!

But his ire abruptly drained away. He was tired of fighting her and bored with their constant conflicts. He simply didn't have the interest or energy for another squabble.

"If it bothers you so much, I'll stop," he said.

The team's heads rose and gaping looks were shared among them.

He sat down and dropped the juggling balls over the side of his armrest, one by one. In the shocked silence, the soft, quiet *thump, thump, thump* of the bean-filled sacks hitting the deck was plain to hear.

An almost inaudible giggle came from Kekoa's direction, but he maintained his dignity and ignored it.

"Lorcan?" asked Iolani.

"*Yes?*"

"I've been here for months now and I haven't seen the *Balor* or the *Banba* yet. Is it okay if I take a shuttle to go and check them out?"

Do what you like.

"By all means," he replied. "I have no objection."

"Thanks." She rose to her feet and walked over to stand in front of him. "Would you like to come with me?"

He looked up at her, surprised. "I beg your pardon?"

"I was just wondering if you would like to visit your other ships too. I noticed you hadn't in all the time I've been here. I thought it might make sense, if I was going, for us to go together and save on shuttle trips."

Now he thought about it, he realized he hadn't been to either of the *Bres's* sister ships in over a year. He received regular reports from the supervisors who oversaw their construction and nothing he'd read had given him any cause for concern, so he hadn't bothered with seeing the progress for himself. He'd been too caught up in Earth affairs and the business with Hale.

"Perhaps that would be wise," he replied.

"Great. There's no time like the present. Shall we go now?"

Feeling uncomfortably like a puppy following its new master, he trailed her as she left the control center. At least it looked as though she wasn't going to insist on bringing her actual dogs.

∼

LIKE THE *BRES*, the *Balor* and *Banba* were constructed in the shape of corkscrews. The interiors consisted of zones: cryosuspension sections, accommodation centers, habitats, agricultural sectors, leisure modules, hospitals, shuttle bays, science and technology divisions, and a whole host of other districts. Magalev rails connected the areas, which alternated in type around the spirals. Though it was more expensive to build the ships this way, it meant that, if any part of the vessel failed for some reason, perhaps mechanically or due to an impact, the effects of the disaster would be mitigated. The damaged area would seal itself off and no ship would lose her entire complement of passengers or everything she held stored, for instance, unless she was completely destroyed.

At the center of the spirals sat long, columnar engines that would compress spacetime in front of the vessels and expand it to their rear, propelling them faster than light. Probes were already traveling to prospective colony planets using the same engines, so there was no question the new technology worked. But no nation or business entity had been able to come up with the funds to build full-scale models until the foundation of the Antarctic Project.

When the probes arrived they would transmit data that would help Lorcan decide where to send his ships. They had already sent back plenty of information as they came within closer scanning range of their targets, information he had begun to sift through, though it was still years before he would have to pick his ships' destinations. The probes were also assessing their own functional status, helping to inform the engineers building the starship engines.

"Which one leaves first?" asked Iolani as the shuttle brought them closer to the *Banba*. "Have you decided? Or will they all leave at once?"

"All three ships will complete test runs over several months prior to departure," Lorcan replied. "I anticipate there will be teething problems that will delay one or more of them. In the unlikely event they're all entirely operational, I imagine the *Bres* will lead the way. Call me narcissistic if you like, but, after all these years of effort and expense, I feel I've earned the privilege of leading humanity to the stars."

"A little narcissistic maybe, but I don't begrudge you that. I don't think anyone could deny the amount of work you've put in. It's really been a labor of love, hasn't it?"

He didn't answer. Something about the question or her tone

put him on edge. She was starting on one of her niggling, annoying probes into his psyche. He decided to turn the tables, for once.

"Have you thought about what you'll do when the Project departs the system? Will you go back to Suriname?"

"Hmm. I haven't decided for sure. That's a long time away. But maybe not. I think I'd become too used to living alone in my own little world. I was content there. The world and everything that was happening to it was too much for me to handle. I wanted to help, to change things for the better, but I didn't know how. So I retreated to the jungle and my work. Contributing to scientific understanding of life on our planet was my way of helping, I guess. But in my time working with you and the team, I've come to realize I can do more. I think I've made a difference, haven't I?"

Her quiet, honest, open-hearted words sent a shiver of shame through his being. He'd dragged the woman, unconscious, from her home, imprisoned her on his ship, and nearly placed her in cryonic suspension before taking her billions of kilometers from Earth. And in return she'd brought to light potentially disastrous flaws in the Project, recruited world specialists to devise ground-breaking solutions, and uncovered child exploitation in one of his subsidiary companies.

Her attitude had left him seething plenty of times, but she could hardly be blamed for that after what he'd done. Why had he hated her so much? He was sure the Lorcan of thirty years ago would never have behaved as he had toward this innocent person.

What had he become?

"You...you have made a difference, Iolani. A big difference. And I am grateful for it."

She turned toward him, her eyes widened, but she didn't respond to his answer. Instead she said, "Have you made a decision about the Alliance's proposal?"

"No. Not yet."

For the rest of the journey to the *Banba*, he felt calmer than he had in a long time. Something had changed. It was as though a great weight had slipped from his soul.

13

Abertawe Town Hall was a modern structure. Taylan vaguely recalled hearing about its construction and opening when she'd been a teenager. She didn't know a lot more about it than that. Gazing up at the series of tall, curved sections that made up its frontage, she wished she'd paid more attention. Maybe she would have learned something that would help her sneak inside and find Hans Jonte.

The security guards at the entrance would never allow her in. Why would they? What possible business could a raggedy fortune-teller have with the mayor? And, masquerading as morally compelled not to speak, she couldn't even try to persuade them.

If it had been nighttime, she might have stood a chance of killing them both without raising an alarm, but it was broad daylight and the street was full of people celebrating the mayor's inauguration. Also, the thought of murdering the two men turned her stomach. She was sick of all the death and pain she'd seen. Surely there would come a time when it had to stop?

She leaned on one of the curved, tiled walls, sheltering from a cold wind that had started up, and watched the guards checking passes and allowing visitors through the entrance. It looked like some kind of party was going on. The lucky attendees were dressed up, though in the usual handmade Crusader style. The men wore felted wool jackets and pants in matching colors, and the women were dressed in long, heavily embroidered frocks. She was reminded of her first customer, the young girl who dreamed of meeting Dwyr Perran Orr. Of course, she realized, the guards weren't checking passes, they were checking invitations.

The breeze funneling down the street suddenly stiffened, and she put her hands in her skirt pockets for warmth. Her right hand touched her cards.

That's it!

Stepping out from the shelter of the contoured facade, she quickly walked toward the entrance. As she passed in front of it, she threw up her arms dramatically, gave a loud wail, and fell to the ground, taking care not to fall too hard and hurt herself. Her eyes closed, she waited and hoped for a reaction.

She didn't wait long.

"Oh no!" a woman exclaimed.

Footsteps trotted to Taylan's side and she felt the presence of a figure kneeling beside her. Too late, she remembered she was supposed to be hiding her face. In her current position it was exposed. Never mind. It couldn't be helped.

"This woman's fainted!" her rescuer called out. "Can someone bring her some water or something?"

It was time to 'come around'.

Taylan opened her eyes and blinked as if recognizing her surroundings.

A concerned female face with deep green eyes hung over her and, beyond it, two men stood, watching. From their fine clothes, she guessed they were partygoers.

"Some water!" the woman called again. "Sebastian, get her some water!"

One of the men pulled a face before walking away.

"Are you feeling better?"

Feigning grogginess, Taylan sat up and put a hand to her cheek.

The woman squatted down to peer into her face. "You seem okay. Maybe you were a bit light-headed for a minute. Are you hungry? Have you eaten lately?"

Taylan was touched by her kindness. That was the thing that killed her about Crusaders. Most of them were normal and decent—though only when it came to their own kind, she reminded herself. She shook her head and drew a finger across her lips.

When the gesture only elicited a puzzled frown, she reached into her pocket and pulled out the card that explained her condition.

"I see," said the woman after reading it.

Her companion, Sebastian, had arrived with a cup of water. He crouched to give it to her, but Taylan waved it away. Scrabbling inside her bag, she retrieved a piece of paper and a pencil. Her months of practice had improved the speed and legibility of her handwriting. She scrawled a couple of sentences hastily, worried that, now she was 'better', she might lose the attention of the bystanders.

The woman's jaw dropped as she read. "You did?! That's so cool. What was it about?"

Taylan gave a little shake of her head and wrote another sentence.

"I guess that makes sense," said her rescuer, reading as Taylan wrote. She looked disappointed. "I'd ask you to whisper in my ear, but..." She giggled, embarrassed.

"What's going on?" asked Sebastian. "What did she say?"

"She didn't say anything. She can't talk. But we need to get her to the mayor."

"The mayor? Why?"

"I'll explain later. Come on, help me get her up."

He hesitated, looking doubtful.

"Sebastian! Help me."

Taylan supposed her attempts to look frail and helpless had to be working. The two Crusaders gripped her elbows and gently lifted her to her feet. As they escorted her to the town hall entrance, she pulled her headscarf forward so it hid her face. The guards might have seen her image when Dwyr Orr was searching for her.

The woman whispered to the guards as they checked her and Sebastian's invitations. They didn't look convinced, and Taylan feared they wouldn't let her in. But then they looked her up and down and apparently concluded a sickly fortune-teller couldn't do any harm. One of them handed back the invitations and gestured for the group of three to step inside.

Wall hangings depicting figures worshiping the former Dwyr in her horned headdress decorated the walls in the party room. Taylan guessed there hadn't been time to replace them with ones showing the new Dwyr yet. Thickly scented smoke from candles, incense, and weed had turned the atmosphere hazy. She could also smell barbecued meat and some kind of alcoholic spirit, maybe rum or brandy. The party was in full swing. The Crusaders were flushed, relaxed, and getting touchy with each other.

In the intervening time between seeing the mayor on his float and finally being admitted to his presence, Taylan had begun to second guess her conviction that he was Hans Jonte, former high official of the BA Government. But seeing him up close took away all her uncertainty. Even if she hadn't recognized him without his beard, the man had a way about him, a confident, charming manner, that was distinctive and hard to forget. She was surprised no Crusader had recognized him, but, then again, the cult followers were cut off from the world's media. They probably couldn't have picked Queen Alice out of a line up when she'd been alive. It was an excellent method of control, with obvious downsides.

She watched her rescuer approach the little knot of people fawning over the mayor, politely ease her way through, and lift her lips to his ear. The woman seemed known to him already as he didn't balk at this intimate behavior. Jonte's gaze met Taylan's across the crowded room. In different circumstances, it might almost have been romantic, but romance was the last thing on her mind. This man could hold the key to finding her children.

He appeared to demur. The woman insisted. Unable to hear what was said, Taylan felt like she was watching a mime show. His barrel chest heaved in a sigh, and he smiled graciously.

He agreed!

But, after bowing politely to his friends, he left the group and headed out of the room.

Her heart sank. He hadn't agreed after all.

"Don't look so glum," said the woman as she returned. "Joseph wants to hear what you have to say. Only not here. He's gone to his office. He'll see you there."

In her excitement, Taylan almost asked where it was. The question must have been obvious on her face, for the woman said, "It's okay. I'll take you to him."

Her curiosity mildly piqued as to who this woman was who was so close to Hans Jonte, Taylan followed her through the building. When they reached an ornate, solid door made from dark wood, she didn't knock before opening it. After ushering Taylan inside the room, she backed out and closed it.

Jonte sat behind a wide desk, a pained expression on his face. He had clearly only agreed to see her on sufferance, perhaps as a favor to the woman who seemed to have a close connection to him.

"Please take a seat," he said. "I can give you five minutes. Then I must return to the party. It would be rude of me to absent myself from my guests too long. I understand you're unable to speak. If you write your vision down, I'll read it later. Naturally, you'll be paid for your services."

What a smooth diplomat he was. It was obvious to both of them that he had no interest or belief in the flash of prophetic insight she claimed had come to her at the steps of the town hall, but he was willing to play along with the masquerade. He knew it was all fake, though he'd inferred the wrong reason. He thought she was scamming him, and, sensitive to Crusader ways, he was allowing her to. Pandering to their odd ideologies was worth more to him than the little money she would receive.

Taylan opened the door and peeked into the hall. It was empty. The woman had gone.

She closed the door and sat down across from the now-puzzled Jonte. She was fairly confident the room wasn't bugged. The EAC wouldn't bother spying on their own side.

She pulled her scarf down and announced, "I know who you are."

Jonte, who had been leaning back in his seat, his legs crossed and his hands clasped on his lap, sat upright. "What? She said...Miranda said..."

"I haven't taken a vow of silence. It's a disguise, like yours, Mr *Fry*."

Jonte's skin paled and he rubbed his chin, but he was taking the revelation in his stride.

"Who are you?" he asked.

"My name is Taylan Ellis. I'm a West BI native and a former Royal Marine."

"I see." His fingertips drummed his desk.

"I recognized you at the parade this afternoon. I know you're—"

"Shhh!! I don't want to hear it, and if you know what's good for you, you'll never mention your suspicions to anyone."

"Do you deny it?"

"Do you understand how dangerous it could be for you to be throwing around that kind of assertion? Imagine I was who you suppose me to be. How would you prove it?"

Taylan had a sudden sensation of uneasiness. "I would tell the Crusaders to check old news reports."

"Such information is not easily available to members of the EAC. And what makes you think I would let things get that far?" He fixed her with a glare. "Why would someone in my position allow it?"

Apprehension settled on her. He was right. He had all the power. She had none. She'd thought she could walk in and threaten to expose him if he didn't help her find her children. That had been stupid enough, but, worse, she'd revealed herself to him. If he didn't already know the significance of who she was, a cursory search of Crusader records would turn up her name in no time.

She began to get to her feet. Could she make it out of the building without being captured? Could she recall the way back to the entrance?

"Sit down," said Jonte. "I'm only trying to make you understand the dangerous path you're treading. Are you with the Resistance?"

"No. I..." She hung her head, remembering. "I was, but I... I've lost touch with them."

"Pity. I've been trying to get in contact with them, but it's hard. The higher you go in society, the more closely you're watched." He put a finger to his lips and frowned as he thought.

"Mr...Fry. What are you trying to do? Why are you here?"

"To answer that would require more time than we have. I

cannot stay away from the party much longer, and, besides, it's probably better that you don't know. But I could ask you the same question. You've winkled your way into my presence with your silly story of a vision concerning my future, but why? Was it only to make your accusation?"

"No. I was here when the invasion took place and I got separated from my kids. I've been trying to find them ever since."

"And you thought I could help you with that?"

She nodded.

His gaze remained on her, but his eyes became unfocused for several beats before he abruptly snapped back to attention. "Perhaps I may be able to uncover some useful information for you. But I want something in return. I want you to be my bridge to the West BI Resistance."

"But I don't know if I can—"

"That's my price. Take it or leave it. It shouldn't be too hard for someone in your position." He paused then exclaimed, "Ha! The vow of silence. It's because you can't do the accent, isn't it?"

"That's right. And you can?"

"Two of my grandparents were born in Berline. I speak the language, so the accent's a doddle."

"Lucky you," Taylan muttered.

"I must get back to the party. What do you say? Find the Resistance for me, and I'll try to find out what happened to your children. Is it a deal?"

"Do I have a choice?"

"Excellent." He pulled a drawer open and took out a wad of banknotes. Peeling off a few, he said, "These should make life a little easier for you." He slid the notes over the desk. "I'll have an usher show you out. Come back the same time next week. You can be my personal seer. The Crusaders will love it."

14

When Kala Orr felt on the edge of hysteria and utter despair, she would plan an event to celebrate the triumph of her return to glory. Crusader celebrations were always extravagant, but this one would be on a scale never before attempted and never to be repeated. She would imagine a breathtaking setting, such as a vast plain overlooking an ocean, and she would decide every aspect of the event down to the smallest detail; what luxurious and unusual dishes would be eaten and when, what innovative and mesmerizing entertainment would be provided, what drinks and drugs would be served to bring the participants to a fever of excitement and abandon. No item was too small for her attention.

Thus, unmeasured time passed in her sleepless nightmare of imprisonment. During moments when she couldn't block out unwanted thoughts regarding her position, she acknowledged that Morgan could not have thought up a crueler punishment. Not only was she cut off in every way from the real world, there was no foreseeable end to her sentence. She had no means to kill herself and escape her new and dreadful existence. She imagined Morgan must be keeping her body alive to prolong her mental agony.

Yet, despite everything, she was not cowed. She didn't fear her enemy. Her captivity within the walls of her mind had only nursed her flame of hatred until it was white hot. If she were ever given the opportunity to have her revenge, she would take great pleasure in exacting an equal and fitting retribution for what she'd suffered.

She was imagining the pyrotechnic display that would cap the event celebrating her return to power. Each effect and color had to be carefully thought out, as well as the sequence of the fireworks. A river of golden sparks would signal the commencement, rolling and bubbling over the ground. Fountains would rise up from the river before transforming into mythical beasts: a dragon, a unicorn, a gryphon, a phoenix, and a basilisk. The firework creatures would rise into the air, shedding shining embers, until, when they reached their zenith high in the atmosphere, they would shudder and explode, raining down in glittering, multi-colored showers before evaporating into mist and smoke.

Something touched her.

For the first time in an eon, she had felt a touch.

Instantly, she was forced out of her imagination and flung back to the terrible nothingness that was her existence.

Had she imagined it? Were the hallucinations starting up again? She had felt the touch on her shoulder, but she could not move to look in that direction.

"Hello?"

Deprived of hearing, she only felt her chest move and the faint vibration of her vocal cords as she spoke. In the beginning of her incarceration she had spoken often, hoping Perran might be able to hear her and he could persuade Morgan to set her free. But the experience of talking yet not hearing herself had been so disorienting and strange, she'd given up. Now, she had a feeling her voice was nothing more than a hoarse whisper.

"Hello," she repeated, more forcefully.

Sounds.

She could hear noises: rustling and a low, soft hum, almost too quiet to detect.

The darkness began to lift. It took on a deep red hue, highlighted with spots of brightness.

Next came the sensation of cloth on her skin. She was lying on her back, underneath a sheet.

"You did it," someone said. "She's waking up!" It was a man and he'd spoken in an unfamiliar accent. His voice seemed to come from her right.

"For all the good it'll do," said another man. His accent was different yet she still couldn't place it. "It's a waste of time," he went on.

Her relief and joy at being brought out of her horrifying ordeal overwhelmed her sense of confusion. She had no idea who these people were. Where was Morgan? Surely only she could have undone the curse?

She didn't care. It didn't matter. Nothing mattered. She was free at last.

A hand touched her shoulder. It had to be the same person who had touched her before, but the fingers felt small and the skin soft—a woman's hand.

"Can you hear me, Kala?" she asked.

The hand left her shoulder and then took Kala's hand in her own.

"If you can hear me, squeeze my hand."

"Ugh," said the second man who had spoken. "There's no point in any of this. Let's go. We have better things to do."

With a huge effort to activate her long-unused, weak muscles, Kala managed to move her hand a little.

"I think I felt something!" said the woman. "I think she can hear me."

"The two are not necessarily related. Some twitching of her muscles is to be expected, but—"

"Uhhhh..." Kala was attempting to say *I can hear you*, but all that came out was a voiced outward breath. She realized that when she'd been saying *Hello* before, she couldn't have been saying anything at all. It had been a figment of her isolated mind.

"You see?" the woman said. "She *can* hear me."

"Extremely unlikely."

"I don't know why you would say that. I've nursed several people back to consciousness who'd been in a coma. It takes them some time to return to full health, but they do eventually. There's no reason to think Kala won't do the same."

"There's every reason to think it," said the second man. The first had remained silent throughout the spat. "The people you've treated who were in a coma were unconscious most of the time. They may have dreamed a little, but that's it. This woman has been fully conscious for months while deprived of the input of all her senses. *Months*. She hasn't even slept. If you'd looked at her brain scans you would know that."

"That's not possible."

The first man finally spoke. "When it comes to the bewitchings of Morgan le Fay, anything is possible."

"Not quite," said his companion, "but in this case, that's what has happened. Imagine it. Utterly cut off from the outside world. No sights, sounds, tastes, smells, or sensations, no notion of the passage of time, not even the sense of your own body's spatial position, without pause and without the hope of escape. How long do you think *you* would last before losing your mind?"

The woman didn't reply.

"This is all moot now," said a fourth voice, another woman

older than the first. "Thank you for your efforts. The medical team can take over from here."

"Good luck to them," said the second man dismissively. "It would have been kinder to kill her."

There was the sound of a starship door opening and closing. *That* was what the soft hum was. It was the noise of the engine. So she was still aboard the *Belladonna*? In which case, who were these people? Who was the man who appeared to be the one responsible for restoring her to a normal state? Whoever it was, he was wrong. She hadn't lost her mind.

As the conversation had been going on, she'd been trying to open her eyes. At last, she succeeded. Everything looked unbearably bright and blurry.

"Uhhh...Wh..." She wanted to ask where she was, how long she'd been locked in her senseless state, who the people in her attendance were, but all she could utter was meaningless sounds.

"I'll get something to moisten your mouth," said the woman Kala now understood to be a nurse. "That'll make it easier for you to speak."

"How long will she take to recover?" asked the older woman.

"Depends what you mean by recover. That guy who brought her out of it had a point about her state of mind, but I *did* look at the brain scans and there's no sign of actual damage. Now she's getting better, she'll slip in and out of consciousness for a week or two, each time staying awake longer. We should have an idea about her mental fitness in three or four days. Physically, it'll be two months minimum before she can walk normally again. We do our best to keep the muscles exercised but some wastage is inevitable."

"Two months? We don't have that long."

15

"Opening valves, sir," said Jeong over the CUV's comm.

"Copy that," Wright replied.

Seawater began to pour into the chamber, swamping the deck and quickly rising up the sides of the CUV.

The *Resolute* carried four Uncrewed Underwater Vehicles but only one Crewed Underwater Vehicle. The boat was simply too small to hold any more. All the vehicles were stored in a chamber toward the stern that could be flooded for launches. The two-seater, transparent-hulled CUV was clamped to the center of the deck, while the UUVs were secured to the bulkheads.

Wright had decided to lead the mission to investigate the newly blasted, small harbor Ford had discovered. The lieutenant would be in charge during his absence. Strictly speaking, he should have sent his subordinate and remained on the boat himself, but since being sidelined due to his mental health crisis, sticking to the book didn't seem important anymore.

Besides, he reasoned, obtaining permission to deviate from protocol would have taken too long. If they were to catch the smugglers in the act they had to move fast, and the vessels they'd been tracking had disappeared from sonar readings a day ago.

He'd picked Abacha as his partner. The man was easy-going and had a calmness about him that indicated he wouldn't be rattled by a crisis. Wright didn't have much of an idea what to expect. The smugglers—if that's what they were—would outnumber the tiny crew of the *Resolute*, so any attempt to curtail their activities was out of the question. The plan was to conduct reconnaissance, but information on the terrain in that remote location was almost as slim as their knowledge of the foe they might be up against.

"Releasing clamps," said Jeong.

The chamber had filled to the overhead and the exit hatch was cranking open. With synchronized clunks the clamps opened. The CUV bobbed gently free. Wright started the engine and piloted the vessel out into the cloudy water of the Coral Sea.

"I've never been in this part of the world," Abacha commented. "It reminds me of home."

"And where's that?"

"A small island in the Caribbean. St. Kitts."

"The Caribbean? You must be glad we got it back."

"Yes, though..." Abacha gave him a sidelong look.

"What?"

"It doesn't matter."

"You can speak freely, Corporal," said Wright. "Nothing you say will go any further."

The Alliance probably had no interest in either of their opinions anyway.

"Life under the BA is better than life under the EAC, but the people of the islands would prefer to have no master."

"I thought it was something like that. Don't worry. That isn't news to me. I met plenty of Resistance fighters on Jamaica who felt the same. But without the Alliance, could the Caribbean protect itself?"

"That's the problem. In the current state of the world, we're too weak. But what has the BA done to build us up? It suits its purposes to keep us at a disadvantage. That way, we'll always need Alliance help, and its leaders will always be able to exploit us."

Sunbeams glittered through the water above them. Wright had been taking them higher, planning on getting a visual on the mysterious vessels if he could find them. The CUV's scanners were not currently registering anything out of the ordinary.

"I don't know what to tell you," he said. "I signed up because I'd decided the Alliance was a force for good, and all I had to do to make the world a better place was to follow orders. But lately I've come to realize things aren't so simple."

"That's right, they're not. For me, enlisting was my way off the island, and it meant I could send money home regularly to help my folks. But if I had a choice, I wouldn't fight. I would have done something else with my life."

"Like what?"

"Who knows? I never really thought about it. No point."

"Is there money in xiangqi?"

Abacha grinned. "Now there's an idea. There might be, if the world is ever at peace."

"You could be a grandmaster. Whoa, I think we have something." As Wright had been speaking, a shape had appeared in the scanner display. "What do you think that is?"

The little CUV's computer couldn't interpret the data in the way the *Resolute's* could.

"It's too pointy for a whale," Abacha replied.

"Let's take a closer look."

Wright turned their vehicle south-west and even higher.

The scanner readings said the object was sitting at or just beneath the surface.

"It's gotta be a boat," he muttered. "And it's heading away from the harbor Ford discovered, out to sea."

"That leaves three still in port."

"Yeah, unless they left before we got here."

"Wouldn't the sonar have picked them up?"

"Not necessarily. I think we were lucky to find them in the first place. The passive sonar stations on the seabed never registered anything before. It might have been only because the *Resolute* was looking in the right place at the right time that we noticed them."

"Or it's their first run."

"If it is, I want to make it their last."

The water grew clearer the nearer they got to the surface. Fish appeared on the edges of their visual range, hastily flicking their tails and swimming away at the CUV's approach.

"What was that?!" Abacha exclaimed as a large gray shape passed into and out of view.

Before Wright could answer, the creature reappeared: a dolphin. It swam boldly closer and peered in through the transparent hull. Then it began to keep pace with their vehicle's progress, circling, passing beneath them and coming up the other side.

"Ha," said Abacha. "Looks like we made a friend."

The dolphin suddenly veered away and was gone.

"I spoke too soon."

"Look at that," said Wright.

In the distance, hanging below the waterline, was a ship's hull. Ford had been correct. She was wooden, the planks overlapping and festooned with barnacles. According to the scanner readings, she measured 24 meters long, so not a small ship. How had she evaded detection by Alliance satellites, which tracked all shipping in Oceania's waters?

According to the scanner data, the ship was moving at six knots and heading out to sea. Extrapolating from her current trajectory led to the same gap in the reef the original four ships had passed through. She must have unloaded or picked up her cargo and was now returning home, wherever that was.

"What are you going to do?" Abacha asked.

The CUV was unarmed, so sinking the smuggler's ship was off the table. Wright wasn't sure he wanted to anyway. If attacked, the smugglers would just restart their business somewhere else. For a long-term solution, it would be better to find out more about their operation. They had to be bringing in or taking out contraband. If he could find out what they were smuggling, then the Australian authorities could tackle the problem inside the country.

"This," he replied, pressing a button.

A projectile flew from a small launcher on the side of the CUV. The tag hit the bottom of the ship, its barbs biting into the wood. Nothing would dislodge it now, not most inquisitive fish or the roughest seas. Wright checked the CUV's interface. A regularly repeating blip appeared on the screen. Thousands of kilometers above, Alliance satellites would be recording the same signal. Wherever the ship went, the BA would be able to track it.

"Now let's check out that harbor."

16

Hugging her knees for warmth, Taylan squatted under a small tree. Its branches hung down to the ground. Though many of the leaves had turned autumn colors, enough remained clinging on to obscure her presence from any except the keenest observers. Not that there were many people about in the Preseli Hills. She guessed the area had retained its cursed reputation, due to the number of Crusaders who had gone 'missing' here.

Raindrops dripped from the canopy, hitting the centuries-old leaf mold in steady *plop plop plops*. The tree offered only partial protection from the downpour, and Crusader clothes were shit at keeping out the rain. She wistfully recalled the travel gear the Resistance had lent her the first time she'd set off to find her children. The West BI men and women had been generous despite the scarcity of their resources. Now she had to see them again, she didn't think her reception would be so friendly.

How long had she been waiting? She guessed it had to be three or four hours. In another hour it would be dawn and she would have to find somewhere to wait out the day. The Resistance did most of their work at night.

Her leg muscles were cramping and her hands were turning numb. She stood up and stretched, then rubbed her hands together to bring some warmth into them. A fat raindrop made it through the canopy and slapped into the top of her head. The icy trickle ran down her scalp.

Ugh.

She shivered. She didn't fancy another night of this. It rained so much this time of…

What was that?

Above the sound of rain the soft tramp of boots could be heard. Three or four people were walking along the track on the rise beyond the tree.

She whistled, hoping she got it right. She'd been practicing but she was doing it from memory. The whistle was like bird song, only no bird made that sound.

There was a murmur of voices, and one set of footsteps split from the rest.

She peeked out. A dark, lanky figure was approaching, taking long strides down the slope.

Yes!

The man's companions were walking on, but slowly. She didn't dare risk coming out of hiding until they were out of sight.

"Taylan?" Marc whispered.

"I'm here. Under the tree."

He lifted a soggy branch.

"Come in. I don't want to be seen."

Marc was hooded against the rain, but she could make out his young features in shadow. The sight of him gladdened her heart. He was whole and healthy. Merlin had kept his promise and healed him.

"It's good to see you," he said.

"And you, more than you know. I didn't think you would recognize the call."

On their trip to Ynys Môn to sabotage the Crusader festival, Marc, his brothers, and Taylan had devised a birdlike whistle to use if they were ever separated.

"I nearly didn't. I just thought it was early for any birds to be singing, and then I thought, that bird sounded like it was being strangled too. It was then I knew it had to be you."

Taylan laughed quietly. "Come here." She hugged him. "It's good to see you're better. I'm so sorry—"

"No. It was my decision to help you gather up the incendiaries, and going for that last one was my own stupid fault. Don't blame yourself."

She didn't know what to reply. She *did* blame herself, and she knew she always would no matter what he said.

"And I was healed by the great Merlin and got to meet King Arthur!" Marc went on. "So everything turned out all right in the end."

He was making light of what had happened. She'd witnessed the agony he'd endured, and would have had to endure for the rest of his life if she hadn't happened to have a bargaining chip with the alien.

"It's good to see you, Taylan. But what are you doing here? I can't stay long. I told the others I had to answer a call of nature."

"Who's with you? Some of your brothers?"

"No, they're all at the hideout. We changed location, by the way. If you'd gone to the old place, you wouldn't have found us."

"I'm not sure I'm looking for you now."

"What do you mean?"

"The reason I came to find you on the trail was I thought if I turned up out of the blue at the hideout I might be lynched."

"Oh, come on, Taylan. As if anyone would do anything like

that." He paused and considered before continuing, "Well, maybe Medwyn might." His teeth flashed white in the pre-dawn light as he grinned. "Only joking."

"*Marc!*" A voice softly called. One of the men had walked back to where Marc had left the trail. "What's keeping you? Shitting your guts out?"

"I'll be with you in a minute," he replied. To Taylan, he said quietly, "I have to go. But...come with me. I'll introduce you to the fellas. It'll be okay. No harm was done in the end, and what happened at the midsummer festival is old news now."

"But will everyone trust me again after what I did?"

"What *we* did."

"Yeah, but your brothers think I put you up to it, don't they? They think I was a bad influence on you."

His silence confirmed her fears.

"I need them to trust me."

∽

THE WEST BI RESISTANCE in that part of the country was holed up in a church's crypt deep within the Preseli Hills. The church itself was little more than ruins. The rosy dawn that had followed the rain shone through skeletal, glassless, arched windows and an absent roof. But the crypt had survived intact, along with the tombs of priests who had died thousands of years ago and gravestone coverings of bodies buried directly in the floor.

One of Marc's companions, a man named Tom, had given the password that allowed him, Taylan, Marc, and the third man, Alun, into the hideout. After Marc explained who she was, Tom and Alun hadn't spoken much on the journey to the crypt. She had the impression they didn't approve of Marc's invitation to her. It was the custom in her culture to be friendly to strangers, and she wasn't even a stranger, strictly speaking.

She was one of them. Only, she supposed, they might not see it like that anymore.

Her arrival had caused a stir. The people in the hideout hadn't been slow to notice that the party that had gone out to watch the comings and goings at a Crusader military camp—with a view to stealing some equipment—had returned with an extra member. Quiet settled on the large stone chamber as gazes turned to check out the newcomer.

"Not that bitch!"

Taylan would have recognized Medwyn's voice anywhere, even without the hatred for her in it.

There was a flash of movement, and she just had time to duck. His fist swept the place her head had been a moment before. She leaned sharply to one side as his other fist came swinging toward her face.

She did not want to fight this man, let alone hurt him. She genuinely didn't wish him any harm, despite the animosity he'd displayed ever since they'd met, but also, it wouldn't help her image here.

Catching the man's wrist, she said, "Calm down! I only want to—"

His other fist headed for her jaw. She deflected his arm and, grabbing it, stepped behind him, twisting it up his back. Medwyn roared and struggled.

"No fighting in the hideout!" a voice yelled. It was Meilyr, oldest of the siblings. "Taylan, let him go. Medwyn, if you try to hit her again, I'll knock you down myself."

She released her hold. With visible effort at controlling himself, Medwyn turned his attention elsewhere.

"What the hell do you think you're doing bringing *her* here?!" He pushed his face close to Marc's. "She's got you under her spell again. What did she do? Flash her tits at you? Or did you get further this time?"

Marc's fist shot out and connected with Medwyn's chin, catching the older man by surprise and flooring him.

"You're disgusting!" Marc shouted, standing over him.

Medwyn was rubbing his jaw, but he quickly leapt up and was about to retaliate when Meilyr restrained him.

"That's enough! Marc, apologize to your brother."

Medwyn was struggling in his grip, red-faced, probably with both anger and embarrassment.

"But he insulted—" Marc protested.

"Apologize!"

With reluctance, Marc murmured, "Sorry, Medwyn."

This seemed to mollify him a little. Meilyr judged it safe to let him go. When he was released, Medwyn stalked to another corner of the crypt, where he kicked a pile of clothes stacked on the floor.

"Taylan Ellis," said Meilyr. "I see you've come to sow discord among my family again."

She hung her head. It was exactly the greeting she deserved, though nothing of what had happened between the brothers had been her intention.

"That isn't fair," Marc protested. "I've told you all often enough I helped her of my own free will and I would again. She was right when she—"

"Why don't you shut up and let her speak for herself?" asked Madog as he sauntered over. He took a bite from a piece of bread and glared at Taylan expectantly.

Marc clenched his jaw and turned away.

"I have an apology to make too," she said. "I didn't get a chance on Ynys Môn. It was too soon after the accident and I was hurt. Then we all left. We wanted to get out of there as soon as we could. I'm not sorry for what *I* did, but I regret Marc being dragged into it all and injured. I regret that a lot, and I was glad I had the chance to fix my mistake.

"I know you must all hate me for preventing the sabotage, yet I can't stand here and say I wouldn't do it again because I would, in a heartbeat. I won't hurt Crusader children, and I'd think twice about hurting the civilians. I've been living among them for weeks now. They're just people, like us. They have some strange beliefs and customs, but they aren't that different from you or me."

"All right!" Meilyr interrupted angrily. "You've said enough. If you've come here to plead the Crusaders' cause, you can—"

"I haven't! Let me finish. Even if they are only ordinary people, they have no right to be here. I want them out of the BI the same as you do. And I think I know the way. I met someone who can help you. He's working in secret on behalf of the Alliance and he wants to get in contact. That's the only reason I'm here. Otherwise, believe me, I'd never show my face again."

"Why hasn't he come here himself?" Medwyn growled from the shadows.

"He can't. He's in a high position. Someone would notice."

"Why should we believe you?" asked Madog.

"I don't know. I don't know what I can show you as proof. You know Crusader society. They don't have the technology to—"

"Then you can piss off," said Medwyn. "You're a traitor, as everyone knows. We'd be mad to trust you again."

Taylan looked at Meilyr. As the oldest brother and one of the founders of the Resistance along with his mother, Angharad, his siblings and the other Resistance fighters generally let him have the final say.

Before he could speak, however, she said, "You told me once that we shouldn't act alone, that the only way we'll get our country back is if we act together, as a group. I'm bringing you the opportunity to join forces with someone who has real power in the Crusader world. He's tapped into their inner circles and has inside knowledge. Let me help you work with him."

17

There they were: three wooden ships riding at anchor just outside the harbor. At first, Wright had wondered why they hadn't entered the harbor and docked. But closer investigation revealed the space wasn't even large enough to accommodate one of the wooden sailing ships. It was also rocky and dangerously unstable, the result of hasty and inexpert blasting.

He was getting a strong impression of who was responsible for the illegal activity, but he still had no clue what exactly it was they were doing.

"What now?" asked Abacha.

The three hulls hung above them, bobbing on the swell, their long anchor chains stretching out to the sea bed.

"If we had scuba equipment we could climb aboard one of them and try to find out what they're carrying," Wright mused, speaking partly to himself.

Abacha didn't reply. The impediment was obvious—with or without scuba equipment, they couldn't open the CUV without flooding the vehicle with water, thus disabling their ride back to the *Resolute*. The only alternative seemed to be to leave, to return to the patrol boat with the intelligence they'd gathered and send in a report. Then await orders on how to proceed. Perhaps the Australian authorities would decide to tackle the problem at their end, and the *Resolute's* involvement would be over.

The possibility he might have no more to do with this intriguing mystery galled Wright. It was the most interesting thing he'd done for a long while, and since they'd been following the smugglers' ships, he hadn't had a single flashback or nightmare about his time in Jamaica. He didn't want to hand over the reins if he could help it.

He squinted upward, checking the level of daylight glowing through the waves.

"It isn't long until sunset," he said.

Abacha checked the CUV's control panel. "Seventy-two minutes."

Wright also consulted the figures displayed. "We have plenty of oxygen left, and the tide's on its way in. I have a risky idea, but if you don't like the sound of it, I won't make it an order."

Abacha's left eyebrow lifted. "Sounds like fun."

∼

BEACHING the CUV was harder than he'd anticipated, and dragging it up the sand was even harder. Though the vehicle was small, it was surprisingly heavy, and, unsurprisingly, it wasn't designed for maneuvering out of water. Eventually, they managed to get it under the palm trees that fringed the beach and covered with fallen fronds. By the time they finished, they were wet with seawater and sweat.

Wright looked ruefully at the long trail they'd left all the way down to the water, a mixture of their footprints and lines drawn by the protrusions on the base of the CUV. The Moon was already up and nearly full. Anyone with half a brain could follow the trail and find the vehicle.

"Come on," he said reluctantly to Abacha. "We have to get rid of that before we leave."

They dragged palm leaves over the dry sand, obscuring the evidence of their presence, but it was harder to erase the trail through the wet sand. Anything they did to it still stuck out in the otherwise smooth expanse.

Wright paused in his efforts and swept the surroundings with his gaze. The forest was dark and still in the breeze-less night, and though it wasn't silent, none of the noises sounded like they were made by humans. He looked out to sea—and sucked in a breath. The smugglers' ships should have been visible from the shore, but he couldn't see a sign of them.

Since they'd beached the CUV, he'd been preoccupied with hiding it and covering their trail. He hadn't thought to check out the ships.

"Abacha," he said. "Can you see anything out there?"

The tall man lifted his head. "No, Major. Not a thing. I guess the ships haven't lit any lights because they're trying to hide."

"But we should be able to see *something*. The night isn't dark."

"Uh huh. Yeah, we should." Abacha's brow wrinkled. "Maybe they sailed away."

"Shit." Wright threw down his frond. But after a moment of frustration, he said, "It doesn't matter. We've done what we can to cover our tracks. Let's go take a look at that harbor."

They walked up the beach and stepped into the forest. Once they were under the trees, the heat and humidity became intense. After ten minutes' effort, both men were drenched in sweat and panting. The going was tough. The area was uninhabited, and clearly nothing large lived in the forest to create passages between the trees. They were forced to wade through chest-high undergrowth, using only their bodies to clear a path.

They were also quickly disoriented once they were out of sight of the Moon, and had to halt regularly to get their bearings and avoid walking in circles. Sounds of animal life scattering at their approach came from the vegetation. Wright tried to not think about the venomous snakes and spiders native to the area.

The harbor sat less than three kilometers from the beach where they'd left the CUV, over a forested headland, but he contemplated giving up. He'd realized how quickly his little expedition could turn into a disaster.

Just as he was about to call it a day—or night—they burst into an open space. Ever since they'd set foot in the forest, it had been a constant battle against the vegetation. Now, suddenly, there was emptiness, though the jungle quickly closed in on the other side.

"A track!" Abacha blurted.

Stretching into the forest to their left and right was an unmistakable trail. No animal prints marked the channel through the leaf mold and, from its orientation, one direction led to the harbor. The other led west into the interior.

They set off toward the harbor.

The humidity and rich odor of woody decay remained the same, but the heat decreased just a little as they went forward. Air was moving up from the sea to higher ground through the gap in the forest, evaporating some of the sweat that coated them.

The track led sharply down and soon the sound of waves on rocks could be heard over the nocturnal calls of animals. Their first sight of their destination was a gigantic rock that barred their way. The rock was jagged and its surface not weathered, as if it had been recently dug—or blown—from the ground. Yet vegetation had grown up around it lush and tall. Wright guessed it must have been there two or three years at least. The trail led around it.

On the other side, a vista opened up.

They were standing twenty meters above the sea. The path dropped out of sight along a cliff edge that led down to the water and a chaotic mess of rocks and sand. The inexpert blasting had created a hollow in the coastline but not much more than that. It was no surprise the smugglers didn't trust their ships to the turbulent flow and sharp edges of the space.

Wright's suspicions were confirmed. "There's no way this is anything to do with the AP. This kind of bodge job is Crusader work."

"I don't get it," said Abacha. "They could anchor out at sea and come to shore by rowboat. They could land on a beach, the same as we did."

"I don't get it either," Wright agreed. "But as they seem to have left, we aren't likely to find out anything more. We should head back."

"Wait," Abacha hissed. "Look!"

The moonlight was glinting heavily on the waves, turning them into a mass of sparkles, but it was just possible to discern a disturbance in the display. Something was coming through the harbor entrance. Wright peered down more intently.

It was a rowboat, bucking and rolling on the heaving water.

The smugglers hadn't left.

"Maybe they moved their ships farther out to sea?" Abacha offered.

"And given themselves more work to row in? None of this makes any sense."

The rowboat swept into the harbor, the flowing tide aiding its progress.

"Great," said Wright. "Maybe we can see what they're smuggling. Let's get out of sight."

They found a patch of thick undergrowth on the forested side of the large boulder from which they could watch the trail. Wright had considered watching the goings-on below after the rowboat landed but he didn't want to risk even the slight chance they might be seen. Instead, they waited in the darkness and closeness of the vegetation. *Things* were crawling around them and occasionally on them and they were entirely at the mercy of mosquitoes endlessly plaguing them.

An eternity seemed to pass in their uncomfortable vantage point before they were finally rewarded by the sound of people approaching. There were no voices, only the soft tramp of feet. Wright leaned forward. He could see about two square meters of track. He'd already concluded that whatever the contraband was, it had to be fairly portable, something light the smugglers could carry up or down the steep trail. He expected to only see bags or boxes being transported, though he hoped he might get a glimpse of something more.

What he actually saw when the people passed by flummoxed him. He watched until the party had traversed the section he had in sight and then waited until they would be out of hearing range.

He asked, "What did you see, Abacha? Tell me I wasn't seeing things."

"No. I saw them too. Kids. The Crusaders are trafficking children."

18

The revivification process had taken hours. Xiao, head of Cryonic Suspension, was present to oversee the procedure, the first in a range of tests to be completed before the colony ships departed. The problem was, though the breakthrough in the science of cryonics had been made two decades ago—the discovery of a solution that could replace water in animal cells and not swell and burst the cell walls when below freezing—no subject had been held in suspension for longer than twenty-six months before being revived. The long journey to the stars could entail much longer periods of freezing if the colonists were not to grow old and die before they reached their destination.

Despite the momentous nature of the occasion and the fact he was only witnessing the final stage, Lorcan was growing bored. Part of his success in life had been due to his short attention span. He was always pushing for something new and better and could hold many concepts in his mind simultaneously. Standing and watching the reanimation of the first test subject to be revived after fifteen years of suspension was tedious. He would much rather have continued his inspection of the *Banba*, only Hale had wanted to witness the event and he guessed Xiao probably wanted him there too, as recognition for the man's admittedly exceptional work.

First, the body had been warmed to an internal temperature of thirty-five degrees C, a little below normal temperature, by irrigating its cavities with warm water and running the solution in its veins through a warming device. Then the slow process of replacing the cryonic solution with water had begun. Now that all the solution had diffused out, it was time to replace the water running in the circulatory system with warmed artificial blood. Using artificial blood was easier than storing the blood removed from the body when it entered suspension.

"Internal temperature thirty-six point five," Xiao read from the display. "Nearly there."

"When will you start the heart?" Lorcan asked.

"If the temperature stabilizes, another hour or so. I prefer to be cautious, especially with these long-term patients. The blood is already circulating so the cells are receiving nutrients and oxygen. Hopefully, the other organs will begin to show signs of life soon."

"Have you had any failures?" asked Iolani.

"We have seen some organ failures. The kidneys seem the most susceptible to damage, but we can grow new ones in a couple of weeks and transplant them. Cognitive function is tricky to measure in these subjects, of course, but the brain seems to endure the process well, perhaps due to its high fat content. No deaths since the early days, thankfully."

"Xiao is the best," Lorcan commented. "That's why he's here."

"How does it make you feel," Iolani asked him, "knowing this will be you one day?"

He regarded the pig and the masses of tubes and sensors extending from it. After being taken from its suspension chamber a blue, stiff, corpse-like body, the creature now looked as fresh and healthy as it must have the day it was frozen. Yet, as Xiao had said, determining the effect on the brain was difficult. Human subjects had come out of a suspension of two years mentally unaffected, and apes had been frozen for longer with similar undetectable effects. The human volunteers aboard the *Banba* had entered their chambers ten years ago, but no attempt to revive them had been made.

"I confess I'm not entirely comfortable with the prospect," he eventually replied. "I see it as a necessary risk and inconvenience if I am to live out the remainder of my days on an alien world. Once we've arrived, I doubt anyone will be hurrying to start up cryonic suspension again. The initial drive behind its invention—the possibility of future cures for incurable diseases and the desire to see the future—these won't apply on the colony planets. For the first few decades, life will be about survival and establishing humanity's new homes, and people will be living in the future, not wishing for it."

"I wonder if Camilla and Anders would change their minds if they knew exactly what was involved?" Iolani mused.

The two scientists had recently agreed to join the Project as colonists, much to Lorcan's delight. He'd been a little foolish regarding his feelings for Camilla. Her likeness to Grace had made him sentimental and nostalgic, but now he knew she and Anders were a couple, he'd put all that to one side. The presence of two such intelligent and capable people—especially the people who were responsible for key elements of the Project—would be invaluable.

"For the human patients, the process would naturally be more dignified," Xiao explained, "and they would never be brought to consciousness in this state. Even this subject will spend a couple of days recuperating before we bring her out of sedation. All the colonists will be aware of is going to sleep in a regular hospital bed and then waking up in a similar bed years later. Perhaps they'll feel groggy and disoriented for a while, but hopefully nothing worse than that."

"I suppose it all depends on your perspective," said Iolani.

Lorcan had given up hope that Hale might agree to becoming a colonist. He no longer asked her, not even jokingly. He'd accepted that she loved and cared for their home planet too much to leave it.

"Perhaps we could return later to witness the reawakening?" he suggested. "I have a few other things I'd like to see before we move on to the *Balor*."

"Go ahead," Xiao replied. "Nothing interesting will be happening here for a while."

The three colony ships were not identical. Lorcan had realized long ago that many of his customers wanted to live aboard a starship as much as, or even more than, they wanted to live on a new world. He knew he had to sell the experience of traveling to the planets as well as the colonization. So he'd created a unique profile of facilities and configurations for each colony ship.

The *Banba's* selling point was her observation dome. Each ship had an observation deck—what passenger could resist the prospect of looking out upon strange stars and constellations?—but the *Banba's* dome was something special. For some time, it had seemed the vision of a 50-meter-diameter circular room with an overarching, transparent roof could not be achieved. No combination of material and supporting structures could be found that would withstand the air pressure and the potential impacts of space debris, as well as protect the occupants from the deadly rays of interstellar space. Then had come the invention of a ceramic created with aluminum compounds that, triple-layered with water sandwiched between the layers, could achieve the desired effect.

When Lorcan and Iolani arrived at the dome, it was nearing

completion but hadn't been sealed yet. To observe the work, they had to wear EVA suits.

"This is a first!" Iolani remarked as she stepped into the legs of a suit.

They came in different sizes and she'd selected the smallest one, yet it was still a little too big for her. When she pulled it over her shoulders and fastened the front zippers, it sagged down between her legs.

"And it might be a last," she continued. "Don't they make any smaller ones?"

Lorcan kept a straight face. "Starship technicians are generally bigger than average. Even with drones, they frequently end up having to haul things around."

Iolani gave a disgruntled look as she reached for a helmet. "Let's make this quick. There can't be much of interest to see out there."

Suited up and the READY sign on their HUDs signaling it was safe to step out into the vacuum, they walked into the airlock. Two minutes later it had depressurized. The outer hatch opened and on the other side the section's chief engineer waited.

"Ua Talman," he said via comm. "It's a pleasure to see you here. I have your tethers." A-grav hadn't been activated inside the chamber yet, in order to make the transportation and securing of the heavy transparent roofing blocks easier. The engineer held up two extendable leashes with locks at the ends. "I'll fasten yours first, Ms Hale."

He attached the lock to a ring at the front of Iolani's suit, but she wasn't paying him any attention. She was staring at what lay behind him, her mouth hanging open.

"And now you, sir," said the engineer.

"Thanks," said Lorcan.

"Please stick to the rails. If one of you got loose we could probably catch you again before you floated off into space, but I'd rather not have to try."

Their tethers were attached to handrails that ran around the inner surface of the nearly completed roof. The workers got around by releasing propellant from nozzles on their wrists and a pack on their backs, but it took time to learn how to control one's motion in this way, hence the tethers for visitors.

Iolani was already pulling herself along a rail, heading up toward the top of the structure.

Above them, a brilliant canopy of stars shone down. The technicians had lights focused on their work, but the drones moving the blocks didn't require any. Naturally, there was also no atmosphere between them and the stars. The stellar night had little competition.

When the dome was finished, it was certainly going to be spectacular. Lorcan began to wonder if he should travel aboard this ship and not the *Bres*.

"What do you think?" he asked, catching up to Iolani.

When she turned to him, he was surprised to see through her visor that her eyes were shining and her cheeks were wet.

"I had no idea..." she breathed. "I never imagined..." She didn't, or couldn't, go on.

They pulled themselves to the top of the structure where they hung for some minutes, looking out into space. Lorcan explained how to use the HUD to identify the planets and stars. He enjoyed watching Iolani's face as she gazed in wonder almost as much as he enjoyed seeing the starscape himself. In the months since making her acquaintance, his experience of her had been mostly negative. He'd never seen her show such delight and wonder. Being next to her reminded him of his own feelings during the early days of the Project.

Xiao comm'd to let them know he was about to move onto the next stage of the revivification process. They began to make their way back to the airlock. Only about one-eighth of the roof remained to be fitted and all work seemed to be progressing well. Lorcan thanked the chief engineer and congratulated him on the efforts of his team.

"Thank you, sir," he replied. "I'll pass your comments on."

As Lorcan and Iolani were getting changed, he said, "You know, I think I've decided I will commit some of the Project's resources to the Alliance's scheme."

"That's great. If you can help them, it'll make a big difference."

"I know. It's risky and I'm not confident they'll win, but it seems the right thing to do."

"It *is* the right thing to do," said Iolani. She didn't follow up with a lecture, however, for which he was grateful.

By the time they returned to the cryonics section, most of the sensors and several of the tubes had been removed from the pig. She lay on her side on the stainless steel platform, eyes closed, tongue lolling, pink udders jutting from her belly.

"We start the heart," said Xiao, "then extubate. Breathing should re-establish soon after."

Electrodes were already attached to the animal's skin in the region of her heart. Several medics stood by. Lorcan wondered if any farm animal ever received so much attention.

Xiao pressed his interface, and the pig jerked.

"Hmm," the scientist commented, frowning at the screen, "usually works first try." He pressed again. A tense couple of seconds passed. "Ah yes. Good. Let's move on to extubation."

19

Hans lay back and relaxed in his chair as the barber draped a hot, scented, steaming cloth over his face.

"Just the usual today, Mayor?"

Beneath the cloth, Hans smiled. He was still getting used to his new honorific.

"Yes, just the usual."

"Then I'll be with you in a moment."

The barber's footsteps retreated as he went to do something while the warm steam from the cloth took effect.

Hans breathed in the sandalwood odor and exhaled deeply, enjoying this respite from his busy day. Being Mayor of Abertawe was surprisingly taxing. He'd thought the role was mostly ceremonial and he would have plenty of time to use his position to push even deeper into the EAC's circles of influence, but actually he'd found there was always a meeting to attend, a new venue to officially open, or some other business to attend to. The event he was waiting for, which would allow him to introduce himself to the new Dwyr, had not appeared on the horizon yet.

He could bide his time. He'd made amazing progress since

walking ashore with only a fake identity and a few coins sewn into his turn ups. Crusaders were easy to beguile, and the fact that they'd only invaded the country a couple of years ago had made it easy to assimilate. The incomers had arrived from all over the continent, so strangers were nothing new. As long as you had the right accent and espoused the right opinions, no one questioned your story.

He'd had fun making up the tale of his background, refining and embellishing it at every telling. He was the fourth and last son of a wealthy wool merchant. His father's business had been passed to the first son, and the second and third had inherited key, lucrative roles. Nothing had been left for him, so he'd set out to the new lands of the Britannic Isles to make his fortune. It was like a fairy tale, but that was no problem. Such stories deeply appealed to the Crusader psyche, and in a society that employed almost no technology, it was nigh on impossible for anyone to verify.

When he'd understood his fabrication had hit a resonating chord, he added a younger sister, a widow with four children to support. She'd fallen out with the other brothers because they'd disapproved of her choice of husband and now they refused to support her. So it was down to her only other sibling, Joseph, to keep the family housed and fed.

The Crusaders ate it up. Generosity to those less fortunate than themselves was a key aspect of the culture. He'd soon found himself showered with offers of work and accommodation. Some individuals even slipped him money now and then, *to send to poor Eva and the kids*. Had Eva existed, she would have done very well. As it was, the donations had helped to smooth Hans's rise to prominence in the small city.

The cloth was suddenly whipped from his face. Deep in his recollections, he hadn't heard the barber return. A fat brush full of shaving cream was pushed into his cheek and rapidly circulated over his face. The brush disappeared, and then the barber began to softly hum a tune as he drew the razor over Hans's skin.

"Joseph!" a female voice called. "I'm so sorry to disturb you, but may I come in?"

It was Esme Weber.

Hans waited for the barber to pause and lift the razor away from his face before replying, "Of course, Esme. It's always a delight to see you."

Nothing could have been further from the truth. The woman had developed an obsession for him and was always making up excuses to see him in person, bothering him at all hours with her inane chatter. Ordinarily, he wouldn't have minded too much and, in an Alliance-held state, he would have gently steered her toward a mental health professional. But in his current guise, anyone as close to him as Esme wanted to be was a liability. He wasn't so good an actor that he might not one day forget his fake name and not answer to it, or make another slip that might jeopardize his schemes. He couldn't afford to allow anyone to get to know him too well.

On the other hand, Esme was connected to a network of powerful people and, even more importantly, she'd brought Taylan Ellis to him. Ellis, West BI native, in her weird, ridiculous costume, could end up being the most vital connection he would make in his effort to return the Britannic Isles to its people. When he'd helped to achieve that goal, his influence within the BA would be strong. He would be the prodigal son returned to take his rightful place, and to set the Alliance on the road to becoming a republic.

Esme stepped into view.

Her eyes were striking: intensely green with a hint of madness.

The barber gently pushed his nose to one side and scraped the razor down to his upper lip.

Esme seemed excited about something. "Your receptionist

was being very stubborn. I had to argue with her for five minutes before she would let me in."

In an irritated tone, the barber asked, "Would you like me to come back later, sir?"

"No, please finish. Esme, could you excuse me for a moment?"

"It's fine. I have something to tell you. Your barber can work while I speak."

With a barely audible tut, the barber pushed Hans's nose to the other side and shaved under it.

Esme settled herself down on a chair and smoothed her skirt. "I have some wonderful news. That's why I'm here so early. I wanted to tell you right away."

Hans lifted his chin for his neck to be shaved as he listened.

"You remember I told you Sebastian was going to pay a visit to his mother last week?"

His ears pricked up.

"Well, he got back this morning. He took the overnight coach. He was exhausted, poor man. But he didn't want to wait, and I'm so glad he didn't. He arranged it! He said there's to be a meeting of the BI High Council in ten days, and you're invited. The letter should arrive today."

"Excellent," he murmured, barely moving his lips.

The barber scraped the razor down from his left sideburn, and then rinsed it in a bowl of water. He took a warm, wet towel and wiped the remaining shaving foam from Hans's face as Esme chattered on.

"Is there anything else I can do for you, sir?" he asked, raising his voice to compete with Hans's visitor's. "A cologne, perhaps?"

Hans hesitated. "No, not today, Becker. That's all, thanks."

The barber noisily tidied up his metal bowls, comb, brushes, and scissors before leaving in a huff, apparently annoyed at his morning ritual with the new mayor being disrupted. He was an overly sensitive man, but he did a good job.

After he'd left, Hans sat up and asked Esme to repeat what she'd just told him. Without missing a beat, she set off on her ramble again. If he'd learned one thing about her, it was that she loved the sound of her own voice.

"So after Sebastian found out about the meeting, he naturally suggested it would be a good idea for you to attend. His mother was reluctant to do anything at first. She said if your name wasn't on the list there wasn't anything she could do about it, that it wasn't up to her who was or wasn't invited, it was up to the Dwyr. But, he's just a child! How would he know who he wanted in his Council?"

Esme's husband's mother was seneschal at the estate where the new Dwyr was currently residing. Hans guessed she was being honest when she'd said she had little influence over the Dwyr's decisions. Asking Sebastian to intercede on his behalf had been a long shot, but it looked like it had paid off.

"Anyway, Perran isn't the true power there, as Sebastian quickly found out. It's a woman. We think she's related to him, but it isn't clear. She might be a cousin of the former Dwyr. There's a silly rumor that Kala Orr brought her back from the dead, resurrecting her from her grave, but that's nonsense, right?"

She looked questioningly at Hans.

"I would say that's extremely unlikely."

She nodded. "That's exactly what I thought. So this woman is kind of the Dwyr's regent, though not officially. Sebastian's mother says she seems to guide him in everything he says and does, and she—"

"What's her name?"

"Morgan."

"Morgan what?"

"I don't know. That's the strange thing. She doesn't seem to have a last name, or at least, no one knows it."

Morgan?

Hans searched his memory for high-ranking members of the EAC who had come to SIS's awareness in the old days. He couldn't remember anyone with that name. Was she keeping her surname a secret? That didn't make sense. She would only have to make another one up, as he had.

Esme was off on another stream-of-consciousness babble. "It's lucky she was there when Dwyr Orr was killed, don't you think? To help Perran, I mean. The poor boy must have been devastated. I still find it hard to believe the Alliance murdered her in cold blood. No trial. Nothing. Just shot her. Monsters."

Considering the death and destruction Kala Orr had wreaked upon the world, it wasn't so surprising the BA simply executed her when they stormed the *Belladonna*. But he did find it somewhat odd. It wasn't really their style, and, when he'd been head of SIS, it hadn't been the game plan if they had ever managed to capture the EAC's leader. A broadcasted trial would have been much better in terms of public relations, maintaining the Alliance's image as a fair and just organization.

There was a knock at the door.

"Come in," Hans called.

His receptionist poked her head into the room, scowled at Esme, and announced, "Your seer is here, sir. Should I send her in, or...?"

"Ah yes. Please do."

Esme's eyes widened. "Is that the woman I—"

"Yes."

She was being disingenuous. She must have known he'd put Ellis on the payroll after her 'miraculous vision' outside the town hall on the day of his inauguration. In a world where little real news existed, gossip spread like wildfire.

The new arrival stepped into the room, her scarf pulled low, hiding her face. She'd done the same at the party, though he wasn't sure why. It wasn't like the Crusaders could tell she wasn't one of them just by looking at her.

"Thanks for coming to see me," he said to Esme. "And please send my thanks to your husband. I appreciate everything he's done and I won't forget it."

Warm pleasure suffusing her features, she rose to her feet. "It's no problem, Mayor. We all help each other, right?"

"Exactly. Now, if you wouldn't mind...?"

Ellis was standing at the door, her head down.

"Of course, of course. I'll leave you to it. I hope...I expect you'll hear something favorable."

She hesitated as she reached the newcomer as if she wanted to say something to her, but then, probably remembering the fortune teller's vow, she continued on out the door.

Ellis closed it. Pulling down her scarf, she strode over to Hans. "It's on. They agreed to work with you."

20

"No." Kala folded her arms over her chest.

She felt weak, weaker than she'd ever thought possible. And, imprisoned aboard their starship, she was entirely at the Alliance's mercy. But she would never agree to doing their bidding. She would rather return to the endless nothingness Morgan had sentenced her to and live out the rest of her existence in dreams than side with the BA against her son.

Two military officers and two civilians faced her across the table.

The female officer with short, gray hair and a stony expression asked, "What makes you think you have a choice?"

"If I have no choice, why are you asking me?" Kala retorted.

"It would make things easier for both of us if you were in agreement," said the male officer. He was a short man, someone high up in the ranks, according to the number of stars on his shoulder straps. "Face it," he went on. "Your empire is lost. You will never be Dwyr again. The EAC will fall, and you will be executed for war crimes. Agree to our terms, and you can live out the rest of your days in comfort and a measure of freedom."

"I wouldn't call exile freedom," Kala remarked.

"I would call it a far preferable alternative to public shaming and death."

"My people would never blame me for anything I've done, and they are the only people whose opinions I value."

She glanced at the two civilians present. Why were they here? Were they not going to speak? They were an odd pair. One slim and graying but with a youthful face, the other a bear of a man with flowing red-gold hair and beard.

As if prompted by her look, the slim one said, "Kala, we've made a bad start to the negotiations. May I begin by saying how pleased I am to see you recovered so well from your ordeal. Frankly, I didn't think you would be anything other than a gibbering, mindless wreck when I brought you back."

She gave a little gasp as a realization hit. This was the man who had been complaining at her bedside when she'd returned to consciousness. "It was you who woke me?"

"Yes."

Though her body continued to suffer the ill effects of her months of inactivity, her mind remained sharp. This new piece of information set off sparks of significance and connections in her understanding. If this man had managed to reverse the charm Morgan had placed on her, it meant something critical.

Assuming the large man had been his companion when she'd woken, they knew about Morgan. He'd said something about her 'bewitchings'.

"Who are you?" she bluntly asked.

The short officer replied, "It isn't necessary for you to know—"

"I am Merlin," interrupted the slim man, "and my friend—I believe you may have heard of him—My friend is called Arthur."

The short officer grimaced and said between his teeth, "I thought we agreed...Oh, never mind."

Arthur!

A wave of emotion hit her. Shock, wonder, and fear washed through her, leaving her reeling. This was the man who she'd spent years searching for. This was the man who Morgan had warned her about, the man who could kill her.

"I see you do know of him," said Merlin evenly, watching her with a steady gaze.

"I do," she spluttered, all her reserve destroyed by the revelation. "And you!" Her focus switched to Merlin. "I have read your name too, in the old books. You...you..."

He was another powerful figure from the past. So that was why he'd been able to bring her back to wakefulness. Was he the one who had imprisoned Morgan deep below ground for thousands of years? He had to be the person her enemy feared!

"Now the introductions are over," said the female officer sourly, "maybe we can get back to business."

Everything had changed. She was sitting in a room with the only man who was capable of killing her. She felt as though she was growing smaller. Her confidence and anger melted away, and she felt very, very vulnerable.

The female officer was watching her closely. "Do you require medical attention?"

She shook her head.

"Arthur no longer wishes you any harm," said Merlin.

"Huh?" said the short officer. "I thought she was unconscious when you found her. How could she know...?"

"She knows enough," Merlin said, his gaze not leaving her.

The Alliance's threat of execution for war crimes had suddenly become real. This man, this Arthur, could kill her. Not only could she lose her life, she might never see Perran again, never have the chance to wrest his affections away from the dreadful bitch who had taken him from her.

But the new information had opened up other possibilities. When the officers had put their proposal to her, she'd never imagined the Alliance could achieve its desired outcome anyway. There had been no point to her agreeing to play her role in their plan. Morgan was too intelligent and too powerful, and in ways the BA couldn't even imagine. They would never defeat her.

Now she knew they had Merlin on their side, that changed everything.

"I need time to think," she said.

"We don't have time," said the female officer. "We need an answer. Our forces are nearly in position."

"Then your forces will have to wait," Kala spat. "This plan of yours won't work without me, and I *won't* be rushed. I'm returning to my quarters."

She grabbed the edge of the table and used it for balance and as a prop to help her get to her feet. Her wasted leg muscles ached with the effort.

"Let me help you," said Arthur, speaking for the first time.

She knew his voice. Her deduction had been correct. He *had* been the other person in the room when she woke up. His tone was soft and smooth and he had an odd accent. He didn't *sound* like a killer, though he must have been that man who had approached her platform at the launch ceremony, cutting a swathe through the crowd with his sword. At the time, he'd been wearing a helmet so she hadn't been able to see his face, and his hair had been red with the blood of her people. But he was the right build. Morgan had assured her that, were he ever in her company again, he would make a second attempt.

He stood up and walked around the table to her side.

She shrank from his outstretched hands.

"Don't touch me!" she hissed.

"I'll comm a medic for you," said the female officer.

"I don't want a medic!"

She leaned on the table as she walked unsteadily toward

the door. After staggering the few steps it took to cross the open space, she rested against the door jamb.

She could feel them watching her, and she knew how she must look: thin, weak, and frail under her horrible, printed ship's clothes, her hair, once thick and lustrous, now dull and missing in patches. But she didn't care. She couldn't care less what they thought of her.

When she'd gathered her strength, she stepped out into the passageway. As she walked away, using the bulkhead as support, she overheard the female officer ask,

"Shouldn't we request a guard to escort her?"

Her superior replied, "Ha! No need, Colbourn. She's hardly going to escape or take over the ship in *that* state."

21

It had been easy keeping up with the party of Crusaders and children as they hiked through the Australian wilderness. What had been hard was not being discovered. As the night had worn on the nocturnal noises had faded, and then the jungle had given way to desert. In the strong moonlight, Wright and Abacha had been forced to stay far behind to avoid detection.

The Crusaders were armed. Not with much, just a couple of pulse rifles and long, whip-like sticks for hitting the kids. It had been all Wright could do to control himself the first time a child had been struck for going too slowly. He'd wanted to smash the living daylights out of the bastards. Abacha must have felt the same. He'd growled his disapproval so loudly Wright had feared the Crusaders would hear them.

But it would have been stupid to approach them. Wright and Abacha were only carrying regulation beamers. The hand weapons were no match for pulse rifles, and the smugglers outnumbered them ten to two. More importantly, killing or taking the men and women into custody would mean they would never find out where they were going. Crusaders were notorious for never giving up intelligence, preferring to take the first chance they had to kill themselves.

Wright didn't know how far they'd walked, following the group of trafficked children. By the time dawn had arrived, he'd been tired and very thirsty. He couldn't imagine how exhausted the kids were. Some of them looked no older than five or six. At least the Crusaders had allowed them brief stops for water along the way.

When the sun had risen, his hopes had died. A bleak, dry, dusty landscape spreading all the way to the horizon had been revealed. They could not go on. Not only were they suffering a raging thirst, they couldn't expect to follow the smugglers any farther without being detected. If they kept them in sight, they would also be visible to anyone who happened to glance back, and the trail was almost undetectable on the bare, rocky ground.

They were forced to abandon the pursuit and turn back. After sending a brief report to Central Command and logging his position, he'd begun to retrace his steps with Abacha, heavy-hearted.

The thing that killed him wasn't only that he was leaving children in the hands of insane cultists who had stolen them away from their parents, it had also become clear to him almost as soon as he'd seen them that this must have been what had happened to Taylan's kids. It explained perfectly why she hadn't been able to find them. All the time she'd been searching for them in Ireland and West BI, they'd actually been transported across to the other side of the globe.

If he could only have found out where they were going. What wouldn't he give to be able to tell Taylan where her children were?

Not that he knew where *she* was any longer. She'd disappeared into West BI to carry out a new plan she'd thought up. He didn't know what it was. And she must have had her implant removed after the attack on the *Belladonna*, so there was absolutely no way to trace her.

"Is it much farther, do you think, sir?" Abacha asked. The man's voice was croaky with dehydration.

Wright replied in a whisper, his tongue thick in his mouth, "We just need to get through the forest and find the CUV."

Assuming it was still there. It was unlikely anyone had found it and taken it away, but if it was gone, they were sunk. He wasn't sure they would even make it back to the beach. Within an hour, the sun had risen to shine down a brilliant, blistering heat upon them. The rays reflected from the sand and rocks surrounding them, doubling up the assault on their eyes, skin, and hydration.

The Crusaders and children had all been swathed in long, baggy clothes and wearing hats, and when the new day came it hadn't taken him long to realize why. Daytime in the Australian desert was no joke for the unprepared.

Desert vegetation—short, gnarled trees with gray-green leaves and scrubby, spiny bushes—had been increasing for an hour or more when, like a miracle, a line of deep green trees appeared on the horizon, shimmering in the heat haze. If they could just reach them and get out of the desiccating heat of the sun...

Abacha went down. At first, Wright thought he'd only stumbled, but when he tried to get up, he couldn't. Wright grabbed him under his armpits and hauled him into the shade of a boulder, propping him up against it.

"Sorry, sir," he mumbled.

"Don't be dumb," Wright replied. "This is my fault."

He comm'd Central Command. He'd avoided it up until now because he didn't want Alliance helis or other rescue vehicles in the area. The Crusaders might get spooked and abandon the access route to the interior, and then they might never find them. But he wasn't going to risk Abacha's life over it.

"Copy," said the comm officer in reply to Wright's explanation of their situation. "Stand by."

As he waited for the response from Central, he stood up and gazed at the forest. It was only about a kilometer away. If they could just have made it that far, they might have been okay. He felt like an idiot for underestimating the severity of the climate and for endangering the life of another Marine. A scene flashed into his mind. He was back in Jamaica on the top floor of the department building, catching Patel with her ruined face as she fell backward into his arms. Now he was opening his eyes after the explosion of the stadium and seeing the dead and dying young Marines scattered around him.

"Major Wright?" said a voice over his comm. "This is Colonel Rioli. We can get a heli to you in four hours."

"*Four hours!*"

"Australia's a big place, Wright," the colonel replied testily, "and you've picked the arse-end of nowhere to get lost in."

"We aren't lost, we..." He was too exhausted to continue.

"I know it's a long time," Rioli went on in a more kindly tone. "Look, I wouldn't normally recommend this—the usual advice in your situation is to stay put—but I can see on the map there's a small creek about half a klick east of your current position. If you're feeling up to it, you could try to get some water for your companion while you're waiting. Dehydration kills fast and it sounds like he's in bad shape."

Water five hundred meters away? He had nothing to carry it in.

"I'll try," he said.

"Good man. We have a lock on both of you, so don't worry if you can't make it back to him. We'll find you."

During the short conversation, Abacha had rolled onto his side. His eyes were closed and sunken and his lips dry, cracked, and bleeding. Wright didn't know if he would last four hours.

He murmured his intention, but Abacha didn't seem to hear.

He set off.

On the way, imaginary conversations ran through his head.

Hey Taylan, I think I might have found out what happened to your children, but, by the way, I had to kill your best friend to do it.

Taylan, great to see you. What's that? Oh, Boots is doing fine. Abacha, not so much.

What a surprise. Who'd have thought we'd ever meet again? You heard about what happened to Abacha, right? Oh, you didn't? Well...

He tripped on a rock and fell to his knees, tearing cloth and skin on sharp stones.

Cursing, furious with the universe and himself, he clambered to his feet and continued on. The trees he'd seen in the distance had to line the creek. If they both could have made it that far they would probably have been okay.

He staggered on, the sun like a red-hot iron pressing down on his back. His vision was swimming. The trees seemed to approach and then move away from him.

Then, before he knew it, he was under them. The cool air felt like a balm on his skin. He could feel moisture in it, taste the humidity. A mild breeze stirred the leaves and it was like a blessing from heaven.

The ground sloped downward. Through the greenery, something glinted.

Water.

∼

ABACHA HAD COME AROUND by the time he returned. He was sitting upright again, propped up by the boulder.

"Man, I'm glad to see you," he said. "I thought you'd gone somewhere else to die."

"Tip back your head," said Wright.

"What?" Seeing what he was holding, Abacha's eyes widened.

Wright squeezed his sodden shirt into the man's mouth. Heavy drips flooded out. When the shirt would yield no more water, he said, "Give me your shirt and put this one over your head. It's still a little wet."

The drink appeared to have done Abacha the world of good. He was already looking much more alert. Wright returned to the creek, feeling much better himself. His first taste of the water had been like nectar. On the way back, he managed a slow jog.

This time, Abacha managed to wring the shirt out himself.

"The river is that way?" he asked.

"Yeah. It's only small, but the water looks clean."

"I think I can make it there myself."

"Maybe you can, but I don't want you to try. A rescue heli is on the way."

"It is? When will it get here?"

"About three and a half hours."

Abacha's left eyebrow lifted.

"Apparently we're in the arse-end of nowhere," said Wright.

"Sir, if I can just get to the water and rest a little more, I'm sure I can make it back to the boat."

"No. I'll wait here with you for the heli, then I'll return to the CUV alone. You need to recuperate."

They argued it back and forth, but eventually Abacha persuaded Wright he was okay to go on. Wright comm'd Central again, canceling their rescue.

The comm officer linked him to Colonel Rioli again, who said, "I'll recall the heli if you're sure, but if you die on me I'm going to be bloody pissed off."

"No intention of dying, Colonel," said Wright and explained his concern about an Alliance heli being spotted by the smugglers.

"Yeah, we're looking at your report now. All right. Good luck, Major."

22

The last thing Taylan imagined would happen when she returned to West BI to look for her children was she would become a go-between for Hans Jonte.

Joseph Fry.

She hit her forehead with the heel of her hand. She had to think of him as Joseph Fry, or she might slip up and mention his real name. Even the ignorant Crusaders, cut off from current affairs of the rest of the world, might have heard of him. Yet she wasn't supposed to be able to speak anyway, so...

She'd arrived at the meeting place.

She loitered at the alley entrance, casting surreptitious glances up and down the street. When no one appeared to be looking her way, she stepped in.

Tall, windowless concrete walls rose five or six stories high on each side, cutting out the meager sunlight. At the end stood a woman. The light that spilled in from the farther street silhouetted her, but from her outline it was clear she was dressed in lumpy, coarse Crusader clothes. To wear anything else in the middle of Abertawe was madness.

Taylan walked down the alley, her heart beating faster at

each step. There was a chance she'd been set up. If the city's Resistance group had been uncovered, or if it harbored a mole who had divulged the secret meeting to the Crusader authorities, she could be on her way to her doom.

She glanced over her shoulder. Pedestrians were passing across the alley entrance. No one seemed to be taking any notice of her or the other woman. She stepped closer.

Her supposed contact in the Abertawe Resistance was young and pretty—beautiful, even. She wore the usual shawl and long dress, and her wavy chestnut hair was unfettered, falling in graceful curls below her shoulders. She didn't speak, only watched until Taylan reached her.

Her throat tight, Taylan took a breath.

Here goes nothing.

"Speak well of your friend," she said.

The woman replied, "Of your enemy say nothing." Then she smiled. Dimples appeared on her cheeks. She could not have looked cuter or more harmless if she'd tried. She had the kind of face people warmed to. It was no wonder she'd managed to survive so long among the Crusaders. No one would ever suspect her of deception.

"I'm Seren."

"Taylan." She wanted to hug her, partly with relief that she hadn't fallen into a Crusader trap, and partly because she was so glad to meet a fellow native of West BI who didn't see her as a traitor.

That makes two of you.

But she couldn't afford to waste time on pleasantries. After reporting to Jonte—*Fry!*—that the West BI Resistance members in the Preseli Hills had contacted the other branches and they'd agreed to help him, now she had to establish a connection with the local members in Abertawe. These would be the people who could help him with day to day subterfuge and they would be his conduit to the national group.

He couldn't speak to them face to face. It would be far too dangerous. That was Taylan's job.

"You look...different from how I imagined," Seren said.

Did she mean the disguise, or had the tale of what happened at Bryn Celli Ddu reached her?

"To be honest," Taylan replied, "so do you. What do you do for a day job?"

"It's better you don't know. Any news from our man?"

"He's got himself an invitation to the next High Council meeting."

"He has? Marvelous! We've needed someone like him all along, but getting into positions of power is so hard in their society. It's all based on networking. It's *who* you know that counts, but, for us, making friends with Crusaders is dangerous. You never know when you might say the wrong thing or your accent might slip."

"Well, he's great at schmoozing and his accent is perfect. Do you have anything you want me to tell him?"

"We'll need time to figure out what he can do at the council meeting to help the cause. That'll take a few days. I'll meet you again at..." She gave Taylan another place and time for their next rendezvous. "But for now you can tell him this: we've been contacted by the Alliance and told to prepare for something big. We're to scale down current operations and stock up on weapons and ammunition."

"Is the BA going to try to take back the island?"

"They haven't said so explicitly, but that's the feeling."

Taylan had the urge to hug her again. She had to make do with a mutually shared grin. A free Britannic Isles would be a good thing in itself, but, more importantly, it might make it easier to find out what had happened to her children.

"I'll pass the message on."

"Are you surviving okay?" asked Seren. "Do you need anything? We can get you food and some other supplies. We don't have a lot, but we would never let a countryman go hungry."

"I have plenty. In fact, let me give you this." Taylan reached into her pocket and pulled out a roll of the banknotes Fry had given her.

Seren's eyebrows rose. "Where did you get all that? The fortune-telling business must have been good lately."

"It's my wages from you-know-who, but I don't need it. I earn enough for my needs, and it would look suspicious if I were found to be carrying all this money."

"No, it's too much. I can't take it."

Taylan grabbed her hand and thrust the cash into it. "It's for the cause. I'm sure you'll find a way to use it."

Seren bit her lip. "I *can* think of a few good uses for it."

"I'm sure you can. I'd better go. It's been good meeting you, Seren. Wait, is it wise to use your real name?"

"I don't go by my real name among Crusaders."

"Of course not. Me neither. I'll see you next time. I hope you'll have more news from the Alliance."

Taylan turned, and then nearly jumped out of her skin. Two men were walking down the alley, staring straight at her and glowering.

"Go," she hissed at Seren.

"No, I don't want to—"

"Go!" Taylan pushed her into the street.

Seren hesitated before running off.

One of the men lunged at Taylan and grabbed her arm to prevent her from doing the same. But she had no intention of trying to get away. She wanted to delay the men and give Seren time to get away. Whatever was about to go down, there was no point in both of them being caught up in it.

"You're right," said the man holding her to his companion, "it is her! It's the Mayor's silent seer." He thrust his face into hers. "Only you're a big liar, aren't you? We saw you talking to that girl! You're coming with us, you charlatan. Let's see what the justice has to say about you!"

She balled her fist, readying to punch him. It wouldn't be too hard to hurt them enough to allow her to escape. She could even kill them. She had a knife in each boot and the alley was empty. But there were too many people nearby, and though she could make up something about them attacking her, the story of a fortune-teller who managed to kill two grown men in self-defense would attract exactly the kind of attention she didn't want.

She allowed her arm to go limp.

As the man dragged her away, she thanked her lucky stars she'd given the money to Seren.

23

One condition of Kala's agreement to go along with the BA's plans was she had to be allowed full access to intelligence reports on the Britannic Isles. She swiped the interface screen to open the latest she'd been given, and immediately tears started into her eyes.

The vid was shaky and grainy, but it was unmistakably of Perran at his oath-taking ceremony. His little face looked proud and brave as he stood in full Dwyr regalia, heavy gown sweeping to the ground, horns curving over his head.

He was so young. Too young for the weight of responsibility of the position.

Behind him stood Morgan, small and slight, fading into the background as always. No one in the crowd would have known the strength of her influence over the new Dwyr or the malignity of it.

It had come as no surprise that Morgan had announced the death of Dwyr Kala Orr as soon as she and Perran had arrived in the Britannic Isles. The intelligence reports contained no vids of her funeral rites, but no doubt they had been lavish and spectacular. Who or what had been burned on the pyre? And how had Morgan managed to keep the funerary attendants from preparing her corpse? Perhaps she'd told them her body had been destroyed in the attack on the *Belladonna*.

Perran raised his hands and his lips moved. The recorder hadn't picked up his words, only the noise of the crowd. She remembered the oaths so well, though it had been many years since she'd recited them. And in all the time since she hadn't broken a single one.

A well of sorrow opened up deep inside her. She'd lost everything. Her dominion, her son, her people. *Everything*.

The crowd was surging around Perran on his dais like wheat in a field on a windy day.

Where had Morgan held the ceremony? She didn't recognize the place, but, according to the report, it was in West BI. Her enemy had maintained the presence of the Dwyr in the place where the Crusaders were least established and most in need of the leader's presence. She was a good strategist.

Was she good enough to withstand the might of the Alliance?

Her door chime sounded.

With some relief, she closed the screen. The next stages in the oath-taking ceremony were not suitable for someone of Perran's age, and she feared discovering if he had taken part in them.

"Enter."

In the open doorway, filling it, was Arthur.

Kala stiffened, every fiber taut. Had he changed his mind and come to finish his task? She had no guards to call. The military leaders held her in such low regard they didn't perceive her as a threat. She also didn't carry the implant they used to speak to each other. All she had was the interface. She swept her fingers across it, trying to figure out how to summon help.

Arthur stepped into the room. "I mean you no harm, my lady."

She clenched the interface between two hands. "Then leave."

"Begging your leave, I would rather stay."

The door had slid closed and he stood between her and it. Even at full health and strength, she would never get past him and out of the room.

"May I sit down?"

She didn't answer.

He walked to her narrow bed and sat down, facing her diagonally.

The large man rested his elbows on his spread knees, his shaggy hair hanging down. He seemed troubled by something. But whatever was on his mind, whatever he wanted to unburden himself of, she didn't care.

She rose to her feet unsteadily.

"Please," he said. "You would do me a great service if you would remain here with me."

Her legs already aching from the small exertion, and weighed down by her emotions, she relented.

"Thank you," he said as she resumed her seat.

"I don't want to alarm you," he went on. "When we met before, and now, too, I did not bring Excalibur with me. I have come to offer an apology."

She gazed at him in silence. Excalibur? The name rang a bell. She must have read it in her books. But she couldn't remember who it was. Another person had survived from his time? That made four: Arthur, Morgan, Merlin, and Excalibur.

"I feel..." His features twisted, as if he were in discomfort or perplexity. "I think I may have almost committed a great sin, and it is only through another's actions I was prevented."

"What kind of sin?" asked Kala, her interest piqued. In the

Earth Awareness Crusade, the only sins were those that caused harm to the world's spirit, but she knew other religions thought differently. In other ways of thinking, behavior that was normal and natural, like freedom of intimacy, was outlawed.

"You don't remember?"

"Oh," she replied, understanding dawning. She continued, acidly, "You mean that time you tried to kill me."

"Both times," said Arthur sadly.

"*Both*? You mean you tried a second time?!"

"On the *Belladonna*, when you were unconscious I don't think I'm supposed to tell you this, but I was about to strike you when Taylan Ellis stopped me."

"She..."

For a moment, the overload of revelations rendered Kala speechless. Here was the man who twice tried to murder her apologizing for it, and apparently the other person who wanted to kill her had saved her life.

Arthur was shaking his great head. "I always believed Merlin. I always trusted him. When I was a baby, he saved my life. And then, when all the barons were against me, he helped me win their support. He saved my country from invasion and ruin. But now...now I don't know what to think of him."

It suddenly occurred to her that she didn't need her old books to find out the truth about Merlin and Morgan. Someone who had been alive at the time was sitting right here before her, a living source of ancient knowledge.

"Arthur, tell me, was it Merlin who locked Morgan away deep below ground?"

"I don't know. I don't know what happened to her after I killed her son. I was wounded and carried from the field of battle. I fell asleep, and when I woke up, I was in this time, aboard a ship in the stars."

"But is he Morgan's enemy?"

"Yes. Morgan le Fay and Merlin have been mortal enemies all the time I have known them."

Hope lifted her heart. "And Merlin has great powers too." It wasn't really a question, only a deduction. If she was right, she might see the end of her usurper and regain her child.

Arthur nodded before his expression returned to brooding introspection. "Merlin said Taylan is playing out a feature of the pattern he didn't see. He said because I didn't kill you, the conflict has turned in our favor. You will be important to the Alliance's victory. I understand that. What I don't understand is, how could he have been so wrong?" He looked at her as though expecting her to answer.

"How would I know?" she replied irritably. "I only hope he doesn't make a similar mistake again, regarding my life or the upcoming battle."

"If I'd done as he asked, your death would not have been righteous." He seem to be speaking to himself. "My sin would not have been forgiven."

"Certainly not by *me*," Kala muttered. Then, exasperated by this moping giant, she added, "If you came here to ask for forgiveness, you won't get it. Why would I forgive your attempt to murder me, twice?! Even if it was due to bad advice, that's no excuse. I was...I *am* the Dwyr. According to global law, all political leaders accused of war crimes are entitled to a fair trial at the very least. Now, your presence is making me uncomfortable. Please leave."

Arthur slowly got to his feet, looking downward. "You are right. I cannot use misguidance as an excuse for my actions. I should have thought for myself. I am the keeper of my soul, not Merlin." His gaze shifted to her. "You may not be willing to accept my apology. Nevertheless, I give it, and if I ever see Taylan Ellis again, I will tell her she was right."

He plodded toward the door. Before he reached it, however, it opened.

Two armed soldiers stood outside. The gray-haired female officer stood behind them.

"Kala Orr," she said. "You are to come with us. It's time to board the shuttle."

24

Heavy footsteps sounded outside Taylan's cell. She looked up. She'd been stuck in the tiny, dirty, cramped room for hours, crammed in with four other inmates. A burly man arrested for brawling had taken the entire single bunk for himself, forcing the rest of them to challenge him for it, stand, or sit on the cold concrete floor. Deciding she was in enough trouble as it was, Taylan had elected to sit, and now her backside was chilled and sore.

The cover over the barred window was slammed open, revealing the guard's unibrowed face.

"That the one?" he asked an unseen companion, his gaze on Taylan.

"If I could see inside...?" suggested a deep, resonant voice diplomatically.

Fry.

She sagged with relief. After she'd finally convinced her cell mates she really couldn't speak by shoving her card repeatedly in their faces, they'd insisted she read their fortunes for them. Regrettably, the card stated her trade too. Only she didn't have any paper or a pencil to write down the predictions and the guard refused to supply any, so she'd had to resort to miming to get her meaning across.

It had been a very entertaining experience for everyone but her. She'd heard of captive audiences before but never captive entertainers. After the first couple of hours, she'd wondered if it was some kind of karmic justice for all the times she'd taken advantage of the Crusaders' gullibility.

"Yes, that's her," said the mayor.

The guard unlocked the door. The cells were pre-invasion and could be secured electronically, but the jailers used the backup, mechanical locks and keys instead.

"Mayor Fry has backed up your claim," said the guard, "so you're free to go. But if you're found to be practicing your craft fraudulently, it'll be a custodial sentence for you." As Taylan edged passed him in the doorway, he added, "Remember that!"

She kept a straight face though mentally rolled her eyes. Fortune tellers preyed on the stupid and credulous who wanted to hear a happy tale of a brighter future. The entire profession was fraudulent.

When she'd been taken to the city jail, it had been hard to defend herself while also pretending she couldn't speak, but she'd managed to convey that the men who had brought her in had been mistaken. She written on the guard's notepad that her friend had been speaking but she hadn't said anything back. None of the officers had believed her. She didn't really blame them. Her excuse was pathetic, and if she'd been anywhere except in Crusader-controlled territory she would have been screwed. But they had no database to check her name, fingerprints, retinal pattern or any other identifying features; no way to establish she wasn't who she said she was. And to secure her release, she'd done what everyone in that society did if they could: she'd used a connection with someone powerful.

He didn't speak to her until after they'd left the jail and climbed into his carriage. The driver started up the horses with slaps of the reins, and the carriage trundled into motion. The horses' hooves clattered on the road, adding to the general noise of the street. After closing the blinds, Fry said quietly, "That was probably more attention than we want."

"I know. I'm sorry. The Resistance suggested the place, but they don't know I'm not supposed to be able to speak. I'll be more careful next time."

"You learned your lesson. Good. I had a few trainee agents who weren't so quick. They didn't last long."

Taylan wondered what he meant by 'not lasting long'.

"What did you find out from your contact?" he asked.

"They had a message from the Alliance telling them to stockpile weapons and ammunition and cut down on their current operations. It sounds like the BA's planning an attack, right?"

Fry's expression turned thoughtful.

"Right?" Taylan pressed.

"Perhaps," he replied grudgingly. For some reason, he didn't seem happy about the prospect.

"So, what have you found out about my kids?" she asked. She'd fulfilled her part of their bargain. Now it was time to get paid.

"Nothing." He frowned as if puzzled.

"What?!" Taylan had been facing forwards. As she spoke, she turned to stare at him. "What do you mean, nothing? Nothing at all?!"

"It takes time to build confidence and trust. If I ask sensitive questions right now, at the beginning of my term, people will become suspicious. I will find out the information you need, but you must be patient."

"Patient! I've been searching for my kids for months! They're just little children. They can't, they can't..." Her throat closed up and her eyes flooded with tears. She swallowed and continued in a strangled tone, "If the Crusaders treat them like they've treated the natives of all the other countries they conquered, they won't survive long."

Sudden, hot fury flashed up. "I did what you asked," she growled. "I traveled all the way to the Preseli Hills and back. I made the contacts you asked for. And what have you done for me? Fuck all."

"What I have done for you is I've cemented my position among the Crusaders," he replied evenly. "The information you seek is confidential and not something someone in my position is privy to. To learn these facts…" He sighed. "I can't explain the entire process of intelligence gathering to you within a few short minutes. Please be assured I am not taking your efforts for granted and I will fulfill my obligation to you. But when we spoke, we didn't agree a timesc—"

"That was because I thought you understood the urgency!" Taylan exclaimed. "Don't you know anything about children? Don't you have any yourself?"

"No, but—"

"They can't wait for you to 'cement your position'. They need help *now*. They need *me* now."

"I'm sorry I've disappointed you. That wasn't my intention. I should have been clearer about what you can expect."

"You tricked me to get what you want," she said sullenly.

"That isn't true. We both want freedom for the Britannic Isles."

"You don't get it, do you?! What I want is freedom for me and mine. That's more important than any of the rest of this bullshit. Tell your driver to stop. I want to get out."

"Let me take you back to the town hall, where we can talk and sort this out."

"No. I've done enough talking. Tell your driver to stop or I'll get out anyway and take my chances." The carriage didn't seem to be going fast, maybe fifteen K an hour. She couldn't bear being in the same space as the two-faced bastard.

He relented and picked up a brass-knobbed stick to rap on the back of the driver's seat.

As the carriage slowed, Taylan said, "I have another meeting lined up with the Abertawe Resistance. I'll come to see you afterward, but I'm not going to give you any more information unless you have something helpful to tell me in return. And *I'll* be the judge of what's helpful."

She swung open the carriage door and hopped out, though the vehicle hadn't quite stopped. After running a few steps to slow her momentum, she took stock of her surroundings. She was in a run-down area of Abertawe that looked as though it had run down a bit further since the last time she'd been here.

She heard the carriage door slam shut, the "Gee up" of the driver, and the clopping of the horses speeding up as they carried the loathsome Fry away.

What an arsehole.

He'd used her and her love for her children to get what he wanted. It was like being in the Royal Marines again. No one gave a shit about her. She was just a soldier in a game of xiangqi, to be sacrificed for someone else's benefit.

Fuck them all.

She wasn't going to let anyone use her again. She would find her kids, no matter what obstacles others threw in her way.

25

By the time Wright had forced another path through the rainforest to reach the hidden CUV, dragged it out to sea, and piloted it back to the *Resolute*, he was at the end of his strength. Knowing Abacha was probably in worse shape than he was making out, he'd insisted on going first through the undergrowth and bearing the brunt of the labor. As he waited for the pumps to empty the launch chamber, he slumped in his seat, wondering if he'd ever be able to move again. He was also dreadfully thirsty once more. He'd drunk his fill at the creek, but he'd soon sweated all the water out again in the extreme heat.

The chamber was empty. The hatch opened and Lieutenant Ford appeared. His lips were moving but the sound was muffled by the hull of the CUV. After he opened the vehicle from the outside, a torrent of cursing flooded in, abruptly ceasing when he realized Wright could hear him.

"You both look like shit," he said.

There was no doubt they did. As well as being dehydrated, they were sunburned and covered in wounds from their encounter with Australian vegetation, most of which seemed either covered in thorns, barbs, or stingers, or harbored insects to do its job for it.

"I'll comm Krol," Ford went on. "Might as well wait here." The boat had no sick bay, though it carried a limited amount of medical supplies.

"Krol?" Abacha asked hoarsely.

"She's our de facto medic," Wright croaked back. "Used to be a nurse."

The reduced number of personnel had meant the *Resolute's* crew had to double up on some roles.

"So she does people as well as engines?" asked Abacha.

Wright didn't have the energy to reply.

The dour engineer soon arrived bringing water with her. She pinched their skins and glared into their eyes. When Abacha took a gulp of water, she barked, "Sip it!"

After prodding and poking them some more, she gave her diagnosis. "You're not going to die yet. Go to your quarters and I'll bring some medication for burns."

Tutting and shaking her head, she left.

Ford appeared to be equally annoyed with them. "If I'd known you planned on going on an expedition into the bush, sir," he said in a pained tone, "I would have warned you what to expect. Pardon my language, sir, but you can't fuck around out there."

"Point taken," Wright replied. He was beginning to regret allowing respect for higher ranks to slip aboard his boat.

While Ford helped Abacha walk to his bunk, Wright made his own way to his cabin. The first thing he looked for was Boots, but the cat wasn't there. The crew must have been taking care of him. Wright felt a twinge of jealousy and hoped the animal hadn't become attached to someone else. He collapsed on his bed, wincing as his burned skin made contact with the bedclothes.

Krol must have had as good an understanding of the

human body as she did engines because he didn't die. Pleased he wouldn't piss off Colonel Rioli, he returned to duty the following day. Abacha also showed up, but he sent him back to his bunk.

He went to speak to Lieutenant Ford in the control room.

"What happened with those Crusader vessels while I was gone?" he asked.

"One of them left but the other three are still there."

The one that had departed must have been the one he'd attached a tracker to. He was surprised the others hadn't left too. There had been no sign of them from the beach. "I wonder why they're sticking around."

"Maybe they're still taking on or offloading cargo?" Ford suggested.

"I thought they already did what they came here to do."

"What was that?"

Wright realized he hadn't told his lieutenant what he and Abacha had seen. As he explained, the man's jaw slackened. "Kids?! Whose kids?"

"I'm pretty sure they weren't their own. There were too many for the number of adults, and the way they were treating them...well, you'd be a monster to do it to anyone's children, let alone yours. My guess is they're from one or more of the countries the EAC invaded. Most likely the most recent invasions, so the Caribbean or the BI. I stuck a tracker on the one that left so maybe we'll find out soon. Central are keeping an eye on where it goes."

Ford breathed out a barely audible curse. "And they were taking them somewhere in the outback? Poor bastards."

Wright mentally agreed. But sympathy for the children wasn't going to help them. He itched to sink the Crusader ships. The *Resolute* wasn't heavily armed, but it wouldn't take much to put a hole in a wooden hull. Yet the same problem applied as before: he didn't want to alert the EAC that their operation had been discovered and trigger them into changing their route into the country. And there was a chance the ships were still carrying some trafficked kids.

What else could he do?

"I want to launch two UUVs. Jeong, maneuver them to, say, to about three hundred meters from the Crusader vessels. One to the north and the other to the east. I want to get visuals on them."

"Aye, sir."

If the Crusader ships hadn't changed position, he and Abacha should have been able to see them from the beach. Visibility had been good. He wanted to find out if they were similarly hard to see at a closer distance.

The UUVs were controlled via a direct mind/machine interface. It took Jeong a minute to set up the system and integrate with it via his implant. Then two screens lit up on the control panel displaying the visual feeds from the underwater vehicles. The interior of the launch chamber appeared, filled with quickly rising water. Then the pictures wobbled as the UUVs detached and moved out into the ocean. For a while, all that could be seen was slightly murky water, lit by beams from above.

Jeong's eyes were closed as he concentrated.

"I've never figured out how he controls two at once," said Ford quietly. "Must be ambidextrous."

Jeong smiled as he overheard. "I can pat my head and rub my stomach too, and my missus says—"

"Just concentrate on the job, Jeong," interrupted Wright.

"Yes, sir. Nearly there."

The vehicles' coordinates and depths appeared in the corners of the displays, rapidly altering as they moved along. Then the coordinates became stable but the depth figures began to decrease. When the UUVs were a meter below the waves, they stopped their quick decrease and hovered within a fixed range of roughly twenty centimeters. There was hardly any swell.

"Raising periscopes," said Jeong.

The water near the surface was very clear. Blue water rippled with sunlight moved slowly across the displays until it disappeared, replaced by air.

"So that's how they're doing it!" Ford exclaimed. He was looking from the sonar readings to the screens showing the visuals from the UUVs.

Wright had to admit, the Crusaders' solution to avoid detection by Alliance satellites was simple but ingenious. The wooden ships had been constructed in the ancient style, high-prowed and three-masted with sails. But as well as the sails, long swathes of material hung from the beams. Light-weight and a shimmering blue, from a distance they would baffle human and machine eyes into thinking they were looking at the ocean. He guessed when he and Abacha had looked out from the beach, the material had been hanging down in the windless air, obscuring the ships unless you knew exactly where to look.

"I was going to say I'm surprised that stuff doesn't get ripped to shreds in a high wind," said Ford, "but they must only deploy it when they're within our waters, and they must only come in during this time of year, when there's hardly ever any storms."

"Jeong," said Wright, "record what we're seeing for a couple of minutes and send the recording to me."

He would forward it to Rioli. A detail like this could help put an end to the Crusaders' terrible trade.

26

Lorcan had always stayed well out of harm's way whenever the Project's military wing engaged in action, remaining safely aboard the *Bres* for the duration of any armed conflicts. Not only did he see no point in endangering himself with a closer involvement, his focus had been outward, toward the stars. He'd had no interest in what happened on Earth, providing she continued to yield her resources to him.

But something had changed. This time, he was curious to see at a closer hand how the upcoming battle played out.

It was a trip Iolani didn't wish to participate in, unsurprisingly. If her veganism and choice of living situation hadn't already convinced him of her deep-seated reverence for life, his months of working with her would have confirmed it. She reminded him of the Jains, whose religion dictated they should brush insects out of their path to avoid stepping on them.

Hale wasn't quite so fanatic and she didn't push her beliefs on anyone, yet her sensitivity about death wasn't difficult to see if one paid any attention to her. He'd been spending more time than usual in the ship's refectory lately, and he'd noticed she often ate by herself if steaks or other large meat items were being served. And she'd entirely avoided involving herself in the plans to bring farm animals to the colony worlds.

It felt odd to not have her accompanying him on his trip to Earth. Perhaps it was only that he'd become used to her always hanging around. Since she'd come aboard the *Bres*, she'd involved herself in almost everything he'd done. It had irritated him at first, but then he'd found it didn't bother him so much. And now, on the shuttle, he even missed her a little bit.

"How long until we land?" he asked the pilot over comm.

"Four hours twenty minutes, sir. It'll be six thirty in the evening when we get there. Your residence has been prepared for your arrival."

"Thank you."

His tantalum mine in Old France was the perfect spot from which to observe the offensive. Close enough to feel a part of the action, but not so close as to be in danger. And if by chance the conflict did spread wider than was expected and things began to look threatening, he could depart the place quickly.

It had been years since he'd been there. The mine had been started before the EAC had swept into the country and taken it over. Luckily for him, Crusaders were easy to bribe with goods and knick knacks that weren't available under their chosen regime. The mine had continued to operate without scrutiny or impediment from the higher echelons of the cult. Such a bunch of hypocrites, secretly enjoying forbidden items while decrying them in public.

Yes, the relationship with the local Crusaders was cozy and he shouldn't expect any problems from that quarter during his visit. He'd even received gifts from them in the past. The champagne he'd served Dwyr Orr at their first meeting had been one of them. That had been somewhat of a slip up. He'd grown complacent and forgotten where it had come from. Never mind. Kala Orr was now in the hands of the Alliance, neutralized.

Four hours until landing.

How to pass the time? Usually, he would read or listen to reports and mentally rehearse the many and varied Project plans, checking for details he might have missed and thinking up new ideas. If he couldn't stomach any more Project business, he might allow his imagination to roam to his journey to the new worlds and life upon them.

But neither the Project nor dreams of the future appealed. He looked out of the small window. A tiny blue and white orb stood out among the field of stars. Perhaps Iolani had a point. There was something special about the place, sole home of life for billions of miles around. Her argument that the colonists would need somewhere to return to in case of disaster had made sense, but maybe Earth was also worth preserving simply for the sake of it.

A leaden hand seemed to close around his heart and, not understanding why, he was suddenly thrown back to one terrible day more than two decades ago. He inhaled a great breath and exhaled heavily. Prickles were running across his skin and behind his eyes and sweat wet his skin.

What was wrong with him? He was grateful for the empty passenger cabin, relieved Hale hadn't wanted to join him for this journey. He would have hated anyone to see him like this.

Compelled by an unknown force, his hand moved to the interface on the bulkhead in front of him. With trembling fingers, he opened it. He could link to any database on the *Bres* from here, including his personal files. He could not bring the impulse under control. His digits sought out the pictures automatically. He hadn't looked at them in years. He hadn't been able to bring himself to. Now he was on automatic. He had no choice.

Grace appeared first. He felt the same response at the sight of her that he always had: pure love. Next came the boys, Oran and Tiernan. They'd been playing football when the picture had been taken and they were unaware of the camera. It had captured all their vitality and energy, their lust for life. Finally, there appeared—

No!

He could not look. He would not look.

He swiped the screen closed and forced his gaze out of the window again. The small blue dot had grown slightly larger.

"Pilot," he said. In his confusion, he'd forgotten the woman's name.

"Yes, sir?" she asked smoothly.

"There's been a change of plan. I want to go to Antarctica."

"Antarctica?!" All her professionalism couldn't keep the note of surprise from her voice.

"Yes. I'll send you the coordinates."

He knew them by heart.

"Thank you, sir. Should I inform your residence in Old France that you won't be arriving today?"

"That would be good. Tell them..." *What?* When *would* he get there? "Tell them to stand by."

He passed the remainder of the journey in a state of trepidation. His entire being rebelled against what he was doing, yet he couldn't help himself. A battle was being waged within him. On one side stood the adamantine protection he'd built up, his safeguarding against pain. On the other side was a burgeoning force, a pressure welling up, to face the reality of what had happened.

For the first time in a long time, he was out of control and he had no idea what the end result would be.

A gray-green mass lightly dotted with white came into view through the shuttle window.

Two millennia ago, Antarctica had been a sheet of ice, hundreds of meters thick, spreading out from the continent over the ocean. Then the climate had warmed and the ice had begun to melt. Great ice bergs cleaved from the mass and floated out across the seas, becoming shipping hazards until they finally melted away. The ice sheet grew thinner, gradually revealing the mountains, plains, and vast lakes unexposed to the atmosphere for tens of thousands of years.

More frozen water from the North Pole, glaciers and high mountain ranges had also melted, adding to Antarctica's contribution of fresh water to the salty deeps of the world. Sea levels had risen, flooding the coastal cities. Historic capitals were engulfed, forcing the building of new metropolises farther inland on higher ground. Now, the old cities were nothing more than memories in ancient vids and the province of intrepid divers.

None of this had particularly mattered to Lorcan. To him, Antarctica had been only one of his most lucrative mine sites. After the initial one he and Grace had started, they'd created four more in other parts of the continent as well as the operations they opened elsewhere in the world. The country's confused legal status as a nation had been ripe for exploitation. He hadn't looked at old pictures of Antarctica as it had once been with any sense of regret or nostalgia. He hadn't been responsible for what had happened to the land and, after all, humanity had adapted to the global changes, adapted, and moved on. Millions had died, it was true, but that had all been a long time ago.

Antarctica hadn't meant much to him except in the sentimental sense of it being where his and Grace's business had started up. Now, it meant everything.

"Sir," came the pilot's voice over the comm, "the spaceport seems deserted. The location identifier is no longer recognized and there's no air traffic control to contact."

"Is that a problem?" asked Lorcan tensely. "I believe I still own the land."

"I guess not," the pilot replied uncertainly. "Only...if the landing pad hasn't been maintained, touching down could be dangerous. Antarctica is famous for—"

"I'm all too aware of what the country's famous for."

"Yes, sir. Of course. I'm sorry, I wasn't thinking." Again, her professional demeanor had slipped. She sounded embarrassed and uncomfortable.

Previously, he would have been irritated and would respond with something acid and cutting, but today he could only answer, "If you don't want to take the risk, fly to the nearest alternative landing site and I'll make my own way across country."

After a pause, she replied, "I think it'll be fine, sir. I'll take you directly there."

27

Picking up a bagel, Wright yawned and scratched his beard with his other hand. Ever since getting back from the Australian desert he'd let his beard grow, but he guessed he'd probably have to shave it soon. Something big was coming up and he might have a face-to-face briefing with a senior officer.

The *Resolute* was gliding over the Indian Ocean at maximum knots on her hydrofoils, smoother than a baby's bottom. They were leaving Oceania. He'd been given the coordinates of their new destination but no one had told him anything else. Not that he really cared right now. He'd just woken up. Morning was not his favorite time of day.

He chewed morosely on his bagel, wondering why he couldn't see very well and why his eyes hurt.

Abacha sat across from him in the mess. The *Resolute* was too small for a separate wardroom for officers. Everyone ate in the same place. Wright preferred it this way. The crew felt like more of a team. Though, at the moment, he kind of wished everyone could eat a bit more quietly.

Abacha was watching him. Noticing Wright meet his gaze, he asked, "Everything okay, sir?"

He grunted something approximating an affirmative.

Then he realized. It was the sun. The sun was shining through a porthole and hitting him square in the eyes. So *that* was why he couldn't see properly.

He chewed and thought some more.

He comm'd the bridge. "Jeong?"

"Yes, Major?"

"Could you shift our heading..." he squinted at the sun "... two degrees south. Thanks."

He closed the comm.

Slowly, the bright circle of light slid off his face. He blinked. He could see again.

Across the table, Abacha was grinning at him. He gave a half smile back and took another bite of his bagel.

~

HALF AN HOUR LATER, when he'd properly woken up and told Jeong to return the *Resolute* to her original course, he went to the port gunwale to look out across the cobalt ocean. There wasn't a lot else to do, except to wonder what lay in store at their destination, and hope the Australian authorities would find the location of the trafficked children.

When he'd received the new orders, he'd taken the opportunity to ask Colonel Rioli for an update. The colonel reported that a thorough search had been made of the area where Wright and Abacha had been forced to turn back, and nothing had been found. There was nothing but desert for hundreds of kilometers. The only lead was the highway that passed through it, running north and south. The traffickers had most likely been walking the children to the road, where they had been picked up and taken somewhere else.

The good news had been that, now the authorities were aware of what was happening, a permanent watch would be kept on the trafficking route. As soon as another party of traffickers and children arrived, they would be followed. But the wet, stormy season was on its way and, considering the Crusaders' method of camouflaging their ships, no more might arrive for months.

"Sir," said Ford as he approached from the bridge.

"Yes, Lieutenant?"

"Jeong's running a competition and the crew were wondering if you'd like to join in."

"What kind of competition?"

"I think you call it a sweepstake in the BI. We're betting on the number of words Krol says at one time before we dock."

"Hm, I'll have to think about that."

"I should tell you, all the best numbers have been picked from the hat already. Abacha's got three, I've got two, and Hadley's got four. We've excluded one because that's stupid. Even Krol says one word now and again. What do you think? Are you in?"

"So only numbers higher than four are left? I'm basically betting our engineer will say more than four words in a row within the next week?"

"Not exactly," Ford replied ruefully, "Not everyone's drawn their ticket yet. You might get an even higher number. I admit your chances aren't good, but you never know."

"All right. Whatever. I'll do it."

28

The memorial site was magnificent. Four crystal monoliths stood fifty meters apart in a square and rose to slender points at a great height.

One for each of them.

Between the monoliths sat a tall, wide, elegant glasshouse. Even at a distance, the verdant vegetation and large, colorful flowers were plain to see. A moat surrounded the site crossed by one narrow, arching bridge.

The small town was deserted. The factories still and derelict. Slow-growing, gray-green native mosses and plants had begun to reclaim the area. In the bleak Antarctic landscape, the memorial was a precious jewel among dull stones.

Behind Lorcan, the shuttle engines quietened to silence. The wind was the only sound. The endless wind. He'd grown so used to it in his years in Antarctica he'd ceased to hear it.

Grace had...

His heart convulsed.

He gasped.

Could he do this?

He'd never been here. He'd planned the structure, paid for it all, oversaw the building of it virtually, but he'd never been able to bring himself to visit.

The architect had done a marvelous job. He'd taken shock, despair, and grief, and transformed it into something beautiful, an homage and tribute to the lives lost. He had realized Lorcan's dream. Yet it was not enough. Or perhaps it was too much.

He took a step forward, and then another. Automatically, his footsteps continued, one following the other, though he didn't consciously will it.

Did anyone still come here anymore? The memorial wasn't strictly only for his family, but also for everyone who had died. How many? At least a hundred. He hadn't read the reports at the time or since. He actually couldn't remember the period directly after the disaster very well. He could recall receiving the news and then...nothing. Not for days, perhaps weeks.

He hadn't seen any pictures of it, but the sinkhole had swallowed about half the little mining town, as he understood. Swallowed his family. Swallowed a part of him, irretrievably. By then, he was already fabulously wealthy and living a luxurious and powerful life. Yet the insignificance of all that had been demonstrated to him in one devastating second, when everything that really mattered had been ripped away.

Like an automaton, he had tottered closer to the memorial. In all the desolate ruins that remained, it was the sole place that continued to be looked after. The crystal and glass shone in the wan sunlight and the water moving lazily in the moat was clean and clear. The glasshouse plants were growing strongly. Some person or team of people was still faithfully performing the work.

He stepped onto the bridge. As he reached the top of the arch, he saw into the glasshouse more closely.

It had been Grace's love of gardening that had inspired him

to create the living reminder of her life. Yet, now he looked at it with new eyes after the passage of many years, he was struck by how the scene of beautiful flowers and plants protected from a harsh climate was rather like one of Kekoa's habitats.

Had this been where his idea for the Project had begun?

He paused, taking in the view. He was vaguely aware of the bite of the icy wind, but he didn't pay it any mind. He was awestruck by the beauty of the place he had created and then never visited for so long.

Feeling stronger, he walked the rest of the way across the moat and along the gravel path that led to the glasshouse doors. Two of the crystal monoliths rose to dizzying heights to the right and left of him. Their interiors were not uniform, though their surfaces were smooth and polished. Cracks and irregularities ran through them, catching and refracting the daylight, breaking it into rainbow colors.

One for each of them.

He faltered.

Hesitating, he stood a few paces from the glasshouse doors, clenching and unclenching his hands. He felt unsteady on his feet and feared that if he took another step he would topple over.

He had to do this. He had come so far, and not just in terms of distance.

As if weighed down by a ball and chain, he dragged himself forward.

The glasshouse doors slid smoothly open and warm, humid air billowed out, enveloping him in rich scents of aromatic flowers and foliage underlit by the subtle scent of vegetative decay.

He stepped forward.

Sitting at a desk to the left of the entrance was a middle-aged woman. She'd looked up from her interface as he'd entered. Her expression had been of mild surprise as though she hadn't expected anyone to come in, but then her mouth dropped open. She'd recognized him. She hastily got to her feet and brushed crumbs from her skirt. A half-eaten piece of cake on a plate sat on the desk.

"Ua Talman!"

She grabbed the plate and tried to find somewhere to put it, but the only available alternative was the floor. She held onto it, awkward and flustered. "I wasn't expecting you, sir. Did I miss a message? I'm very sorry."

"I didn't send any advanced warning. Please sit down and finish your cake."

"Oh no. Let me take you on a tour of the site. We also have an interactive guide, or you can listen to a commentary."

"I won't need any of that. But I would prefer to be alone. Do you have any other visitors?"

"No. Not today. Not usually, in fact. Not for a long time. I..." She put the cake down. "I'll leave and lock the doors. When you're ready to go, you can unlock them from the inside by pressing the release."

"Thank you. I appreciate it."

"No problem, sir." She moved around the desk. "I-I just wanted to say, I'm so glad to see you here. It's a beautiful place. It's a shame hardly anyone comes to see it anymore. I suppose it's only to be expected, considering it's so far off the beaten track. But the people deserve to be remembered, right?"

"They do indeed," he replied tightly. His capacity for small talk, never large at the best of times, was being stretched to its limit in his current state.

The woman seemed to sense this as she said, "I'll go. Please take as long as you like. I'll know when you've left because I'll get a notification about the release being activated."

She stepped past him. The doors swished open and closed, and then, finally, he was alone.

Steel grid paths led through the planted areas. As he walked along, his footsteps quietly echoed. Somewhere, water was playing from a fountain or trickling along a stream. Above, an orchid sprouted from a branch curved over the walkway. Orchids had been Grace's favorite flowers.

He found a bench and sat down.

29

Putting his hand in his pocket, Hans was surprised to feel a piece of paper in it. He pulled it out. It was a note, folded in half.

Dear Joseph

Please forgive my forwardness. I have asked your laundress to put this among your best clothes, the ones you will wear for the High Council meeting.

We, your Abertawe friends, wish you luck and success in your endeavors. We know you'll do your best to represent our interests, and you'll be an invaluable support for the new Dwyr.

Warm regards,

Esme

He read the note through twice and then threw it on the fire.

Politely deflecting Esme's heavy-handed hints that she wanted to accompany him to the Dwyr's castle had tested his powers of diplomacy to the utmost. He'd sensed she put her husband, Sebastian, through the same trial whenever he visited his mother. Not because she ached to see her mother-in-law. Esme was of a type Hans had met many times during his career in intelligence. She was a hanger-on, a groupie, fascinated by and in awe of people who wielded power. She longed to be a part of the scene, but she lacked brainpower, perception, discernment, and charisma, so she scrabbled for crumbs. Simply being present among the ones she idolized fed her spirit. She was a fool. She saw glamour and mystique where in truth there was only deception and danger.

He'd managed to deny her wish without offending her and severing their connection. He might need her in the future.

He took a final look in the mirror. If he'd been in his former role with the BA, anyone would have thought he was about to attend a costume party. Fashionable clothing for men among the Crusaders currently consisted of corduroy breeches, stockings, a long jacket, and high-collared linen shirt. His suit was a deep green and his shirt pale yellow. Though he looked ridiculous, his attire was, he had to admit, extremely well made, especially considering the textiles were hand woven and the clothes hand sewn.

The heavy wooden door to his chamber resounded with a knock.

"Come in."

It was a female servant, dressed in the plain gray dress and white hat and apron that signified her low rank. Living among Crusaders was like returning to feudal times.

"I beg your pardon, sir. I was asked to inform you the meeting will begin in five minutes and to guide you to the room."

"Thank you. I am ready."

As I'll ever be.

He'd attended countless meetings in his life. He'd met with royalty, prime ministers, presidents, CEOs of multinational corporations, tyrants, and genocidal murderers, but he'd never met the Dwyr of the EAC. Also, he hadn't been informed about who else would be in attendance. He had no idea who occupied the highest positions in the cult. Neither did anyone else outside the close-knit circles of influential Crusaders as far as he was aware. It had been one of the mysteries SIS had failed to crack.

As he followed the woman through the castle corridors, a sense of unease crept over him. He hadn't questioned the fact that Sebastian's mother had managed to secure him a place at this high level meeting, but maybe he should have. On the face of it, he was only a mayor of a large town, one of many in the BI. Why should he be invited to attend the High Council?

Had his cover been blown?

His footsteps slowed and the servant began to draw ahead.

Had Taylan Ellis informed on him? She'd been angry he hadn't been able to give her the information she wanted. Had she found a way to take her revenge?

No. That didn't work. He'd received his invitation to the meeting *before* he'd told her he hadn't been able to discover anything about the whereabouts of her children. Still, she might have informed on him since then.

The servant had noticed he'd fallen behind and halted to allow him to catch up.

He was deep within the Dwyr's castle with no idea how to get out and entirely surrounded by Crusaders for hundreds of kilometers. If the Dwyr did know who he was, he wouldn't stand a chance. He'd heard the cultists did terrible things to their prisoners.

He increased his pace. He was being ridiculous, losing his cool. He couldn't allow his nerves to get to him. He'd been in worse situations. Trapped inside a cage and close to death, for instance. He'd been given a second chance and he was going to take it. And he had to move fast. From what Ellis had told him, it sounded as though the Alliance was about to launch an attack. That was all well and good, but if the BI was to be reclaimed, he wanted a role in the process. The Alliance needed to step away from its monarchical roots and become a republic, and it would only do that if influenced by someone who had played a large part in the significant victory. He had to be *involved*, not a bystander who happened to have snuck back into the country before it was liberated.

"Here we are, sir," said the servant.

She twisted the iron latch on a set of double doors and pushed one of them open.

As he walked past her, she inclined her head.

He almost shivered in revulsion.

Crusader ways disgusted him to his core. People should be equal. Why should this woman live out her days in drudgery while others basked in luxury?

He carefully set his features to a neutral expression in his lifelong practice of never giving anything away.

He was not the last to arrive. Three chairs were empty around the long, polished table. A slim, dark-haired boy dressed in a deep blue suit—Hans judged him to be thirteen or fourteen—sat at the farthest, narrow end. Wooden panels covered the stone walls and a mullioned window looked out over the central courtyard.

"Mayor Fry, welcome to the High Council. Please take a seat."

A woman he guessed was Morgan sat on the boy's right. She was dark-haired too, pale, and small. She didn't look at him. A bony, ruddy-faced man was at the boy's left. More officials ranged down each side of the table. Including the Dwyr and himself there were nine in total. When the two remaining attendees arrived, the number would be brought up to eleven. An odd number prevented a hung vote. Perhaps that was one reason he was here.

He sat between a heavy-jowled man in early old age and a nervous-looking woman who was picking at a hangnail. The man nodded graciously while the woman offered a quick smile.

The Dwyr suddenly grimaced and put his fingertips to his forehead. Then he looked at Morgan questioningly. She gazed at him in return, but she appeared to be the master of the inscrutable expression. Hans prided himself on his ability to read faces, but in hers he read nothing. Why had the boy grimaced?

"Master Heirophant," he said to the man on his left. "Please introduce the Council to the mayor."

"Yes, Dwyr."

He cleared his throat. "Mayor, if I may introduce—"

The sharp sound of metal clanging against metal made Hans jump. The chamber door flew open and the woman who had brought Hans there rushed in, her white cap awry.

"Forgive me, Dwyr," she blurted, "but the seneschal has received a message that planes have broken through our defenses!"

"Planes?" The boy's large, dark eyes grew round. "What sort of planes?"

"It's thought they're Alliance planes, sir. I don't know what type."

Morgan stood. "You should all go down to the cellars. Dwyr, come with me."

With that, she swept from the room, the boy following in her wake.

The remaining attendees appeared frozen in shock.

"If you would like to walk this way," said the servant, "I can show you to the cellars."

Inside, Hans was cursing. The Alliance had begun their attack and he wasn't ready. He could have done so much to smooth the path of the assault. He could have helped to coordinate the Resistance, persuaded key people like the ones at this meeting to rethink their allegiances, relayed vital intelligence, and now the opportunity was to be snatched from him.

The officials were quickly filing out of the room. Hans

mentally dragged himself back to the crisis. The castle might be bombed.

Fear seized him. Memories of the bombing of General Council in the Caribbean were flooding back. The dreadful explosions. Fire raining down. The conflagration he had only escaped with Josephine's help.

The last person had left the room. If he wanted to shelter in the cellars, he had to hurry. But did he want to do that? If the castle were bombed, he could be trapped under a mountain of rubble. Would anyone bother to dig the officials out? Did the Crusaders even have the equipment to do it? Morgan and the Dwyr weren't going to the cellars. They were going someplace else, somewhere better and safer.

He couldn't face the possibility of being entombed and slowly dying of thirst or hunger.

If the Alliance was going to strafe the place, he would take his chances outside, in the open.

He ran from the chamber.

The others had already disappeared.

How to get out?

The sound of footsteps was coming from one end of the corridor. That way lay the stairwell he'd come up. He needed to go another way to find the front entrance. These old places usually had two or three sets of stairs.

As he raced to the other end of the corridor, he heard a droning noise. The air seemed to vibrate. The planes were already drawing near.

An arched opening and narrow stone steps descending in a spiral appeared.

He bounded down them, two or three at a time, pressing his hand against the outer wall for balance as he careened around the curves. When he reached the bottom, he was in an open, airy space. It took him a moment to recognize it. He'd come directly to the entrance! The formal wooden staircase he'd ascended when he'd arrived stood in the center. He must have come down the secondary, servant's stairs.

The double doors stood open, but two men were in the process of closing them.

"No!" Hans yelled, running toward them. "Wait! I'm leaving."

"It isn't safe, sir," replied one of the men, raising his voice over the noise of the approaching aircraft.

The planes did seem to be preparing to bomb the castle. They were flying too slowly for anything else.

Not bothering to answer, Hans forced himself through the closing gap and out onto the lawn.

There they were.

Flying in a wide V below the clouds were three airplanes. Snub-nosed and wide winged, they had not been built for speed. Hans guessed the planes that had done the fighting to allow these three into EAC airspace were far away, somewhere out to sea.

The castle doors thudded as they closed and the bolts slid into place.

As he watched, transfixed, the two outer planes peeled away, off to drop their terrible cargo on other targets. The point of the V flew on. From its trajectory, it would fly directly overhead.

He tore his gaze from it to glance at his surroundings. A driveway cut through the lawn, but, aside from that, the nearest hundred meters were flat and featureless.

He could go nowhere, do nothing, except—

The belly of the craft was passing over him. It was so close, he saw a hatch open in it.

He was about to be blown apart.

But what came out was...

Confetti?!

Open-mouthed, he watched thousands of pieces of paper

flutter out, billowing and scattering in the turbulent air. The paper fell like snow, obscuring the departing plane. The noise of its passage softened.

He was shaking. He'd gone from staring death in the face to...what?

What the hell was the Alliance doing?

Some slips of paper were drifting to the ground. He glimpsed writing on them, and it was then he understood.

Someone in the BA was very smart.

He strode to the nearest sheet and picked it up.

30

CRUSADERS, YOU HAVE BEEN LIED TO
Dwyr Kala Orr lives!
She has a new consort, the ancient king and rightful ruler of the Britannic Isles
She will return soon.
PREPARE FOR HER ARRIVAL

Taylan frowned as she read. More of the notices were scattered all over the street. Like the rest of the population of Abertawe, she'd thought the town was about to be bombed, but instead the plane had dropped these.

So Orr must have woken up. But had she really agreed to help the Alliance win back the BI? She didn't seem the type of person who was content with being only a figurehead. If the BA expected her to do as she was told, it was treading a dangerous path.

Taylan scrunched up the paper and tossed it on the ground, unsure if the confirmation of the impending battle was good news. Returning the country to Alliance control might free up the information on where her children had gone, but there was no guarantee it would win.

She could see the strategy: a two-pronged attack on the Crusaders' psyches. They were fanatically loyal to their Dwyr, whoever that might be, and the King Arthur myth—truth—played right into their love of legends and fanciful tales. They would lap up the story of the once and future king, and anyone who met him was wowed by him. He was so goddamned charismatic. No one would realize he was the same person as the sword-wielding berserker who had sliced his way through the crowd at the launch ceremony, and no one was going to tell them.

It was a good plan. She couldn't deny it. But the EAC had a new Dwyr now, and there was clearly no love lost between the two. The son had abandoned his mother and departed in the company of the original Dwyr's strange female companion. How would the Crusaders react when they had to choose between the mother and the son? From what she'd learned of them, they would get confused, and confusing them made them angry. They would probably start fighting each other.

There would be bloodshed, disruption, and turmoil. In conditions like that, finding her children would be even harder.

People were coming out of their houses along the little street and picking up and reading the propaganda. She felt safe to return to the place she'd chosen to sleep in last night. Everyone was too distracted to notice her. She walked down the path that led to the back door and went inside.

After passing through the dusty kitchen, she stepped into the tiny square living room with its worn sofa and silent, dark, defunct wall interface. Thank god Crusaders still believed in indoor plumbing. Her sleeping bag lay on the carpet. She hadn't gone upstairs to find a bed to sleep in. Bedrooms were more personal to the previous occupants. It was too depressing.

She'd stuck to her policy of moving to a new abode every evening for safety's sake. It was wearisome to find a different place every night that was empty, dry, and relatively clean, but like the first town she'd plied her trade in, Abertawe was full of abandoned houses. It would be a long time before she ran through them all.

No one would want their fortune told today. The town would be in upheaval after the propaganda drop. She decided to stay in the house, out of sight. She would pass the day practicing her handwriting and making up more drivel to tell gullible Crusaders.

Sitting on the sofa, she took a half-eaten pastry from a paper bag, the remains of last night's dinner, and munched on it. As she chewed, she thought of Mayor Joseph Fry. What did he make of the Alliance's leaflet drop? He had to be at the new Dwyr's castle by now for the High Council meeting. She'd passed on the Resistance's message about the direction he should push the Dwyr in, but she guessed it was all moot now. He wouldn't have time to do much before the Alliance attacked.

With a twinge of guilt and fear, she realized she was already regretting her decision to cut ties with him. Even at their second meeting, he hadn't been able to tell her a thing about what might have happened to her kids. Not a thing! She'd told him that was the last time he would see her, that he could figure out his own way to contact the Resistance from now on and she'd been true to her word.

She'd been so angry. She'd given him plenty of warning and he'd still come up with nothing. He'd tried to spout his spiel about how these things took time, but she'd cut him off, swore at him, and left.

Had she been right?

Now, with the benefit of hindsight, she had to admit she hadn't. Meilyr's words about how people would have to work together if they were to defeat the EAC continued to play on her mind. Despite telling Fry she only cared about reuniting her family, it wasn't true. She desperately wanted her homeland to be free again.

More than that, though, she'd been stupid. Fry might not be fast at getting her the information she needed, but he was her best source. *Had been* her best source. And she'd told him to take a walk.

She put down the remains of the pastry.

Dammit.

She'd lost her temper, lost control of herself, and cut off her nose to spite her face. Fry had all the power and she had none. She would have to go to him when he got back from the High Council meeting and eat humble pie.

A rustling came from outside. It sounded like someone trying to force their way through the overgrown front garden to reach the door. She waited, not moving.

When she'd first entered the house she'd closed the living room curtains so no one would be able to look in and see her, but that meant she couldn't look out.

Rap, rap, rap!

It *was* someone trying to come in. Who the hell would be knocking at an empty house? Were they there by mistake? Maybe if she did nothing they would go away.

Rap, rap, rap!

Shit.

She got to her feet and walked to the living room doorway, which led to the hall. Poking her head out a fraction, she saw a fuzzy figure through the frosted glass of the front door. It looked like just one person. She couldn't tell if it was a man or a woman.

It had to be a mistake. Someone had got the wrong house.

The doorknob turned.

Taylan held her breath.

She didn't know if the door was locked. She hadn't checked. There hadn't seemed to be any point. The lock on the back door was busted anyway. Most abandoned houses in West BI were the same. Crusaders had broken into them to find the people who had been hiding out during the invasion, or just to steal food and clothes.

The front door didn't open.

The figure moved away, their shadow receding from view.

Taylan exhaled.

Whoever it was, they seemed to have given up. But there was no point in taking any chances.

She walked into the kitchen, stood to one side of the back door, and drew her knife from her boot.

If the visitor came down the path at the side of the house, he or she would be here about—

The doorknob on the back door rattled, and the door opened.

Taylan leaned out, reached around the door, and grabbed the intruder's clothes below their neck before dragging them the rest of the way in.

She had the tip of her knife at the woman's throat before she saw it was the green-eyed Crusader who had got her into Fry's mayoral inauguration party.

In surprise, she jerked her hand open. The woman had instinctively pulled backward in response to Taylan grabbing her. When she was released, she staggered backward, her arms windmilling.

"Oh!" she exclaimed.

Taylan reached out and grabbed her again, by her arm this time. Still in shock, she almost spoke, but clamped her lips shut. After she was sure the Crusader wouldn't fall, she returned her knife to her boot.

"Did you...?" asked the woman. Her gaze traveling from Taylan's feet to her hand. "What was that? Did you have a...?"

Taylan tried to smile though she had a feeling it looked more like a grimace.

"I must have scared you. I'm sorry. I didn't mean to. It's taken me so long to find you. Can I come in?"

With a sense of misgiving, Taylan pulled out a chair at the kitchen table. Gesturing the woman to sit, she went to the living room to get her cards, paper, and a pen. The annoying Crusader must have come for a reading.

Since becoming the Abertawe mayor's seer, she'd experienced a big upturn in trade. Her reputation had spread around town, and people approached her in the street. She must have been watched last night when she'd found this house.

When she returned to the kitchen, she almost collided with the woman, who hadn't stayed put.

"I'm Esme." Seeing what was in Taylan's hands, she continued, "I'm not here for that. Can we talk? I mean..." she laughed nervously "can I talk to you?"

Taylan sat down.

Esme sat opposite her.

There was something unsettling about the newcomer. She hadn't noticed at the time of the party. She'd been too focused on making the connection with Fry. But Esme had been at the town hall when she'd gone to see him another time, and then she'd felt a strange vibe from her. Now, the woman's intense stare was setting off alarm bells.

"I'll just come right out with it, okay? I wanted to speak to you about Joseph. I went to see him before he left, and he told me he wouldn't be seeing you anymore. Is that right?"

Taylan nodded.

"He said the decision was yours, not his?"

She nodded again.

"I'm sure you must have your reasons. The Mayor wouldn't elaborate, which I respect. But I'm here to ask you to reconsider. You have a very special gift. Joseph needs you. The town needs you, especially in light of this."

She searched among the folds of her skirt and pulled out a crumpled propaganda leaflet. Spreading the paper out on the table, she continued, "Momentous events are underway. The future of the EAC is uncertain. The guidance you provide will be invaluable."

Taylan nearly laughed. Why waste your time with soldiers, guns, and bombs when you have people who can read the future? She managed to keep a straight face.

"Will you think again about being the Mayor's adviser? It would mean so much."

She shrugged and nodded for a third time.

31

Kala picked up the dress the Alliance had provided her between the tips of a finger and thumb, wrinkled her nose, and dropped it on the bed. Whoever had chosen it didn't have the first idea of how a Dwyr should look.

For one thing, the dress appeared to be *printed*. Made by a machine. Where was the dedication, the work, the artistry? Anyone could use the same program to create a garment that was identical in every way. Even when a seamstress used the same pattern and cloth, the results were only ostensibly alike. There would be differences in the fine detail. Everything made by hand was unique in some way. She wasn't sure she held the same belief as many Crusaders did, that the maker imbued his or her creation with a part of themselves, their soul or spirit, but there was undeniably something personal about handmade products.

How come no one outside the EAC could understand that?
Ugh.
She sat on the edge of the bed. Her legs remained weak,

though each day she was growing stronger. The medics who helped her with her physiotherapy told her so.

She curled her lip at the memory of their patronizing words of support and praise. They spoke to her like she was a child or a feeble old person.

"Mirror."

The wall opposite the bed transformed to a reflective surface.

Dolefully, she turned her head and ran her fingers through her hair. She'd had it cut short. The thin patches were growing back and her face had fleshed out somewhat.

"Mirror, close."

The surface reverted to a plain wall.

It was only recently she'd been able to look at herself. Her image filled her with anguish and gloom. She had sunk lower than she'd ever imagined possible. If she'd known she would one day be a puppet of the Alliance, she might have joined Jon, swinging from his castle window in the breeze.

Closing her eyes, she concentrated.

Perran! Perran, can you hear me?

She winced as pain lanced through her head.

She'd tried to contact him telepathically so many times, even when she'd been locked within her mind, but he never answered. Before, when she'd been aboard the *Gallant*, she hadn't known if it was because the distance was too great. Here in Ireland, she was so much nearer to him. She hadn't discussed with Morgan how close people had to be to speak mind to mind. The subject hadn't come up. Did distance even make a difference?

Disregarding the possibility her efforts were useless, she continued, ignoring the feeling of white-hot needles being inserted into her brain.

Perran, my darling. I don't know what Morgan has told you, but I'm alive and I'm well, and I miss you very much. I'm coming to you.

I'll be there soon. There will be some fighting, but I don't want you to be frightened. You won't be in any danger. When the fighting is over, things will be the same as before. I'll be Dwyr again, and you will be free to do whatever you want. We'll be happy together again. Wait and watch for me, darling.

She slumped onto the bed, exhausted.

∼

WHEN SHE WOKE UP, she was not alone.

The gray-haired female officer was there. She'd learned the woman's name was Colbourn. She vaguely remembered being prodded awake.

"You aren't dressed," said Colbourn. "You were told to dress and go to the front of the building."

"I'm not wearing *that*. It's disgusting."

Colbourn's lips thinned. "You aren't attending a fashion parade. Get up and get dressed. You have five minutes."

When the officer had left, Kala snatched up the dress and threw it at the door.

But following the Alliance's orders was the only way she would get to see her son again and her only hope for a better future. Once she'd been restored to her position she might find a way to throw off the BA's control and resume real power. They would be watching her and try to stop her, naturally, yet she might succeed.

She got up, took off the horrible hospital pajamas and put on the equally horrible dress. Not bothering to check her appearance in the mirror, she exited the room.

Colbourn was waiting for her. Without a word, the officer walked away, expecting Kala to follow her.

The building had once been a hotel but now it was full of Alliance staff. Military men and women hurriedly passed them along the carpeted hallways. From her window, she had also seen troops taking part in exercises in the grounds. The preparations for the forthcoming battle were in full swing. How ironic it was that, not so long ago, she'd been preparing to launch an attack in the opposite direction.

Morgan had to know what was going on here. Crusader spies in Ireland regularly sent reports across the sea. What had she done to protect the Britannic Isles? Did she even know what to do? The EAC's military heads would help her, but leadership had to come from the top. Kala had learned that lesson well previously. When she'd lost focus on military control, things had started to slip.

More importantly, since the propaganda campaign, Morgan had to know she'd told the Alliance everything she could about the Britannic Isles' defenses. That was the reason its planes had broken through so easily. The message on the leaflets would have explained it. All the infrastructure and strategies the EAC had in place to defend the island would have to be rethought and altered.

Would she manage it in time?

"Today you will rehearse your victory parades and speech," said Colbourn. "I assume you've memorized it as you were asked?"

Kala didn't answer.

They'd reached the terrace beyond the entrance to the hotel. Stone steps flanked them to the left and right. They were facing the balustrade, looking out over the green lawns.

"Have you memorized the speech?" Colbourn asked, hardening her tone.

When Kala still didn't answer, she said, "Everything has to go according to the plan you've agreed to. If you deviate from it, you know the consequences."

Yes, she knew. The 'discovery' of atrocities committed in her name, imprisonment, prosecution for war crimes, and execution. Her people would rise up in protest, but by then the BI and the rest of her empire would be filled with Alliance military, ready to quell dissent.

"I understand," she replied sullenly.

Two figures were approaching across the grass. Arthur and Merlin climbed the steps to the left. She hadn't seen Arthur since his visit to her on the *Gallant*. She wondered if he continued to harbor reservations about his companion. He'd seemed to be having some kind of crisis of confidence too. As he reached the top of the steps, his expression was glum. It appeared she wasn't the only one who was unhappy with what they were being told to do.

A flat-bed truck trundled toward them.

"This will serve to represent the vehicle that will carry you through the streets," said Colbourn. "You will give your speech from it before moving on to the next city. We've chosen the fifteen largest metropolitan areas to hold the parades." In response to Kala's sneer, she went on, "Of course, if the EAC hadn't systematically destroyed the broadcast media networks, none of this would be necessary. You would only have to do it once."

"I would rather not have to do it at all."

"Unfortunately, that isn't an option. Climb up onto the truck."

The driver had reversed the vehicle up to the right-hand steps. No railings ran down either sets of stairs, so it was easy to step directly onto the back. A small podium had been set up on it behind a safety barrier.

"Is that really necessary?" Kala asked. "Can't we do it here? We aren't children."

"It is completely necessary. We need to see how you will appear and sound. It's important you create the right impression. And you must be able to stand for long periods of time. Can you do that yet?"

"I believe so. What's more, though this may come as a surprise to you, I have given speeches before."

"We should do as they say, Dwyr," said Arthur. "It will be simpler in the end."

"I don't recall asking for your opinion, *King*."

"You should address him as my lord," said Merlin, "in public at least."

"I'll address him however I like," Kala spat.

"Onto the truck," commanded Colbourn. "Let's get this over with. I think it's safe to say that's what everyone wants."

Stiff with anger, Kala marched down the steps and onto the truck. As Arthur joined her, she edged as far away from him as the space allowed. Whether she wanted to participate in the subterfuge or not, her Crusaders would see there was no connection between them, emotional or otherwise. It wasn't something she could fake, no matter what the Alliance forced her to say.

At further prompting from Colbourn, she woodenly recited the mandated speech.

Whether she would do the same on the day, she hadn't decided.

32

At Dwyr Perran Orr's castle all was confusion and disarray. The arrival of the propaganda leaflets had lit a fire that threatened to burn down the edifice of the EAC, it seemed to Hans. In the days following the air drop, several of the High Council officials had left without a word to anyone, slipping away late in the evening when no one was around to challenge them. Most of the ones who'd stayed were tongue-tied at meetings the Dwyr had held, as if in fear of saying or doing something that might impact on them later.

Hans didn't envy their positions. If the EAC managed to repel the Alliance, those who had expressed loyalty to the boy Dwyr would be rewarded, but if the Alliance won through, their words would be remembered and would come back to haunt them. Kala Orr might forgive her son for his transgressions, but she would not forgive the people who continued to support him knowing she was still alive. Everything hung on the outcome of the impending attack.

"We will break for refreshments," Morgan announced.

It was a good decision. The meeting was going nowhere. Master Heirophant Neuman had been protesting against every proposal made by the military representative, General Lange. Neuman appeared to be one of those relentlessly negative people who only offered problems, not solutions. Lange had arrived this morning, no doubt summoned by Morgan in the name of the Dwyr. The Council official responsible for the defense of the BI had disappeared two days ago.

The people Hans had sat between the day of the propaganda drop had remained and he was sitting between them again. The heavy-jowled man had turned out to be the Keeper of the Dwyr's Purse, Mr Richter, and the nervous woman was Miss Strong. He didn't know her title but, from the comments she made, she appeared to be responsible for transportation within the BI. It was no wonder she was in a perpetual state of anxiety. Her role was essentially impossible. She was supposed to dismantle the previous, electrically powered transportation system and replace it with something that worked just as well but didn't require electricity.

Hans excused himself from both of them and went to the side table, where servants had placed drinks and snacks. Perran was loading his plate with small, sugary cakes.

"I haven't had a chance to speak to you personally yet, Mayor Fry," said Morgan, pouring herself some wine from a carafe.

"I'm honored to have your attention, ma'am."

"I confess I argued against your inclusion in the High Council at first. Someone of your rank wouldn't normally have any input into the decisions of the EAC."

"I understand that, and I am grateful you changed your mind."

"It was only when the seneschal mentioned that you'd gone from complete obscurity and barely a few coins to your name to Mayor of Abertawe within a few months that I became interested in you. The seneschal is one of Perran's favorites too. She spoils him rotten and he holds her opinion highly. But, getting back to your history, it is quite remarkable, especially in Crusader society where having the right friends counts for so much. Were you truly without contacts when you arrived earlier this year?"

"I was, but people were very kind and helped me out. It only seemed fair that I did what I could to repay that kindness and support my city in whatever ways I could."

Hans had a feeling she wasn't remarking on his fast journey to a political position because she admired it but rather because she was suspicious of it. She'd wanted to see him face to face and get the measure of him.

"Well, after hearing your input today, I believe I made the right decision. You've offered many wise and sensible suggestions, even though the Master Heirophant may not think so."

She hadn't lowered her voice to prevent the man in question from hearing her. He turned pink and stepped away from the buffet.

"Thank you, ma'am," said Hans. "I think we would all agree the Dwyr is in a difficult position. Many will believe the Alliance's message and when the assault begins, as it surely must soon, they will feel conflicted. So he could be fighting a battle within the BI as well as on its borders. The message must have been hard for the boy emotionally, too, so soon after losing his mother."

There was no chance of Perran overhearing his words. The boy had returned to the meeting table and was busy stuffing his mouth with cake.

Without even the tiniest glimmer of empathy in her eyes, Morgan took a sip of wine before murmuring, "Oh it is. It is."

"There's really no chance of any truth to the Alliance's assertion?" Hans gently probed.

"Absolutely not. I saw her die with my own eyes."

He was usually good at telling whether people were lying, but with this woman he had no inkling.

"The Alliance troops fired on her as soon as they saw her," she went on. "Perran and I were lucky to escape."

"It was fortunate for the EAC that you did."

"It was. The people need their Dwyr."

"And such a young Dwyr needs an adviser."

Morgan smirked and looked him searchingly in the eyes. He had the sensation she was boring into his soul. Did she suspect he might have ties with the Alliance? She certainly appeared to distrust him. For the moment, however, she was tolerating him, and that was all he needed.

"And this mention of a consort," he said. "An ancient king and rightful ruler. It's strange no one seems to know what that's about."

"It's time to reconvene the meeting," she said, leaving him at the side table.

Hans quickly added a few items to a plate, poured a glass of water, and returned to his seat.

He had no clue whether Kala Orr was dead or alive. The Alliance could be spreading a lie in order to destabilize its enemy or Morgan could be mistaken. Perhaps the Dwyr had been shot but not killed. If the BA *were* telling an untruth, it was a new tactic for them. It was also possible Morgan was lying, though he couldn't think why. It would be cruel to mislead the boy. On the other hand, he didn't appear to be grief-stricken. Was it a struggle for power?

"Dwyr," said Lange earnestly as Hans sat down. "Before we try to pick up from where we left off, can I speak freely?"

After a quick glance at Morgan, Perran replied, "You may."

"I'm the only person sitting at this table with any kind of military experience, and I'm telling you we do not have time for this prolonged decision-making process. The Alliance could be on our doorstep tomorrow. They could be on their way as I speak. I'm going to be frank. Our army, navy, air force, and space fleet are in a state of distraction and bewilderment. The fake announcement they heard about the former Dwyr has unsettled all of them deeply. They need guidance. They need orders. And they need them *now*."

She paused and her expression twisted as if she were trying to figure out a way to put what she wanted to say politely. She sighed in exasperation and seemed to give up. "I've listened to enough bullshit today to last me a lifetime. Concerns about expenditure when our lives are at risk. Hogwash about omens not being in our favor. Who cares what the omens say? Are we going to fight for our way of life, for what we believe in or not?" She turned to Perran. "Dwyr, I beg you. Leave the defense of your realm to the people who know what they're doing. Trust us. Give us your permission to work without your direct approval or oversight. I know it's a big ask. But we've run out of time already. If we wait any longer to develop a coherent strategy, we'll lose. I guarantee it."

Before the boy could answer, the door to the chamber opened. "I beg your pardon, Dwyr, but there's someone to see Mayor Fry and she says it can't wait."

"Who is it?" asked Hans.

"I'm sorry, sir. I did ask, but she wouldn't give her name. Said she must speak to you personally."

"You may leave," said Perran.

Hans didn't want to leave. The meeting was finally getting somewhere. He wanted to hear the Dwyr's answer to the general's proposal, and perhaps to have a say in it too. But everyone was looking at him, waiting for him to go so they could continue.

He stood up, irritated, and stalked out of the door.

"When did this person arrive?" he asked the servant as he followed the man down the stairs.

"Just a few minutes ago. Drove up to the front entrance. I

told her you were in a very important meeting and shouldn't be disturbed, but she said you would want to see her. I believe there's someone else with her too."

They'd reached the entrance hall. One of the doors was open but there was no sign of the mystery visitor. Wracking his brains as to who it could be, he stepped out into the bright sunshine.

The only people who knew where he was were...

Esme Weber stood waiting next to a coach. As he appeared, she grinned broadly and a little maniacally.

"Mayor! I'm sorry to drag you away from your meeting, but—"

"Esme!" He was mustering all his powers of self-restraint, but he couldn't keep the note of frustration and anger out of his voice. "I told you your presence here is inappropriate. I'm in the middle of a very important discussion on the fate of the EAC. I do not have time for this! Please return to Abertawe and I'll see you when I get back."

He turned, not wanting to waste another second on the stupid woman, when she said, "Please Mayor Fry, wait and see who I've brought with me. I know you don't have any use for me, but what about your seer?"

He about-faced. "What?!"

Esme was opening the coach door.

Inside, drooping against her seat and looking totally out of it, was Taylan Ellis.

33

Taylan blinked blearily. The last thing she remembered was sitting at Esme Weber's dining table. She'd accepted the Crusader's invitation to stay at her house for a few nights while waiting for Fry to return. Maybe that hadn't been wise, but she was heartily sick of sleeping on the floors of houses whose previous occupants were either dead or refugees. Now she appeared to be somewhere else entirely.

Where *was* she?

She straightened her back and sat up, putting a hand to her head as her movement caused it to throb. Her throat felt dry and sore, as if she had a cold or had eaten or drunk something...

Fry!

What was *he* doing here?

He looked as surprised as she was.

She was inside a coach in front of a castle. How had she come here?

Esme's beaming face appeared. "You've woken up? Perfect! We're here! You slept the whole way. Can you believe it?"

There was something weird about her expression. Taylan read desperation and fear but of a juvenile kind, like a child who has been caught doing something really bad.

"Where's here?" asked Taylan, her mind foggy.

"The Dwyr's castle, of course!" Esme turned to Fry with a nervous giggle. "I guess she's still half asleep. Should I help you take her inside?" She rose onto tiptoes to peer over the mayor's shoulder and into the castle entrance.

Fry gently pushed Esme aside and leaned into the coach. He seemed to sense something was up.

Something *was* up. The castle had to be a day or more from Abertawe by the Crusaders' outdated methods of transportation. How come she didn't remember any of the journey? Nor did she recall any conversation with Esme discussing the visit.

"You look like you've been drugged," Fry murmured softly. "Is that possible?"

That was it. The bitch must have slipped something into her drink. "Very possible," she whispered.

"I don't want to cause a scene," he said, "so don't say anything. Let me get you to a room."

He took her elbow and supported her as she climbed down from the coach.

"Esme," he said, "it was thoughtful of you to find my seer and bring her here, but misguided. She's clearly unwell and should never have traveled so far."

"Really?" asked Esme innocently. "She seemed fine before we set out. Then she fell asleep and..." She moved closer. Fry stepped between them, pushing Taylan behind him.

"I'm sure the Dwyr has staff who can take care of her," he said. "Leave her with me. You can return to Abertawe."

"Oh, but..." Esme sounded wistful. "Can't I come in?"

Taylan couldn't see her, but she imagined the woman looking with desire at the castle.

Finding where she was hiding out, persuading her to reconsider working for Fry, offering her somewhere to stay, it had all been a ruse with this end. Esme wanted to be close to the Dwyr and his home. She wanted to be involved. She wanted to feel important.

"I must insist you leave now," said Fry. "Go home, Esme. Or, better still, find somewhere safe to hide. Gather supplies and take Sebastian with you. Dark days are coming."

He put an arm around Taylan and guided her toward the entrance. As they stepped into the hall, she caught a glimpse of Esme watching her, disconsolate and forlorn, before the servant shut the door.

Fry sent him away, telling him he would see to the visitor.

"You can wait in my room until the meeting I'm attending is over," he said when the servant had gone. "As you've regained consciousness you should be okay. Stupid woman. I doubt she regularly drugs people—I hope she doesn't. She could easily have given you too much and killed you. Can you walk? Come with me."

Her legs felt rubbery, so he offered her his arm to lean on as he escorted her through the castle.

It wasn't until they reached his room that the danger of her situation hit her. A painful fact leapt to the front of her rapidly clearing mind. She was in the new Dwyr's castle, where the woman Arthur had called Morgan le Fay lived. The same Morgan le Fay who had conjured 'phantasms' of her kids and probably knew who she was and what she looked like.

Fry was ushering her into his room when she blurted, "I can't stay! I have to get out of here."

"You can't. It's too late now. Esme's gone. Why do you want to leave?"

She was about to answer, but he continued, "Whatever the problem is, I don't have time to hear it. I must get back to the meeting. Remain here. It's perfectly safe for now. Everyone's too busy to bother about a fortune-teller's arrival. If you pull the rope next to the bed, a servant will come and attend to your needs. I'll be back later, though probably not until this evening."

With that, he was gone.

Shit.

She sat down in one of the velvet-covered chairs. She still felt woozy. Whatever Esme had given her, it must have been powerful to knock her out for so long. She didn't even know what day it was.

If she did ignore Fry's instructions and try to leave, she probably wouldn't get far. She needed to rest.

She relaxed into the chair and closed her eyes.

What had Esme been thinking? Had she really wanted an excuse to go to the Dwyr's castle so badly as to drug someone who was almost a stranger? She was unhinged. All Crusaders were to an extent, but her more than most.

Taylan began to take notice of her surroundings. Dark wooden paneling on the walls, a four-poster bed with curtains, candlesticks, a woven rug on the floor. It was like she was in a historidrama.

Her sore throat nagged at her.

What was it Fry had said about servants?

The rope beside his bed.

It was deep red and silken, feeling wonderfully soft and smooth in her hand. She tugged it. Assuming there was a bell at the other end, it had to be too far away for her to hear it.

She sat on the plump bed and waited.

The servant took about half a minute to arrive, panting. Taylan felt a bit bad. The poor girl must have run all the way.

Taylan remembered her 'vow of silence'.

Damn. Oh, what the hell.

War was coming to the BI. Who was going to remember the

silent fortune teller speaking or her funny accent? Like a servant would care anyway.

"Could I get a drink?" she asked. "Some juice or something?"

"We have apple juice, grape—"

"Apple is fine. And I need something to eat," she added, realizing she was absolutely starving. It wasn't surprising. She hadn't eaten for at least a day.

"Would cheese sandwiches be acceptable, ma'am? Only the cook—"

"I'd love a cheese sandwich. Two or three, in fact."

"Very good, ma'am." The girl began to close the door.

"Wait," said Taylan. "What were you about to say? Something about the cook?"

"The cook left yesterday and the seneschal hasn't found a replacement yet. So we can only offer guests plain fare."

"Do you know why the cook left? Wouldn't she have to give notice?"

The servant's cheeks turned crimson. "I really can't say, ma'am. I'll get your refreshments."

It had to be the Alliance's message. Taylan wondered how many more of the Boy Dwyr's staff had abandoned their posts, believing him to be a usurper. The Crusaders' attachment to their Dwyr wasn't rational or intellectual. It was emotional. They hadn't voted for her based on an assessment of her manifesto. They loved her, worshipped her.

They were reacting to the news she might be alive in exactly the way the Alliance must have hoped. The EAC was beginning to crumble from within.

The servant must have been wary of having to answer more difficult questions because, when she returned with Taylan's food and drink, she put the tray on the hall floor and knocked. By the time Taylan opened the door, all she saw of her was the back of her dress and hat as she went downstairs.

Taylan quickly drained the glass of juice and munched her sandwiches. While she'd been waiting, she'd come to a realization.

Yes, she was in the Dwyr's castle and dangerously close to Morgan le Fay, who posed a serious threat. But she was also in the seat of operations within the EAC. What was more, all the bigwigs were ensconced in an important meeting and the place was probably only half-staffed.

If there was a place and time she might be able to discover where her kids had been taken, it was here and now.

Chewing her last bite of sandwich, she slipped out.

34

"Major Wright, it's good to see you again."

His mouth dropped open.

Brigadier Colbourn's simple platitude spoken by anyone else might not have been meaningful, but coming from her the words were a very warm welcome indeed. In all the years she'd been his CO, he didn't recall her ever being so friendly.

He snapped his mouth shut. "It's good to see you too, Brigadier."

Despite the bad note they'd parted on, it *was* good to see her. The curmudgeonly older woman had a special place in his affections. He understood her. She put doing her duty above all else and he admired that, though lately he wasn't sure he felt the same.

She nodded. "This way, Major."

The Irish climate was a far cry from what he'd become used to off the coast of Australia during the days the *Resolute* had operated on the ocean surface. The cool cloudiness that constantly threatened rain brought back memories of the last time he'd been here, when he'd been on his way back to the

Gallant with Taylan after locating her in the BI. There had been another time too—the Alliance's second attempt on the life of the Dwyr. Taylan had snuck away and disappeared into the darkness, and he'd run after her through a downpour, racing along streets turned into streams. He'd found out about her kids and promised her a discharge.

Where was she now?

Brigadier Colbourn was leading him upstairs in the commandeered hotel. She still hadn't told him why he'd been ordered to bring the *Resolute* to Ireland. It had to be something very hush-hush if she wouldn't tell him about it even among their own people.

"How was Oceania?" she asked him over her shoulder, stepping onto the landing.

"Hot. We uncovered a child trafficking..."

She'd stopped at a door and put a finger to her lips as she opened it.

Inside was a bog standard hotel room containing some extraordinary individuals.

"Wright," said Lieutenant-General Carol, "I think you've met everyone?"

"Yes, sir."

The only time he'd seen Kala Orr close up she'd been unconscious, but he'd recognized her instantly, though her hair was short now. She sat at a dressing table with her back to everyone, her petulant expression reflected in the mirror.

Arthur and Merlin were, of course, extremely familiar. They stood together, Arthur resting his hands on the hilt of his massive sword, which stood on the floor in front of him. The fact he had it with him might not be significant—the massive weapon rarely left his side—but Wright had a feeling that an important part of the Alliance's next plan entailed the king killing someone. It wasn't to be the former Dwyr Orr, clearly, but if not her, then who?

"Major Wright," said Merlin, "it seems we're forced to work together again."

"Is that a problem?" Wright asked.

Carol's eyebrows shot up and he and Colbourn shared a look.

"Not a problem at all, T.J.," Merlin replied smoothly. "At least, not on my side."

Wright's jaw muscle twitched.

Arthur hadn't met his gaze. Something appeared to be bothering him.

"Our guests require transportation to the Britannic Isles," Carol explained. "We need to sneak them into the country and this time a fishing boat won't do. The Alliance is about to launch an attack, and even in the spots where there's no fighting, the coastal defenses will be on high alert. Anything coming across the sea from Ireland will be tracked and targeted. I imagine you can see where I'm going with this?"

"The *Resolute* has the highest stealth capability of the entire fleet."

"Smart man. It was actually Colbourn here who had the idea. She was familiar with the boat you'd been assigned to and so she suggested her. So if you're looking for someone to blame for roping you into this..." Carol laughed uncomfortably. "You must know your command inside out by now, so naturally you're part of the deal. However, if you aren't sure you're up to it, in light of your recent, er, medical crisis, I'm confident we can find another officer to take your place."

"Sir!" Wright spluttered. It was all he could say. How dare the man stand there and insult him, and not only that, in front of others too?

"I'm confident the major will do an excellent job," said Colbourn. "As he always does."

Silently grateful for her support, he asked, "When do we leave?"

"You have a couple of days yet," replied Carol. "We're about to do another propaganda drop. Confuse the Crusaders' already befuddled minds. The attack will begin soon after. Until then, you're confined to this hotel. Your crew will be informed that you'll be returning to your boat shortly and to make ready to depart. We won't tell them any more than that. Loose lips etcetera. I think that's all. If you would excuse me, everyone?"

He left.

"Propaganda drop?" Wright asked Colbourn.

Kala Orr turned in her seat and said bitterly, "They've been telling my people I'm still alive and I'm coming back to rule them again. Sowing discord."

He felt like replying, *Isn't that a good thing?* But her sour face put him off speaking to her. He looked at the brigadier.

"That's the gist of it," said Colbourn. "From the reports we've received from the Resistance, the first drop had the desired effect, so we're repeating the exercise." She paused and then added, "It would be better for us to speak in private."

"I would like to speak to you today too, Major," said Arthur.

"Oh yes," Orr said acidly, "I forgot. They're also telling my Crusaders that *he's* my husband."

The look of sad dismay on the king's face was almost comical.

"It looks like we'll have plenty of time to talk later, Arthur," said Wright.

Colbourn took him to a small room with a single bed and minimal furniture. "You can order uniform items and anything else you might need via the interface on the desk," she said, "but the net is closed. You won't be able to contact anyone externally until your mission is over."

"I understand, ma'am. The lieutenant-general didn't elaborate on what happens after I get the three passengers to the BI. Do I just hand them over to someone else?"

"It hasn't been decided yet. I would say you probably will. When we gain control, the plan is to transport Arthur and Orr around the country and hold victory parades. Crusaders love spectacles and we aim to give them one. If we can get the majority of them to accept Arthur and Orr as their new rulers, our battle will be truly won and without much bloodshed. It's a better alternative than dealing with insurgency for the next few decades. We can manage the repatriation of our displaced citizens peaceably and without too much backlash from the people who stole their homes."

"It seems a good plan, but do you really think Kala Orr will go along with it? She had a face like a smacked arse. Can we trust her?"

Colbourn smiled wryly. "You spotted the flaw. No, we can't trust her, but it will be easier to manage one megalomaniacal narcissist than millions of rebellious Crusaders."

"I'm not so sure about that."

35

Taylan had a feeling she might have visited this castle as a tourist attraction years ago when she was a kid. She wasn't positive. These ancient buildings looked mostly the same on the inside. Whether it had been this castle or another one, walking along the corridors felt very different now. There were no chattering visitors, no kids being told not to touch things or run, no friendly guides to explain the history behind all the artifacts. Everywhere she went was still and quiet.

Where were the servants? Didn't they have any jobs to do in the main areas? Were they all in the basement, or had most of them left, like the cook?

It smelled different now too. Musty. And the scent of burned candles hung in the air.

In some of the corridors the window shutters hadn't been opened, but the sun shone through gaps and cracks in the old wood, crossing the dusty atmosphere with shafts of light.

As she continued to explore the building, treading softly on the carpet runners, her sense of déjà vu increased. She *had* been here before, with Mam and Dad. She must have been eight or nine and it would be fifteen years until the boating accident that took their lives. They'd been bickering that day. The old habit. Mam hadn't wanted to come, saying it would be boring. Then, as they toured the place, she'd rejected all of Dad's attempts to interest her in anything.

"Taylan," he'd said. "You're not bored, are you?"

She'd said she wasn't just to please him, but really the only thing she'd found interesting was...

The library.

All those old books lining the shelves. Visitors weren't allowed to touch them, but you could read the titles on the spines, though some were so faded they were illegible. She'd been fascinated by the place. Crusty leather armchairs and a heavy, polished wooden desk stood behind rope barriers. When the guide had explained that when the castle had been built no one used interfaces and everyone had got their information from books, she'd been amazed.

If the castle had any kind of data storage, even if it was only paper files, it would be in the library. She cast her mind back. The library had been on the ground floor in a corner of the building. She peeked through a gap between two shutters that didn't meet and saw she was looking out over the gardens at the rear. She couldn't remember which corner the library inhabited, but there were only four.

She ran lightly to the end of the corridor and down the steps.

On the ground floor, she heard footsteps approaching. She halted, frozen, at the bottom. Her headscarf hung loose around her neck. She pulled it up and over her head and began to climb the stairs backwards.

The footsteps receded.

She went on.

A door stood ajar, revealing ranks of books. She listened outside for a minute, straining to hear sounds of breathing or slight movement, but there was nothing. She stuck her head in cautiously. The room was almost exactly as she remembered it. No changes appeared to have been made in the intervening decades, except one: there was a hand-held interface on the desk and its screen was lit.

The door hinges creaked as she pushed it open. She winced and looked behind her, but no one seemed to have heard.

The interface displayed a long list of messages. The first was from someone called Justice Wagner of Trefynwy and read,

Dwyr, forgive my direct message to you. I'm sure you must be very busy, but the people of Trefynwy need clarification and assurance. Do you plan on making a statement to refute the claim that your mother still lives? It would help to quell the disturbances and unease among the local population.

The second message was anonymous. It said, *Perran Orr, if you've been lying to us you'll pay. Your mother was a wonderful woman, loved by all. If you've done something to get her out of the way so you can take her place before your rightful time, you'll be punished. Don't forget it.*

"Well, hello," said a soft, smooth voice. "And who might you be?"

The dark-haired woman, Kala Orr's strange companion, stood in the doorway. Morgan le Fay.

How had she arrived so silently?

Taylan ducked her head, thankful she'd pulled her scarf over her face a few minutes ago.

"Sorry," she muttered, her heart starting up a tattoo, "I got lost."

She went to the door and tried to edge past Morgan, but she put out an arm to bar her way.

"What are you doing here?"

"Uhh, I was delivering some, uh, eggs, and I couldn't find anyone to give them to, and when I, uh..."

"Eggs, hm?"

Taylan contemplated making a run for it. But though the castle was half-staffed there were bound to be some guards hanging about. She would never make it.

She had to play her only remaining card. "Actually, that isn't true. I'm here with Mayor Fry. I wasn't sure if I was allowed to wander about but I was curious. I've never been somewhere like this before. I hope I didn't do anything wrong or get the mayor in trouble. He doesn't know what I've done, but he can confirm I'm with him."

She hated to drop Fry in it but she couldn't see any alternative. Plus, she was sure he could talk his way out of a high-security prison if he needed to. Hopefully, he could do the same for her.

Morgan roughly pushed down her scarf.

"I know you!" she exclaimed.

Taylan tried to run, but Morgan seized her arm in a surprisingly powerful grip and then shoved her into the room before slamming the door shut.

The woman's gaze turned momentarily blank then hard as she glared at Taylan. "You are here to assassinate the Dwyr!"

"What? No! I'm just here to…to…"

Morgan was stalking toward her. Taylan had a good twenty centimeters on her, but there was something about the petite figure that was terrifying. Something unearthly. Taylan backed up until the desk separated them. She was reminded of—

"Don't move," the woman commanded. She thrust a long-nailed finger in her direction. "Stay right where you are."

For some reason this triggered Taylan to break and run. She bolted around the opposite side of the desk. Morgan made a grab for her, but Taylan bowled her over. She reached the door, wrenched it open and…collided with a guard.

There were three of them. How had Morgan summoned them?

While Taylan was recovering her balance, the second guard got her in a headlock and the third grasped one of her wrists.

"Get her down!" yelled the man she'd bumped into.

The pressure on her neck increased. She twisted toward her captor to open her airway and then sharply kicked backward at the third guard. A yelp came from behind and her wrist was released. With her free hand, she reached for the face of the man who held her, ready to rake it or jab her fingers in his eyes.

He dropped her like a hot coal.

She lifted her head—just in time to meet the swinging fist of the first guard.

She knew no more.

36

The villa in Old France was well set up to view the forthcoming battle for control of the Britannic Isles. A generator supplied electricity, and the home system was connected to AP satellites that could view the conflict in detail. Lorcan's military had their orders to support the Alliance offensive. Though his army was small, his ships and airplanes had bulked up the BA's infrastructure. It was in space his support would be most valuable, he estimated. His starships would prevent the EAC's from interfering in what was happening on the surface. It wasn't beyond Crusader mentality to target areas populated by their own citizens with pulse bolts from the skies if it looked like the EAC was going to lose.

They were bloody minded like that.

Lorcan had spent the time since arriving from Antarctica re-reading favorite books, listening to music, and cooking. He'd also peeked into files on his home system that he hadn't been able to bring himself to open for years. Images and vids of Grace and the kids, pictures his children had drawn, performances they'd given at school, recordings of holidays. Many times, when he'd finished watching, he'd found his face was wet.

The sadness was inevitable, but it was bearable. In some ways, he almost didn't mind. It reminded him he was alive and he had years of treasured memories he could access at any time, even in his lowest moments.

The villa had a swimming pool and sauna. In the mornings, he would sweat in the humid heat, cool down in the plunge pool, and then swim for half an hour or so before making himself breakfast. He didn't see anyone. The household staff performed their duties in the early hours of the morning while he was asleep, as he'd instructed. He didn't want to be disturbed.

Or he thought he didn't. By the end of the third day of solitude and reflection, he began to feel a little lonely.

So when a packet arrived from Iolani, he was pleased rather than irritated as he usually was.

He opened it.

The scientist's round, cheerful face appeared on the interface.

"Lorcan," she said, smiling, "I know you're going to be obsessing about what everyone's doing while you're away so I thought I'd tell you. It's been one big party all day every day. No one's done any work, Darwin and Banks have taken over your quarters, and—"

A hand he recognized as Camilla's pushed Iolani's shoulder. She chuckled.

"Only kidding. We've all been working very hard. Anders made an interesting discovery he wanted to share with you, but he's decided to wait until you get back. Oh, and Xiao reported that the pig he revived the other day is doing well and showing no ill effects from its years in cryo. Um, what else? Kekoa had a new idea for a habitat on the *Balor*. She wants to create a theme park with rides, hot dog stands, and the rest. She was saying it might be possible to turn off the a-grav to a small area so the colonists can fly around. What do you think? Sounds like fun, right?

"Anyway, I hope you're doing okay down there. I know you aren't close to the conflict zone, but warfare is unpredictable. Maybe have the shuttle on standby in case things get hairy?" She glanced around and then leaned closer to the screen. "In case you're still in any doubt, I think you're doing the right thing. Helping the Alliance right now could be exactly what it needs to put an end to this damned war. I hope so anyway. That's it, Lorcan. Take it easy, and I'll see you when you get back."

The recording ended.

He watched the still screen, unseeing, for a few moments before reaching out to close it.

He was touched she'd taken the time to send him a message. But that was Iolani all over. She was strong in her emotions, whether they were negative or positive; quick to anger and, fortunately for him, warm-hearted enough to forgive the worst behavior, providing the perpetrator's remorse was genuine. His was, and she knew it.

He checked the time. If the Alliance stuck to their initial plan, the attack would begin tomorrow. He needed to arrange his interface set up so he could watch several feeds at once and follow the progression of the battle. He got to work.

37

The *Resolute*'s crew had been running another xiangqi tournament while Wright had been absent. It was obvious from the way they all poured out of the mess at the last second, despite receiving advance notice of his arrival.

Abacha had won the previous tournament in a final match with Krol. It had been a tense game though the outcome had been predictable. Abacha had printed himself a faux-gold medal inscribed Best Xiangqi Player in the Royal Marines. Others had pointed out he hadn't played *every* Royal Marine, but he waved them away. Since then, the game had become everyone's favorite pastime. They were all a little obsessed, in Wright's opinion.

When he boarded with Orr, Arthur, and Merlin, he caught a glimpse of Abacha hastily removing his medal under Colbourn's glare.

The brigadier said a final farewell at the Irish port. She wouldn't be coming along for the trip to the BI. Wright would be solely responsible for the VIPs getting to where they were supposed to go, which was a small, remote harbor on the West BI coast. Their final destination might be changed, however. After the Alliance had taken control, there would be danger spots and incidental conflict outbreaks while mopping up took place.

Wright settled Kala Orr in his own cabin. It was a wrench to give up his personal space, and he was forced to endure her complaints of cat odor while he coaxed Boots out from under his bunk, but he thought it was a better option than subjecting everyone aboard to her presence.

"I hope I don't have to live on this miserable ship for long," she grumbled.

"Boat," he said softly between his teeth.

"What?"

"Nothing. You can comm the galley from the interface if you need anything, though you might have to wait a bit for a response. We operate with a skeleton crew. Everyone has two or three jobs. I think you have everything else you might need. The head and shower are through there."

"The head?"

"The toilet."

The woman had spent time on starships. How could she not know that?

"Ugh." She curled her lip, as if pretending she never used one.

"Right. I think that's it."

"Wait. How will I find out what's happening in the battle?"

"I'll keep you updated if I hear anything relevant."

"What if the BA lose?" she asked, her dark eyes widening.

"Lieutenant-general Carol didn't discuss that with you?"

"No."

"I don't think it's likely. We wouldn't commit to an attack unless the odds were in our favor. But if things go badly I guess I'll be told to bring you back to Ireland."

"Where I'll wither away in solitude," she murmured, not looking at him.

He didn't feel an iota of sympathy. Even if she hadn't been notorious for all the atrocities she'd committed, his short experience of her in the hotel had shown her to be a truly terrible person. She was arrogant beyond belief and utterly lacking in any consideration for other human beings. He'd been reminded of the ancient Egyptian kings and queens, who had believed themselves to be gods. Kala Orr would have held herself as more important than any of them. Just sharing space with her made him want to commit murder and, despite his profession, he didn't consider himself to be a particularly violent man.

He was holding Boots, and the cat began to struggle to be put down.

"I'll leave you to settle in," he said, and made his escape.

While he'd been dealing with Orr, Ford had been setting up Arthur and Merlin in the two-bunk officers' cabin he shared with Jeong.

Wright caught up with him as he was closing the door on his way out.

"Are they okay?" he asked.

"Yeah," replied Ford, looking starstruck. "What a pair. I never in all my life imagined I'd get to meet two of the most famous figures in the history of the BI."

"You've heard of them?" Wright was mildly surprised. He didn't think Australians would know much about the mythology of the Britannic Isles.

"Oh yeah. I loved all that stuff when I was a kid. King Arthur, Guinevere, Lancelot, Sir Galahad, Gawain and the Green Knight, the whole shebang. Lapped it up. And now, here I am, meeting them face to face."

Wright wondered if Ford would be so enamored of Arthur if he knew what the man was capable of when he was in berserker mode. "Enjoy it while you can. I expect we won't have them aboard more than three or four days."

"You think the battle will be over that soon?"

"If not sooner. From what I understand, we're throwing everything we have into it. We have Orr and Arthur's agreement to participate in the plan as well as the support of the Antarctic Project. None of those things are guaranteed forever. The Alliance is going to strike hard and fast. We might not get this chance again."

"What happens after we drop them off? Straight back to Oz?"

"No. I'm to accompany them to their first stop. The *Resolute* is to wait for me out at sea."

Ford pulled a face. "Shame. I miss home already. The northern hemisphere sucks."

Wright laughed. "What difference does it make when you're on a boat?"

"It makes a helluva difference. There, I know it's sunny and hot up top. Here, I know it doesn't matter whether it's day or night, summer or winter, it's pissing down."

"It doesn't rain *all* the time."

"No, I'll grant you that, but it feels like it does."

Abacha appeared at the end of the passageway. "Major, is it okay if Krol and I continue our match now? We were both off duty when you arrived."

"Go ahead."

Wright was thinking he would join them, but at that moment Arthur came out of the officers' cabin. He closed the door carefully before quietly saying, "Could I speak to you, T.J.?"

Ford gave him a nod and walked away.

"Sure." Wright recalled the king had said he wanted to talk to him before, but hadn't managed to for whatever reason. Where to take him? The xiangqi game was going on in the mess and his own cabin was occupied. The control room was staffed at all times.

"This way," he said.

The four-bunk room allocated to Abacha and other crew members was empty and tidy, though it smelled of sweaty socks.

Arthur had left his sword behind, for which Wright was grateful. The hefty ancient weapon was intimidating and Arthur seemed capable of using it on anyone when in a certain state of mind. Wright recalled the cut on Taylan's neck after their encounter at the launch ceremony.

They sat on opposite bunks.

"I would like to ask your opinion about something," said Arthur. "I consider you a friend. I hope and believe you will be honest with me."

"I am your friend, Arthur." Wright had misgivings about things the king had done, but he also found it hard to blame him for them. "I'll try to be as honest as I can."

"I couldn't speak to you before because Merlin stays by my side almost constantly now, and I wanted to talk with you without him present."

Was he finally seeing through his alien companion?

"He won't leave you alone?" Wright asked. "Why do you think that is?"

"I am not sure, but I don't believe it's for my benefit. I think he may fear he's losing control of me."

Alleluia!

"I think you might be right about that," Wright replied.

"T.J., this plan the Alliance has for me, to pretend to be the Dwyr's consort and win the support of the Crusaders, do you think it's a good plan?"

"Will they buy it? I don't know. I don't understand Crusaders very well. But I think it's a good way to take back the Isles without a long, bloody war."

The great man's brow knitted.

Was this what was bothering him?

"I am concerned because the scheme is built upon a lie," said Arthur. "I am not the Dwyr's consort. I would never consent to such a thing. She is beautiful, but she is an odious person. Even if she were not, my heart lies with another and always will. Is it right to trick these Crusaders in order to win their trust? That would seem morally wrong. How can the plot succeed if its foundation is corrupted? I fear we're doomed to fail, and taking part would blacken my soul. Merlin doesn't agree. He says if the outcome is good, what we do to achieve it doesn't matter." The wrinkles on the king's forehead deepened. "He didn't used to be like this. Before, he understood the importance of righteousness, but now he seems to have forgotten."

Wright guessed that expediency was the answer to Merlin's apparently differing attitudes. When Arthur had ruled, everyone had been deeply religious. Now, few people were, unless you counted the Crusaders' fanatical beliefs. Merlin had moved with the times but was butting up against the old king's Dark Ages thinking.

"I'm sorry, Arthur. I don't think I can help you. All I can tell you is that if we win back the BI, we will have righted a wrong. Dwyr Orr's campaigns have killed and displaced millions over the years. The people of the BI deserve to return to their homeland and rebuild. I want to help them. Whether you want to be a part of that is up to you."

38

Mayor Fry's head hit the wall of the cell with a crack that made Taylan wince. The guard slammed the door shut and locked it. When Fry sat up, blood began running through his hair and over his ear.

She took off her scarf and pressed it to the wound. She felt like shit. If she hadn't mentioned the man's name, Morgan might not have made the link between the two of them. Only one servant had witnessed Esme's arrival with her in the coach, and servants were usually ignored. She should have said she'd sneaked into the castle by herself. Fry could have maintained his cover and Morgan would be none the wiser.

The mayor had turned pale green and looked like he might vomit.

"Just keep still for a while," said Taylan. "You'll feel better soon."

"I can do it," he said testily, and moved her hand away from the scarf, replacing it with his own. He also moved himself away, shifting on his backside into the corner of the cell.

"I'm sorry," Taylan said. "Sorry for getting you into trouble too."

"*I told* you to stay in my room!" He seemed too angry to even look at her. "Why were you wandering around the castle? Why didn't you wait for me?"

"I was trying to see if I could find out any information about my kids!" she protested. She didn't think she should bear all the blame for their predicament. "If you'd done as you promised, I wouldn't have been forced to—"

"I was working on it!" he barked. "You aren't the only one who needs help. My role here concerns the entire BA, not just you!"

She clenched her jaw. She was so sick of being accused of selfishness. "And it isn't only my kids who have gone missing! If I do find mine, I'll probably find out what's happened to all the others too. Who's looking for the children, huh? As far as I know, no one. You politicians and the military only care about governments and who has control. You don't give a shit about the people. You'd sacrifice us all as long as you can be in power."

"That isn't true," he replied, his tone softening. "With a just government, the people benefit. We're trying to achieve a just government. Would you prefer to live under a Dwyr or the Alliance?"

"I wouldn't give a shit who I was living under as long as my kids were safe."

"That's a very narrow view."

"Yeah, well I don't care what you think about my view."

He rolled his eyes and then grimaced in pain and pressed the material tighter to his head.

Taylan crawled over to him. "Let me take a look."

He allowed her to move the wadded up scarf away. She gently parted his hair and peered at his scalp. The lighting in the cell was bad. The only light came through a barred window in the door. But she could see a three-centimeter cut, blood welling in it. The blood was already beginning to coagulate.

"I don't think it's serious," she said, taking the pad from him and pressing it to his head again.

"You seem to be hurt too."

He'd spotted her blackening eye from the punch she'd received.

"I've had worse."

"I don't understand what we're even doing here," he muttered. "Imprisoning us just because you were caught snooping seems an overreaction."

"Oh, you don't know! Of course not."

"What is it I don't know?"

"Morgan thinks I'm here to kill Perran."

"Why would she think that?"

"Because I tried to kill his mother."

"You did what?!"

"It's a bit of a long story, but it isn't like we have anything else to do. I told you I used to be a Marine, right?"

She explained how she'd shot Kala Orr while the Alliance was hunting her in Jamaica, and that the former Dwyr had discovered her name through torturing a mission mate. Then she had to explain about the assassination attempt at the launch ceremony, though she left out a lot of details. She thought about also telling him of the attack on the *Belladonna* as, despite saying he was working for the BA, he didn't seem to know, but she decided against it. That would entail telling him about Arthur and Merlin too, and she was too anxious and stressed to go into all that.

"So you see," she concluded, "when Morgan saw me, she recognized me. I'm not sure how she got my appearance as well as my name from Wilson, but she did, and she knows what my kids look like too. Because I tried to kill Kala Orr, she thinks I must be here to kill Perran."

Fry had listened patiently and carefully while she'd talked. "Your concern over your children makes even more sense now. I assume you think Morgan is looking for them too?"

"Yes, I do."

He leaned the back of his head against the stone wall.

Taylan removed the scarf and watched his wound for a short time. "I think it's stopped bleeding."

"We're in worse trouble than I thought," said Fry. "Damn. I thought Morgan was only suspicious of me and, when she discovered you in the library, her suspicions were confirmed. But things are more serious than that."

He climbed to his feet and walked to the window in the door.

"I don't think there's anyone else down here but us," said Taylan.

He stood silently with his back to her, not answering. Minutes passed. His chest began to heave as if he were panting after physical exertion. She wondered if he was crying and trying to hide it.

When he eventually turned around, his face was pale and sweaty but his eyes were dry.

He was scared of dying, she guessed. So was she. She didn't know how they were going to get out of their predicament.

He crossed the cell again and sat down, putting his face in his hands.

What to say to him? She had no words of comfort.

"Forgive me," he said in a strangled tone. "I was in a similar situation once before. The memories are hard to forget."

"You've been in prison?"

His head moved in a slight nod. She scooted on her bottom to his side and put an arm over his broad shoulders. It was hard to imagine how the head of SIS could have ended up incarcerated, but now was not the time to find out.

They sat motionless as the silence pressed in, then, after a while, Hans straightened his back and lifted his head. He fished in the top pocket of his jacket and pulled out a silver necklace between two fingers.

"I was in Jamaica before I came here," he said quietly, looking at the jewelry.

"You were in Jamaica when it fell? You didn't get out in time?"

"Hardly anyone in the government did."

"Yeah, I forgot," remarked Taylan, wondering who the necklace belonged to. "You were lucky to survive. I heard what happened to some of the ministers."

"I suppose I *was* lucky. I thought I was. Now, I'm not so sure."

The bolt on the door to the cells jolted noisily open, making them both jump.

A guard's face appeared at the window. "Now isn't that sweet," he sneered. "They're cuddling up."

"Open it, you gibbering fool." The acid words were unmistakably Morgan's.

She'd brought Perran with her.

The boy's lower lip dropped almost lewdly as he gazed at them.

"This is the woman who shot your mother when she was in the Caribbean," said Morgan. "Do you remember how horribly burned she was?"

"Uh huh."

"And I believe this was the person who killed your mother on the *Belladonna*, though if she did, she will deny it, naturally."

"Kala Orr is alive," said Taylan. "Perran, your mother is alive."

Morgan strode across the short distance between them and slapped her cheek so hard she tasted blood.

"That's a terrible, cruel lie to tell a child!" declared Morgan. "Don't pay any attention to her, Perran. We know the truth, don't we?"

He nodded, not removing his open-mouthed gaze from Taylan and Fry.

"She and her friend, the mayor," Morgan said, "have come here for only one reason, and that is to murder you. They were going to sneak into your room at night and cut your throat. Do you understand?"

The boy's mouth closed and he looked at her before nodding again.

"This is your first real test, Perran, dear. Your first challenge as the new Dwyr. You have to think of a fitting punishment for murderers. What do you think we should do to them?"

With the triumphant look of a student called upon by the teacher to answer a question he found easy, he replied, "Execute them!"

39

The attack had begun.

Alliance attack jets and bombers were taking off from bases in Ireland and aircraft carriers, ready to rain devastation on the EAC's airfields, fuel supplies, military equipment manufacturing plants, and road and rail links to the coast in the BI.

Lorcan couldn't resist a small smirk as he contemplated the fact that he was observing the battle from within the enemy's own territory. What would that smug bastard Perran Orr have to say if he could see him? Lorcan hadn't forgotten the time the little shit had spent aboard the *Bres*, and he would never forgive Perran's invasion of his privacy, sneaking into his suite and snooping in his personal files.

He hoped the new Dwyr was about to get his arse handed to him on a silver platter.

The invasion should be swift and successful, considering the Alliance had Kala Orr herself as a source of intel. He assumed she'd told them everything. She would want to return to her position, even if it meant sacrificing real control and power. She was drunk on the worship and adulation of her

Crusaders, in love with her image in their minds. If she were not Dwyr, life would have no meaning.

Personally, he disagreed with the Alliance's decision to run a propaganda campaign spilling the beans that Kala lived. The EAC was now aware the BA knew its secrets and would have changed whatever it could accordingly. He didn't believe the discord the revelation of the Dwyr's existence would sow was worth the advantage the EAC would gain. It would have been better to stage an unexpected strike and catch them unawares, but that was a strategic military decision and he'd had no input.

The screen of one of his bank of interfaces lit up with a white flash. His satellite had captured a hit. A cloud billowed up from the explosion, obscuring the destruction below.

Time to check in with Admiral Bujold of his space fleet.

"The fighting has begun, sir," she replied in answer to his comm. "The EAC has fired on the *Fearless* and the *Valiant*. Sorry, I was just about to inform you. I think they just realized the Alliance ships are perfectly positioned to defend the BI from an attack from space."

"Ha!" Lorcan exclaimed. "They've been caught with their trousers down. This is even better than I thought."

"Maybe. We're a long way from counting all our chickens, though."

"You're going to the BA's aid?"

"As ordered."

"Excellent. Keep me updated."

He cut the comm.

Another flash from an interface screen. A missile strike. He checked the location. It was a munitions factory within the Midlands. The Alliance had penetrated deep into the interior. The early stages of the assault were progressing well.

It wasn't surprising. Anyone with half a brain could have told the EAC decades ago that it was trying to do the impossible. It could not espouse a return to the technology of the

Middle Ages *and* be a formidable military power. It was simply impossible. All that gobbledygook Kala Orr had spouted about an alternative, deeper layer to the universal laws of physics was absurd, fantastical nonsense.

If the EAC had wanted to regress human civilization to pre-industrial levels, it should have waited until it had control of the entire globe and no powers with superior tech remained. He was glad it hadn't.

The outcome of the battle was inevitable. And once the Alliance had its homeland back, it would head over the Channel to Old France and the rest of the continent would fall.

The end of the war was coming. He only had to watch it play out.

40

The last game of the second xiangqi tournament was in full swing. Krol had made it through to the final again and was, predictably, facing Abacha. His medal hung from his neck as he hunched over the board. No doubt he'd worn it as an intimidation tactic, but it was unlikely to be having any effect on taciturn Krol, who was as expressionless as ever. She would make a great poker player, Wright mused.

Every off-duty crew member was in the mess to watch. Even Arthur and Merlin had taken an interest and were in the audience. Though the atmosphere was tense, it was affable. Morale was good, mostly because Orr rarely left her cabin, reducing her opportunities to inflict her sulkiness, brooding, and rancor on everyone.

Wright was waiting for the order to take the *Resolute* to the agreed West BI harbor. According to the battle plan, the attack should have progressed to the land invasion by now. Amphibious assault craft would have landed on the beaches, troops would have arrived in dropships or been parachuted in farther inland, and the BI Resistance would have risen up and attacked key installations.

The fighting should be over within a day or two. Then the arrival of Dwyr Orr and King Arthur would be the coup de grâce. Most of the EAC military personnel would be dead or taken prisoner, and the civilian Crusaders would be persuaded to accept the new status quo by the return of their precious Dwyr. It should be that simple. He hoped it was.

A collective sigh sounded around the room.

Drawn back to the game, Wright peered at the board.

Krol's general was surrounded. Abacha had won again.

With the merest hint of a rueful look, Krol reached across the table to shake his hand.

"That was harder than last time," Abacha remarked. "I need to watch my back."

"You'd better," said Krol.

Was that a smile on her face? Wright couldn't be sure.

"Time to print another medal," Abacha announced.

"Print a silver one for Krol," someone remarked.

"No," she said, "I'm not wearing stinking silver. It's gold or nothing."

The banter and congratulations continued, the engineer receiving several hearty slaps to the back. The audience began to break up and the joviality quietened to general conversation. People began to wander out.

"I used to play a similar game," said Arthur to Wright.

"Chess?" he asked.

"That's it. Do you know it?"

"Yes, but I haven't played in a long time."

"Merlin always used to beat me."

"I'm not surprised."

"You were an excellent player," said Merlin.

The alien hadn't made the same mistake he'd made when he'd first boarded the boat. Wright hadn't seen him leave Arthur alone once since the king had snuck away for a private conversation. Arthur looked harried and unhappy most of the time. A sea change had happened in their relationship. The alien's hold had become more overt and less consensual. Wright didn't know how to help or if he should. Arthur's part in the Alliance's invasion plan could be vital to its success. Many could gain their freedom if he was prepared to sacrifice his own.

"I'm sure he was," said Wright. "Let me know if you fancy a game some time. The boat's database will have it. I'm rusty, but it could be fun."

"I will," Arthur replied. "Thank you."

Merlin said, "And I would love to—"

A screech echoed through the passageways of the *Resolute*, unbelievably loud and almost inhuman. It seemed to have come from aft. Wright ran in that direction.

The boat's sound-proofing was state-of-the-art, but even so it might not prevent the escape of a noise like that. If an EAC ship detected them they could be in serious trouble.

Several crew members joined him as he ran. Boots appeared raced past them, heading forward. There was no sign of the source of the noise until they reached the propulsion compartment.

It was Kala Orr, sitting on the deck with her knees drawn up, screaming her head off.

Krol was there too.

A kitchen knife lay in a corner.

"She was going to kill the cat!" yelled Krol.

"Pipe down," Wright commanded.

"Sorry, sir."

He grabbed Orr's shoulders. "Shut up! Shut up now!"

But she carried on caterwauling like a banshee. He got behind her and clamped a hand over her face. This reduced the volume of her screams somewhat, but she grabbed his hand and dug her nails in. Ford had followed him into the compartment. With the lieutenant's help, he managed to get Orr onto the deck, where he could put more weight behind his hand on her face and Ford could grab her arms.

Still, she wouldn't stop.

Wright shifted his hand so it covered her nose.

He leaned down to hiss in her ear, "If you don't shut the fuck up I'll suffocate you and tell everyone it was an accident."

Despite the noise she was making, she must have heard because her screeching abruptly ceased.

He waited a few seconds until Orr's eyes began to widen in panic before lifting his hand. The imprints of his fingers were deep and red on her cheeks.

"Should I let her up, Major?" Ford asked.

"No."

"That woman hit me!" Orr exclaimed, her gaze roving until it alighted on Krol. "That bitch dared to strike me. I demand her immediate execution."

"If you think I'm going to execute our engineer," said Wright, "you've got another think coming. Krol?" He craned his neck to see her.

"I caught her with Boots," she said. "I'd come to do a maintenance check. She'd closed the hatch, and she was in here with the cat and that knife. She was going to kill him. I punched her, and that's when she started screaming."

Scratches on Orr's arms confirmed the engineer's story.

In Taylan's words, the woman really was a Grade A bitch.

"The cat stinks," spat Orr. "Keeping an animal on a ship is disgusting. I was doing you all a service ridding the vessel of it."

"There's only one animal we would all benefit from not having around," said Wright, "and it isn't the cat."

"Krol, your behavior is reprehensible," Ford remarked.

"Sorry, sir."

Orr smirked.

Ford continued, "You should have hit her harder."

Orr growled and struggled, but the lieutenant's grip on her was firm.

"You're all vile! When I'm in power again I'll have you hunted down and murdered. I'm going to remember your names. All of them!"

After a few moments' mental debate, Wright decided on the only sensible course of action. He couldn't allow her the freedom of the boat anymore. Boots wasn't safe from her and, in her current belligerent state, the same probably applied to everyone. Nor was she safe from them after threatening the life of the most loved illegal pet in the Royal Marines.

"Ford, help me carry our VIP to my cabin. I'm going to lock her in."

"No!" she protested. "No! I will not be locked up like a common criminal. I refuse!"

Ignoring her, Wright said, "I'll grab her legs."

"Got it," said Ford, beginning to adjust his hold on her arms.

"Major Wright?" Lieutenant-general Carol was comming him.

"Wait a minute, Ford. Yes, sir?"

"You're to proceed to your destination immediately."

"Wilco."

"Is everything all right aboard the boat? No problems with your passengers?"

"We had a little hiccup, but everything's under control now."

"Good. See you on home turf soon."

41

Hanging seemed a cruel and spiteful choice as a method of execution, but Perran Orr was clearly that kind of kid. Morgan and Perran walked to Taylan's left in the procession to the tree, and she could see his eyes shining with anticipation. Morgan appeared pleased too from smug smile on her face.

Taylan wasn't sure how she felt. She didn't dare think about her children, and she couldn't contemplate Fry's death due to her dragging him into her problems. It was all too much. Focusing on what she could do to avoid death right up until the moment it claimed her was the best option, though nothing was springing to mind right now.

The tree selected as a make-do gallows stood alone in the open space front of the castle. Two nooses were swinging gently from one of its lower branches and two stools stood below them. The nearest cover was fifty meters from the tree. Fifty meters of lawn to cross to get to the forest. Unless both the guards were blind, they would shoot her and Fry long before they reached it, assuming they could outrun them. Fry didn't look in the best shape. He was kind of chubby. And they both had their hands tied behind their backs, which wouldn't make things any easier.

"Tell me, Taylan Ellis," said Morgan, "did you find your children?"

"What?"

"It's a simple question. I'm sure you would remember something like that. Did you or didn't you? I confess I'm rather hoping you didn't."

"Why?"

"Because that means they're either already dead or we still have them, in which case I'll find them one day and kill them. It will be a pleasure to put an end to your line."

"What the fuck are you talking about, you nasty witch?"

Taylan was deeply confused. She'd thought Morgan had created holos of her kids and Kala Orr had threatened to kill them in order to make her give herself up. Now the EAC had her, why would they still be in danger?

"Ah," said Morgan. "You don't know."

"Know what?"

"Merlin didn't tell you," she said in an undertone. "I wonder if Arthur guessed. But if he had, I'm sure he would have mentioned it. He and Lancelot were so close."

"What have Merlin and Arthur got to do with me? I haven't seen either of them in months."

"Never mind. It doesn't matter now. It's going to bring me great satisfaction to finally accomplish something I spent many years attempting."

Morgan was obviously off her rocker, so Taylan decided to try to appeal to the kid, though her gut told her it was pointless.

"Hey, Perran. I wasn't lying back there when I said your mum's alive."

His eyes flicked toward her but he didn't slow his pace.

"I was one of the team that boarded the *Belladonna*. I admit I was sent there to assassinate the Dwyr. We found her unconscious, and Arthur was going to kill her but I stopped him. It was hard. He's pretty much unstoppable once he gets going, but I managed it. I guess it must be hard to believe. Maybe Morgan really doesn't believe it. She must have taken it for granted we would kill your mum when we found her, and that's why she left her behind. Because she wanted her dead and you under her control."

"Stop speaking," said Perran.

"It's true. I protected your mother from Arthur."

"You shot my mother!"

"That's true too. I did. You see? I admit it. That's how you know I'm telling you the truth when I say she's—"

"Stop speaking now! Guard, make her stop."

The rifle butt to her head dazed her and made her fall but didn't knock her out.

They were nearly at the tree.

"Get up," Morgan ordered.

"All right," said Taylan, on her knees. "All right. If you have to hang me, hang me. Put an end to my line or whatever stupid bullshit it is you've cooked up in your fevered mind. But let Fry go. He had no idea who I was when I asked to be his seer. He's completely innocent. He's just an ordinary Crusader who's been accidentally caught up in this."

"Another lie," said Morgan. "I'm not sure who he is, but he's certainly no ordinary Crusader. As neither of you is going to reveal any facts relating to him, it's simpler and quicker to execute him alongside you."

"Sorry," Taylan murmured to Fry as she got to her feet.

"Don't blame yourself," he replied equally quietly. "I thought it might come to this sooner or later. I tried. That's all I can say. I tried my best."

Another few steps brought them to the tree.

"One at a time or both at once, madam?" asked a guard.

"What do you think, Perran? We could make one of them watch the other die before facing the same fate themselves."

"I want to do them together," he replied.

She rubbed the top of his head affectionately. "That is the kinder choice. You are a merciful Dwyr." She turned to the guard. "You heard what your master said."

The guard ordered Fry to climb onto the stool. The soon-to-be former mayor complied.

Taylan felt sick. Her intention to only think about how to escape wasn't panning out so well. Her skin was clammy and slick with sweat. The world seemed to recede and sounds grew muffled. She vaguely heard the guard tell her to step onto her stool.

But her feet wouldn't move. Her legs were frozen and her heart threatened to thump its way through her breastbone. It was hopeless to try to save herself, but she couldn't go meekly to her death. She would not.

The guard repeated his order.

She recalled Arthur scything through the crowd at the launch ceremony, a force of nature, unstoppable.

She would be Arthur.

With a bellow of fury, she swung her leg up high and kicked the man in the head, knocking him to the ground. When the second guard lifted his pulse rifle to shoot her, she bent in half and flew at him, aiming the top of her head at his stomach like a battering ram. As she hit him, the air left his lungs in a *whoosh*.

"Run!" she yelled at Fry.

If she couldn't save herself, maybe she could save him.

The two guards were on the ground, one groggy from her kick, the other was trying to get his breath. She kicked the groggy one in the head again and knocked him out cold. The winded one's rifle had fallen from his hands. She kicked it far from his reach.

Morgan ran for it.

Damn.

She hadn't factored in the alien bitch. She'd thought she would run away with the kid.

Morgan reached the rifle.

Taylan glanced at Fry. He was halfway to the forest. He might make it.

She sped toward the alien.

If she was going to die, better to be shot face on than in the back.

Morgan had picked the weapon up. She aimed it at Taylan, and as she did so, her eyes turned black.

Taylan halted in shock. No one else had seen it, but Merlin's eyes had been the same when he'd arrived at the *Fearless*. After also witnessing Morgan dissolve into a black cloud, there could be no uncertainty in Taylan's mind: the two creatures were the same alien species.

What were they doing here on Earth?

What did they want?

"Drop it, or I'll shoot him," said a voice.

Morgan's abyss-like eyes grew wide before reverting to ordinary whites with dark irises.

It was the guard who had been winded. He'd picked up his unconscious partner's rifle and was pointing it at Perran.

"You make us forget, don't you?" the guard went on. "When we're around you, you make us forget we want to kill you. But you can't make me forget to kill him. And I will if you don't let her go. I believe her. Kala Orr lives, and you've been telling us a bunch of lies."

Morgan was smiling. "You're right. I can't make you forget to kill him. But I don't need to. It's impossible for you to kill him. Go ahead and try."

While the stand off between the guard and the alien had been taking place, Taylan had been slowly backing away. It was a long shot, but if they argued long enough, she might even get as far as the cover of the trees.

Morgan was grinning, sadistic enjoyment radiating from her face. Perran looked worried, as if, unsurprisingly, he didn't want her to risk his life to prove a point.

"Okay," said the guard nervously. "Okay. I will! Everyone hates the evil brat."

His finger twitched on the trigger.

At the same moment a gigantic explosion ripped through the air.

Taylan was lifted and blown meters across the lawn. The tree was torn from its roots, but she didn't hear it. She couldn't hear a thing. The blast had turned her deaf instantly. A loud whistle started up in her ears. Chunks of masonry were hitting the ground around her.

The castle had been hit by a bomb or a missile.

Not wasting time on finding out what had happened to the others, she turned onto her front, staggered to her feet, and ran.

42

Lorcan stretched and yawned. Observing the battle over the last couple of days had been engaging and harrowing. He'd barely slept and was ready for his bed, but things were not over yet.

His satellites couldn't capture the nuances of the action but the images had told him the gist of what was going on. The Britannic Isles had taken a massive battering as the Alliance was forced to destroy its homeland's infrastructure to prevent the EAC from mounting an effective defense. Airports, roads, bridges, and railways had been reduced to rubble.

The attacking troops who had arrived via the Irish Sea had faced the toughest fight. It had been as Lorcan feared: the propaganda campaign had given the Crusaders notice that an invasion attempt was imminent, and there was no difficulty in guessing where it would come from. The EAC had concentrated its forces up and down the west coast. Bombing and strafing key areas along the coastline had helped to mitigate the strength of opposition the Alliance soldiers faced, but it had not eradicated it. The sheer number of bodies on the beaches made them easily visible, even from space.

He wasn't often moved by the suffering of others, he had to admit, but the sight had disturbed him deeply. The only consolation was the hope this would be the last time humanity would be so self-destructive, but he had no confidence in that. Perhaps his colonists would be able to learn from the history of their ancestors and not repeat the same mistakes. The Project applicants were screened and excluded for propensity for violence, but he believed that, at some level, everyone was capable of it. Whatever checks he put in place, maybe it was inevitable that humankind would carry its warlike nature with it to the stars.

His own forces had taken a battering in supporting the Alliance. In space, he'd lost one starship and another was out of action. But the combined effort had achieved its aims: the EAC's space fleet had been rendered impotent. It had not had any impact on the surface battle and, according to Bujold, three of its ships were crippled. The Alliance was in the process of boarding and seizing them. His own fleet would take no part in that. His crews were not trained to do it and he had no interest in dealing with prisoners or repairing damaged vessels.

Casualties among his surface forces were greater than in space. He had suffered losses similar to the BA's own. Had it all been worth it? He would probably never know. His primary reason for helping the Alliance had been to provide a failsafe. If the Project failed and the colonists made their way home, he did not want them to return to a world run by Crusaders. That would not be an Earth worth returning to. Yet he anticipated never finding out.

The battle seemed won, but the real test would be the warmth of the welcome Kala Orr received on her return. She was the key that would unlock the door to a peaceful future for everyone. The Crusaders possessed the kind of manic zeal that would perpetuate civil strife for generations. Terrorism, insurrection, suicide bombings, riots, and uprisings would be the order of the day if the EAC cultists believed they were being controlled by the Alliance and not Orr.

Lorcan checked the time. If everything had gone to plan, the Dwyr would be disembarking her vessel in an hour or so along with Arthur and Merlin. An Alliance heli would pick them up and fly them with a small entourage to their first stop, Cardiff, a city in West BI.

The preparations for a victory parade would already be underway. When the Dwyr's resumption of power had been celebrated there, she would fly to another city and another. More importantly, the news of her return would spread by word of mouth. Knowing the Crusaders' mindset, tales of her magnificence would grow in the telling, until her image was once more built up to the fantastical heights she'd once achieved by herself.

He rubbed his eyes. The satellite feeds had mostly gone quiet. It was early morning in the BI. The large-scale fighting had died down and there was not much to observe. If the Alliance's technical engineers had begun to repair and reconnect the net, it might be possible to access a street-level view of the parade, but until then he probably wouldn't miss much if he stepped away from his screens for a while. He could snatch a few hours' sleep before the next significant event.

He stood up. His time zone was two hours ahead of the BI's. The sunlight was stronger here, blazing in through his villa's windows. He'd been awake most of the night.

Yes, a nap would be very welcome.

"Ua Talman, something terrible's happened!" It was Bujold, speaking to him directly via his implant. She was only permitted to do that in an emergency. "There's been an explosion on the *Bres!*"

"What?!"

"One of my off-duty officers just commed me. He didn't know your direct—"

"What's happened?! What did he say?"

"Maybe it's better if you talk to him directly yourself?"

"Yes. Patch him through."

Two seconds of silence followed.

The damned lag.

Then a man's voice burst into his head. "It happened about five minutes ago, sir. I was in my cabin, and I felt a massive shock run through the ship. Alarms are going off all over the place. The emergency seals have activated and no one can leave this section. We've been comming the other areas but it's hard to tell what's going on."

"Where was it? Where was the explosion?"

Another two seconds of lag. The delay was beyond frustrating. "As far as I can tell, it was in the control center."

Lorcan sat down.

Kekoa, Jurrah, Steadman...his entire management team.

"Have you heard if there are any survivors?"

"No, I'm sorry. Crisis teams are working to prevent any further damage. A wide area has depressurized and lost its a-grav, so it must be very unstable. Honestly, I'm cut off here. I didn't know if anyone had managed to get the word out about what's happened. That's why I contacted the admiral."

A notification flashed up on all his interface screens. URGENT URGENT URGENT URGENT

"Thank you..." He didn't know the man's name. "Someone has finally seen fit to inform me directly."

After closing his implant connection he turned his attention to one screen. Opening the comm, he saw Kekoa, dirty-faced and blood running from a cut on her head. Relief hit him like a wave.

"Thank god you're all right."

But she spoke at the same time as him and their words mixed. "Someone blew up the control center, sir!"

When she'd finished, he said, "You speak first. Tell me what happened. Was it an attack?" It was possible an EAC ship had slipped away from the others in high Earth orbit to get revenge on the Alliance's ally.

She paused, waiting for his reply, and then nodded. "We don't think it was an attack. There's nothing in firing range. Something exploded in the control center. I'd gone to the refectory for a snack, or I would have been..." She paused again appeared to struggle to master her emotions. "I would have been there when it happened. It's gone, sir. The whole room is just gone. Blown into space. They're all...all..." She drew in a deep breath.

"Who was there, Kekoa? Who was in the room? What's happening now?"

"The crisis teams are working on preventing any further depressurization. The emergency seals worked, but the explosion fired debris through bulkheads. There are holes everywhere. We're evacuating from this section soon, they tell us."

"Kekoa, who have we lost?"

Her eyes filled with tears. "We were in the middle of a day shift. The place was full of people. All the usual staff and... and..." she swallowed "...Iolani had come in to talk about something. She was still there when I left. I haven't seen her since."

43

The sky was a pale, watery blue when Wright stepped from the *Resolute* onto the quay in West BI, and the sun was shining weakly as it breasted the horizon. Winter was coming. He hadn't been planetside during a northern hemisphere winter in...he'd forgotten how long.

Colbourn and Carol were already here and waiting.

As he walked toward them, Colbourn actually smiled. He almost halted in surprise.

"You'll have time to get that knee fixed now, Major," she said.

He hadn't realized it, but he must have been limping. Now he thought about it, the joint was hurting him a little.

"We really won?" he asked.

"Hard to believe, isn't it?" Carol was smiling too. "It's all over bar the mopping up. Though what the future holds depends on those two."

Orr and Arthur were walking down the gangplank. Orr walked in front of the king, her nose in the air, her fingertips touching the rope gingerly as if she thought it was dirty. Arthur was dressed in his chainmail and carrying his helmet under his arm. Merlin appeared and followed Arthur.

"Those *three*, I think you mean," said Wright.

Here, he would part company with the crew of the *Resolute*. Marines were waiting to be the VIP's escort to Cardiff. His boat would return to Oceania under Ford's temporary command, and he would fly out to rejoin her later. He was already looking forward to it. He liked working with the lieutenant, Abacha, and the rest of the crew, and the relaxed command suited his growing disenchantment with military life. There was a chance he might be able to get involved in the follow up on the child-trafficking ring he'd exposed.

But for now, his earlier involvement in the Arthur saga meant the higher-ups thought it would be a good idea for him to accompany him across the country for the parades. Or perhaps Arthur had asked that he come along. He didn't really know.

His lieutenant had appeared behind Merlin. He saluted the officers on the quay, and Wright thought he saw him give the barest of winks before he disappeared into the bridge.

"The heli's waiting," said Colbourn.

The military style aircraft sat on the empty dock. Like all military vehicles it was plain and bare, and it might even be bloodstained from carrying injured and dying troops. Orr would complain. But then, she complained about everything.

"No time like the present," Carol said.

The majority of the ride to Cardiff passed in silence. It was hard to hear anyone over the noise of the rotor blades anyway. Arthur looked amazed and terrified. He'd probably never flown before. Merlin looked like he was finding everything very amusing. Orr scowled the entire journey. Wright marveled at her ability to hold her face in the same expression for so long.

When Colbourn leaned toward her and bellowed, "You still

remember your speech, don't you?" the Dwyr turned her head away and ignored her.

The brigadier gave Wright a look. What would they do if Orr didn't do as she was told? They would be surrounded by thousands of Crusaders, encouraged into the streets to welcome back their Dwyr. If she rallied them against the Marines accompanying her, they would attack. Pulse rifles could not defend against a mass of human bodies driven by crazed zealotry.

He rubbed his knee.

Colbourn turned to him. "You haven't heard the news about Ua Talman's ship, have you?"

"What news?"

"There was an explosion. About thirty people died."

"No kidding!"

"They haven't figured out if it was an accident or deliberate. We're sending a team of investigators out there to help find out which."

"What do you think it was?"

Colbourn shrugged. "There's no point in speculating. The ship's personnel are evacuating to the other vessels while the investigation takes place, to be on the safe side."

"Any word from Talman?"

"Nothing yet. He was here on Earth when it happened. He's on his way back now."

Wright caught a glimpse of an expression flitting cross Kala Orr's face. Was it a smirk? He couldn't be sure. Was the EAC responsible for the explosion or was she only experiencing schadenfreude? Both were possible.

The crowds had already begun to gather when they touched down. The Resistance activists had done their jobs well. They'd been putting up posters and spreading the word that the Dwyr would be arriving today to claim her victory, won for her with the help of the Alliance. She was about to return and resume her rightful place, and she would arrest the woman who had fooled her son with lies. They were to prepare for a huge celebration beginning with a parade where they would see their beloved Dwyr again.

Curious Crusaders watched from afar as the heli passengers disembarked. Alliance troops stood in a ring guarding the heli pad.

"We've prepared a suite where you may refresh yourselves and wait until it's time for the parade to begin," said Carol. "It's only a short walk from here."

Wright wondered what the onlookers thought of what they saw: a giant of a man wearing mail, more than a head taller than everyone else, with flowing red-golden hair and beard and carrying a gigantic sword, his gray-headed lean companion, and a gaunt woman in an ill-fitting dress and short, dark hair.

"Dwyr?!" someone called out. "Dwyr! Welcome home!"

She didn't respond.

At the suite, Colbourn tried to make Orr repeat her speech, but she refused. She also refused to eat or drink anything. She looked awful. In the few days she'd spent aboard the *Resolute*, she'd gone downhill physically.

Must be all the spite and bitterness eating her up.

Arthur agreed to rehearse his speech, and Wright heard it for the first time. What a sight he was in his armor. His appearance would have a big impact on the crowd.

His words were so characteristic of him Wright guessed the old king had written them himself and the Alliance had given its approval. He spoke about his years of kingship in the old Britannic Isles and the people he'd ruled over; what an honor and privilege it had been to lead them. He explained how sorrowful he'd been to learn the BI had fallen after millennia of nationhood, but that he understood the Crusaders had become accustomed to their new home. He hoped that peace and harmony would prevail now the fighting was over, and he looked forward to sharing authority with their Dwyr over a new BI, populated by shared cultures and ways of thinking.

It was a good speech, but Wright sensed Arthur's heart wasn't in it. He wondered what Taylan would have to say about it if she were here. It didn't seem to have much to do with her idea of the myth of Arthur's return. He thought the king was supposed to vanquish the BI's enemies, not accept the EAC into some kind of warm, fuzzy coalition.

But of course, that wasn't the plan. Once things had calmed down, the Dwyr was supposed to begin encouraging her followers to return to the continent and eventually their homeland. At the same time, compulsory public education would be established all across Orr's realm. The cultists would be free to practice their customs providing they were legal, but their children would be taught science, technology, and critical thinking.

The intention was clear: a return to rationality and the continued progress of human civilization.

Would it work? Wright didn't know. All he knew was he had to get through this day, and that his knee hurt.

~

KALA HATED EVERYONE. Everyone and everything. She almost wished the Alliance had left her in her mental prison, planning every last detail of her victory celebrations. Anything other than this fiasco, this lie, this humiliation. It might have been better to have died under Arthur's sword than to become a nonentity, nothing but a mouthpiece for the Alliance. They'd promised her the adulation of her people, but that was not her deepest need and desire. She wanted control. She wanted her followers to think the same way she did, to believe in the same things. She was being forced to go against all that, and she couldn't stomach it.

She was also cold. No one had brought her suitable

clothing to wear. On that odious ship they'd told her she was free to print whatever she wanted. As if she, the Dwyr, would ever do anything so lowly. The fools had no concept of how to treat someone of her rank. And she'd actually been struck and manhandled! It beggared belief. Her sacred body had been assaulted, and no one would be punished for it. If this was how her life was to be from now on, she wasn't sure she wanted to live it.

"It's time," Colbourn announced. "Get ready to leave, everyone."

The people in the room began to stand and stretch. Arthur picked up his sword and scabbard and fastened it around his waist. His mail clinked quietly as he moved. Kala's stomach turned at the thought he was supposed to be her consort, but she had to give the Alliance credit for the idea. The concept would appeal deeply to her people, especially when they saw him in his armor. Standing next to him she would look unimpressive, which was probably the intention.

"Doesn't anyone have anything warm for me to wear?!" she blurted, vexed beyond imagining by her cretinous companions.

"If you're cold, you should have said something," Colbourn replied.

"There's a blanket here on the sofa," said Major Wright, picking it up and handing it to her, "if that'll help."

She snatched it and put it around her shoulders.

What a sight I must look.

"Let's go," said Colbourn.

An open-backed truck for the parade was waiting outside. The horrible major helped her climb up onto it. Arthur and Merlin joined her along with Wright and several armed soldiers. Colbourn sat in the front with the driver while the other officer, Carol, went off somewhere else. More soldiers were to walk alongside and to the front and back of the truck to keep back the crowd.

The area around the hotel had been cleared of people, but the next street was thronged. According to Colbourn, the parade would proceed down the capital's main streets to the central plaza, where she and Arthur would give their speeches. The process would take about an hour in total, then they would fly to the next city to repeat it this afternoon.

At the sound of the surging crowd, her heart beat faster and blood began to flow into her cold extremities. Some of the old feelings returned. Gratification, joy, delight. She would be loved once more. She would be adored.

A shout went out. "She's coming!" Cheers erupted.

But as the onlookers caught sight of her and Arthur, their yells died away. Their happy faces turned amazed, startled, and curious. Murmuring started up. She could guess what they were saying. *That must be the consort the leaflets told us about. He looks strange, doesn't he? Is that a sword he's wearing?*

She raised her arms, eager to get the attention away from Arthur. "I am home!" she cried. "I am back! Thank you for waiting for me, my people!"

But they didn't respond.

The same occurred wherever the truck traveled. Ahead of them, the crowd cheered and yelled. Then as soon as it caught sight of her and Arthur, quiet confusion fell. They left behind streets of quiet, gawping spectators.

Word must have gone ahead of them because by the time they reached the plaza, the cheering had stopped. Instead, a soft, expectant buzz greeted them.

The truck moved slowly between the temporary railings erected to keep the crowd back until it reached the corner of the open space, where it stopped.

It was time for her to give her speech.

Yet even before she spoke, she knew the plan had begun to go terribly wrong.

44

It was stupid and kinda risky, but Taylan hadn't been able to resist attending the celebration of the return of Kala Orr. Fry had come along too, but not because he was overwhelmed with curiosity like her. He was here because he was drawn to the political stuff. In the days since they'd escaped from the castle, he'd explained at length about his ambition to convert the Alliance to a republic. He'd bored her out of her mind, in fact. It was like that with obsessive people when they got on their hobby horse.

Squeezed into the crowd in the plaza, she was having second thoughts. She wasn't worried she might be recognized. All gazes were on the road where the vehicle carrying the Dwyr and Arthur would approach, and if someone did recognize her, so what? The Alliance had won. She shouldn't be in any more danger. But she could barely move, and she'd quickly been reminded of how, at times like these, Crusaders would go wild. They were hard to be around at the best of times, due to their weird beliefs and ignorance, but when they were off their faces on booze and drugs, they could be unbearable.

As soon as Orr had given her speech, she would leave. Fry could stay if he wanted, and she would meet up with him later.

She was curious to see Arthur too. The posters had said the Dwyr's consort would be with her, a once-famous king of the Britannic Isles, who had returned from the dead. She'd snorted through her nose with laughter when she'd read it. She, more than most people, knew the bit about his resurrection was true, but she'd laughed at the idea of him and Kala Orr hooking up. Arthur would be mortified at the idea, and she guessed Orr would be outraged. It was all a ruse to trick the Crusaders into accepting the new regime, and it might well work.

The crowd was growing quieter, and she didn't know why. She could see right down the street and there was no sign of the truck. Even if there were, she would expect the noise to increase, not go down.

"What's happening?" she asked Fry, who was crammed against her. "Can you see anything?"

He was half a head taller than her and might have a better view.

"No, but I heard someone say something concerning. There seems to be a debate going on."

When she started to pay attention to what people were quietly saying, she heard it too.

Then the truck appeared, and the voices were quelled almost to silence. The whispers continued, but she couldn't make them out.

Was it a respectful hush? She didn't think so.

Marines were walking ahead of the truck and to each side. She suddenly thought of Wright and wondered what he was doing now. She hoped he hadn't been injured or killed in the battle.

The truck pulled in front of her, and then it had passed and she could see into the back.

There was Arthur! He was dressed in his armor as he had

been at the launch ceremony. That seemed an odd decision, given what he'd done there. And Merlin was with him, standing a little behind and to one side.

Wright!

What was he doing there? He must have become caught up in the business with Arthur again.

At the front of all the figures stood a frail-looking woman with short, dark hair, wearing a knee-length dress and a blanket over her shoulders.

That was Kala Orr?

The whispers she'd heard before the truck appeared made sense.

The vehicle had reached the corner of the plaza.

It stopped.

Silence fell.

Someone coughed.

Orr's expression was hard to read. What was she waiting for?

She lifted her arms and drew in a breath, but before she could speak a shout came from the audience.

"You're not the Dwyr!"

She hesitated, arms in the air. She seemed to deflate a little, but then she inhaled another breath—

"You're not our Dwyr! You're an impostor! What have you done with our Dwyr?"

"She's dead," another voice cried out. "She really is dead! The Alliance lied!"

"I am Kala Orr!" the woman thundered. "I *am* your Dwyr!"

"It makes sense," Fry whispered in Taylan's ear. "Look at her. The ones who have seen her in real life are used to seeing her in all her regalia. And the ones who haven't don't have any photos or vids to go by. They have an image of what she *should* look like, and Orr isn't matching it. This is going to mean trouble."

A figure climbed out of the front of the truck. Colbourn. She said something to the Marines who had formed a line around the back of the vehicle, and then beckoned Wright over. He leaned down to speak to her.

Meanwhile, the crowd's angry protest continued. More of them were shouting, and there was additional pressure as people in the back pushed forward to get their voices heard. The barriers began to scrape over the pavement.

Wright said something to Arthur. The king's head shook slightly as if he was disagreeing. Wright spoke to him again, and he gave a reluctant nod.

He stepped in front of the Dwyr.

Stillness descended once more. The intense interest in what this armored man with his ancient weapon had to say was almost palpable.

"Crusaders, if you do not wish to hear what your Dwyr has to say..."

"*That's not our Dwyr*," came faintly from the crowd.

"...perhaps you will listen to me."

This will do it, thought Taylan.

There was something mesmerizing about Arthur's speeches. You couldn't help listening and being moved by him. Maybe it was a power Merlin had given him, like he'd given him his imperviousness to harm.

The Crusaders seemed prepared to hear him out. Of course they were. He looked like he'd stepped out of a fairy tale. She had to admit she'd felt the same awe and fascination once. That was before she'd learned more about the ancient king.

Fry muttered, "Is that really...?"

"Yes, it is," she hissed.

"How can it be? That's impossible."

"It *is* him. It would take me too long to explain. You'll have to take my word for it."

"Remarkable! Well, I'm very interested to hear what he has to say."

He was to be disappointed. At that moment, another voice in the crowd rang out, louder and more powerful than any other. "That is *not* Dwyr Kala Orr! You have been deceived!"

Taylan knew that voice. She swiveled her head to the right. Morgan le Fay was marching down the street, her hand on Perran's shoulder. "This is the true Dwyr! Kala Orr's son. His mother died, murdered by the Alliance. That woman is a fake!"

The calm Arthur had created broke.

Hollers and yells rang out, shouting support for Perran, while others argued they were wrong, that the real Dwyr stood on the truck. Colbourn pointed at Morgan and mouthed a command Taylan couldn't hear over the noise. Six Marines ran out from the rest, heading for her and Perran. People surged forward. The barriers broke and the onlookers who had been standing at them toppled to the ground. The horde burst into the empty space, trampling those below them. The remaining Marines forced the people back with their guns, creating a narrow but open corridor.

"We need to get out of here!" Taylan exclaimed, bracing herself against the buffeting.

"No!" Fry protested. "No, we need to stay."

"We'll be killed, you idiot. The Marines will start firing, and we look like Crusaders."

"Then let's get to the back and watch. We should be safe there."

Taylan wasn't convinced, but she did want to see what happened. She pushed against the flow until they reached the edge of the plaza.

People had formed a wall around Morgan and Perran, protecting them from the advancing Marines. They were ordered to move out of the way. When they didn't comply, a round of shots was fired over their heads. Still, they didn't move. The Marine officer gave them a last warning.

A second later, the Marines fired.

The Crusaders facing them crumpled and fell, but more took their places.

Taylan glanced up to see what was happening on the truck. The back of it was now empty. Orr, Arthur, Wright, Merlin and others were running up the steps of the government building.

When she looked back to what was happening in the street, Morgan and Perran had been seized. Crusaders threatened to attack, but the mean end of a muzzle in their faces soon silenced them. The Marines dragged the two captives along the protected corridor and up the building steps. When they'd disappeared into it, the remaining Marines broke formation and also ran for the steps.

"We have to get in there," said Fry.

"No, we don't."

But somehow Taylan knew that was where they were going.

45

"I tell you I am Hans Jonte, former head of the Alliance Secret Intelligence Service. I demand you let me and my companion in!"

The man's voice was so loud, it thundered down the corridor. And it *did* sound familiar, though the likelihood of it actually belonging to Jonte was slim. Wright remembered him from Jamaica. He couldn't be here in the BI. He went in the direction of the voice. It would only take a second to deny the claim.

He found two Marines were guarding a side door. When one of them noticed him approaching, she said, "It's just a Crusader spinning a story, sir."

Of course it was. An odd story, to be sure, but then Crusaders were an odd people.

"I understand," Wright replied. "I just want to check for myself."

The other Marine, who was blocking the entrance, moved to the side.

Wright locked gazes with the man standing on the step.

Shit! It really is him.

"Mr Jonte," he spluttered.

"You!" Jonte yelled. "I remember you! You're the officer I asked to pass on my message. The officer who *didn't* pass on my message. Do you have any idea of the problems you caused me? You nearly got me..."

Wright wasn't listening to him anymore.

He'd seen who was with him.

She didn't look surprised at the sight of him. She must have known he was here.

"Taylan," he breathed. Then, snapping out of his shock, he said to the Marines, "I know both these people. They can come in."

"About time," said Jonte, stepping through the doorway.

Taylan followed.

The Marines returned to guard duty outside, where Crusaders gawped and jostled each other, trying to get a better look at the people being allowed into the government building. For the moment, the crowds were too confused and disorganized to be a real threat, but the situation was volatile. Enough of the EAC military remained at large to mount an attack and retrieve their Dwyr—whichever one they thought was genuine. Colbourn had commed for backup to ensure a safe passage out for everyone, including their two new prisoners, Morgan and the kid.

What a state of affairs. The Crusaders hadn't recognized Kala Orr. It had been a stupid mistake. They should have dressed her up in her costume. Arthur might have brought the crowd around, but the appearance of Perran had put the kibosh on that.

"Where is your commander?" Jonte demanded.

"The highest ranking officer here is Brigadier Colbourn," he replied. "She's through there."

Jonte stomped off in the direction he'd indicated.

Which left Wright and Taylan alone in the corridor.

"What the hell are you wearing?" he asked.

She was dressed in a weird Crusader get up: an embroidered skirt, torn up one side, frilly blouse, long, sleeveless jacket, and a flowery scarf.

"You don't like it?"

"Uhh..."

She laughed. "How's Boots?"

"He...he's fine. He had a little trouble, but he's okay now. And so is Abacha. Nothing bad has happened to him either."

"Abacha? Are you back on the *Valiant*?"

"No, I..." He looked around for somewhere private to talk. Spotting a door, he walked over and opened it. The room had once been storage for cleaning equipment, but only a few items remained. "In here."

When they were inside, he closed the door.

Her eyebrows lifted. "This is cozy."

"Taylan," he said, stepping closer to her, "I have something to tell you."

"You have? What? Is it something about Arthur? He looked completely miserable up there on that truck. Has Merlin been digging in his claws even more than usual?"

"No, it's..."

As he looked into her gray eyes, he had the sensation he was falling into them. She gazed back, unblinking. For several moments, neither spoke.

Slowly, he leaned in.

She tilted up her chin, closed her eyes, and then they were kissing.

A shock of recognition hit him. It was *her*. He hadn't known he'd been looking for her, but he'd found her. That one person, not perfect, but the right one for him. She was in his arms, and his heart was hammering so hard he was sure she must feel it.

"Major!"

Colbourn.

She must have opened the door and he didn't hear it.

Taylan drew away, and he turned to see the brigadier, furious, glaring at him. "In the entrance foyer. Now."

She slammed the door.

"Damn!" he exclaimed.

"What's the matter?" Taylan asked. "I'm not a Marine anymore, remember? So you weren't caught frater-wotsit. Kissing a civilian isn't a military crime, surely."

"Yes, it is, if you're on duty. But it isn't only that. Colbourn once just about accused me of giving you a discharge because we had a thing going on. And now she'll think she was right all along."

"She thought that?! Well, who cares? She's just a twisted, uptight bitch."

"You don't understand."

How could he explain it to her? She'd never really understood the military. She'd never understood the need to be able to trust and rely on your fellows, to know they were being straight with you, that you were all following the same rules. She would never get how it bothered him that the brigadier thought he'd lied, that he'd let her down.

"I have to go," he said. "But the reason I brought you in here was I wanted to tell you I think I might have found where your children were taken."

"You have?! Where? Tell me!" Her eyes were round with excitement and joy. "Are they okay? Did you see them?"

"Taylan," he said gently, "I don't know what they look like. But I think they might have been taken to Australia." In as few words as possible, he told her what he and Abacha had seen in Far North Queensland.

As he spoke, her face turned stony.

"The Australian authorities are searching for them right now," he continued. "All the children. The smuggling operation has been going on for a while. It has to be somewhere remote, they think, and the area they're searching is sparsely populated, so..." He took in her expression. "What's wrong? I thought you'd be happy."

"You mean," she said between her teeth, "you mean you had a chance to find out where the Crusaders were taking the kids, and you didn't follow up? *You left them there?!*"

"We couldn't go any farther. It was impossible."

"How could you?! How could you come so close, and then just abandon them? How?!" Her chest was heaving and tears were filling her eyes. "My poor kids. Somewhere out in the wilderness. I'll never find them now." She put her hands to her face and her shoulders shook.

"It isn't like that. It didn't happen how you think it did. And the Australians will find them. They're bound to, and soon. I promise."

But she was inconsolable.

"Taylan, I'm sorry, but I have to go. Stay here, and I'll be back as soon as I can. Then we'll talk and I'll explain."

The shame that had hit him when Colbourn had caught them kissing was nothing compared to the wretchedness he felt when he left Taylan crying.

46

Kala Orr was having another tantrum.

"I insist you bring my son out to me now or the deal's off! I won't do another thing for the Alliance, and every chance I get I'll encourage my people to rise up and take back the Britannic Isles."

"You won't get many chances," Colbourn commented dryly. "If you don't do as we say, you won't live long after your trial."

Orr whirled to face her. "Shut up! Your opinion is irrelevant. I demand to speak to your Prime Minister face to face, and I'm not moving from this spot until I do."

In the entrance lobby, as well as Colbourn and Orr, were Jonte, Merlin, Arthur, and a handful of Marines. Wright guessed Morgan and Perran had been locked in a room somewhere else in the building.

"I wasn't aware you'd done anything for the Alliance yet," said Merlin smoothly. "As I recall, you didn't give your speech. Your people didn't believe it was you. I would say you aren't in any position to be dictating terms and conditions. You're nobody."

She clenched her hands into fists and spat, white with rage, "I am *not* nobody! Bring me my son!!"

Merlin's words were the most Wright had heard him say in public since he'd re-encountered the alien.

"Your son, though a child," Colbourn said, "is a prisoner, and he will remain in captivity until his role in the EAC is investigated."

"I would have thought his role was obvious," said Merlin. "He acted as the Dwyr, therefore he is responsible for all the actions of the EAC since he took over the role."

Wright wondered why he was sticking his oar in. He seemed to be enjoying himself, winding Orr up unnecessarily. Colbourn shot an angry glance in Merlin's direction. Was he responsible for Orr's furious state? Had he been winding her up in this manner for a while?

"He's just a boy," Orr protested. "He was stolen from me by Morgan and she's been using him ever since."

Arthur, who had been standing with his head down while the argument had been going on, looked up and said, "Perhaps we should reunite the mother with her child. Morgan le Fay is deceitful and manipulative. She is the instigator of evil in this world."

"That's right!" Orr exclaimed. "She's been behind everything I've done. It was her who gave me the ideas for the EAC. It's been her teachings I've followed. And when I released her, she took over. Then she pushed me aside because I wouldn't allow her to control me. That was when she put me in a coma. And now she's using my son. Neither he nor I is responsible for...for..." She faltered to a stop.

"Oh, please," said Merlin. "Which is it to be? Are you the Dwyr, leader of your people, or are you not? You're going to blame everything you've done on someone who was trapped within the Earth for thousands of years?"

"You!" Orr yelled. "It *was* you who put her there! You *are* the enemy she fears. Then you must be able to destroy her."

"Why would I do that?" he asked sardonically. "I am not judge or executioner here."

"According to Merlin, she's indestructible." It was the first time Wright had spoken since arriving in the room. Orr's words had reminded him of the time when the alien had commented it would be easier to 'kill' a rock than Morgan.

"Then he can lock her away somewhere again," said Orr, "preferably forever."

"Nor am I a jailer."

"But you were once, so you can be again." Orr paused and swallowed before addressing Colbourn. "That's the solution, isn't it? I agree to share power with the Alliance over the Britannic Isles, my son is returned to me, and Morgan is imprisoned somewhere she can't turn into vapor and escape. She can take the blame for everything that's happened. She *is* to blame. You wouldn't have to use deep, sealed underground chambers like Merlin did. You could put her into an airtight container at the bottom of an ocean, where she would never be found."

Colbourn's expression betrayed her horror at the punishment Orr was suggesting, but she only said, "All decisions regarding what is to be done with Perran Orr and Morgan will be made at a later date. For now, we will await reinforcements to facilitate our transfer to a safe holding point. Wright, I want to speak to you."

He followed her to a corner of the hall.

"Major," she said in a low tone, "I'm finding it hard to come up with the words to express how disappointed I am in you. There was a time I deeply respected you as a fellow officer and would happily have trusted you with my life, but I'm sad to say that's no longer the case."

He was about to interject when she went on, "To believe I was actually remorseful about your assignment to the *Resolute*!

I regretted the repercussions of your mental health assessment and arranged Abacha's transfer to your boat so you would have a familiar face around. Then I recommended the *Resolute* for the mission to bring Kala Orr to the BI. And that disgusting scene in a broom cupboard is how you repay me!"

"My feelings for Taylan Ellis are not disgusting!" He paused before adding, "Brigadier." Then he went on, "I know how it must look, but I can assure you—"

"It doesn't matter now. We have more important matters at hand than your dalliances."

He was so angry he wanted to storm off, taking Taylan with him, and desert. It was only by the greatest effort of self-control he didn't. "Which important matters, ma'am?"

Jonte joined them. "If I might say something?"

"Go ahead," said Colbourn.

"Legally, you have to allow Kala Orr to see her son. He's a minor, and he's allowed a visit by a parent or guardian. If you keep them apart until—presumably—one or both of them are put on trial, it will be bad for the Alliance image-wise. The world's media can do a lot with a mother and child story."

"Do we care?" Colbourn asked.

"You should," Jonte replied. "Appearances count for a lot politically. If the BA is to reassert its dominance across the globe, it needs to appear fair and just."

"I see what you mean," said Colbourn, "and Arthur thinks they should be together too. He's been looking like someone stole his puppy for days. I think he's on the verge of abandoning the Alliance entirely."

Wright had to concede she was correct. The life seemed to have gone out of the king. He wasn't sure exactly what the problem was, except it had something to do with feeling the grip of Merlin's control over him. But it was clear he didn't care much about the affairs of this new world he'd found himself in.

If he did decide to go off on his own, there wasn't anything anyone could do to stop him.

He asked, "So you want to follow his suggestion just to keep him feeling involved?"

"I do. But I need you to be on your toes, Wright. After everything that's gone on in Orr's relationship with her son, things could go wrong quickly."

"You don't really think she might try to kill him?"

"I have no idea what she might do. The woman's a powder keg."

Wright thought about Orr's attempt to kill Boots. Colbourn's fears were justified. No one could guess what Orr might do, even to her own son.

"I understand, Brigadier."

She returned to the center of the hall. "Mr Jonte, the major, and I are in agreement with Arthur. We will allow Perran to be with his mother." She ordered two Marines to fetch the boy, and Wright walked over to Orr.

A tense silence stretched out as they waited. Wright was worried about Taylan. He hoped she wouldn't leave.

The boy's light, quick footsteps sounded from the corridors, accompanied by the heavy tread of the two Marines. When he entered the hall, he raced across it into his mother's arms.

"You're alive, Mummy! You really are alive!"

"I am. Morgan lied to you, darling. She's a big liar who wanted to take you away from me."

As they hugged, Perran continued, "I did a great thing, Mummy. Do you want to hear about it?"

"Of course I do. What did you do?"

"I blew up Ua Talman's ship!"

"You...what?" Orr glanced nervously around her. "Tell me about it later."

But the boy continued, "You remember the plans I memorized when I visited it? Well, I told Morgan about them and—"

"Not now, Perran, later."

"She arranged for someone to—"

"Stop talking!" She grabbed his shoulders and shook them.

"It was a good plan!" Perran protested. "And it worked."

"Be silent!" She slapped his cheek.

"Now that's no way to speak to a child," admonished Morgan, strolling into the room.

"What's she doing here?!" Colbourn thundered. She jabbed a finger at a Marine. "You! Take her back to her room."

Morgan laughed. "As if any of your men or women could make me do anything against my will. I was only waiting for an opportune moment to join you all."

The Marine strode over to her, but when he was a couple of meters away, he halted before turning to Colbourn and asking in a confused tone, "What was my order, ma'am?"

"Take that woman to her room!"

"Yes, ma'am. I... Sorry, could you repeat that?"

"They can't touch her," said Kala. "They can't do anything to her. I've tried. She scrambles their minds as soon as they come near. Only *he* can hurt her." She pointed at Arthur. "Kill her," she ordered. "Kill her! That's what you're here to do."

"Not at all," said Merlin. "He's here to kill *you*."

Orr flinched. "But he hasn't tried."

"Not yet," the alien replied, malevolence lacing his voice.

"No one is going to kill anyone," said Colbourn firmly.

"But why is he here to kill me?" Orr asked. "Why? It doesn't make any sense. Why should be come back from the dead to murder someone living thousands of years in the future from his time?"

"It is because you took the Britannic Isles," said Arthur. "But I do not wish to kill you, Kala Orr. I do not wish to kill anyone. I am feeling old and tired, and I have done enough killing in my life."

Orr didn't seem to be listening to him. Her head was bent

and brows knitted, as if she were trying to figure something out. She looked at Morgan. "I am of your line. That's what you said. Your blood runs in my veins."

"Then you're part alien," said a new voice. Taylan stepped into the room. Her eyes were red with crying, and she looked utterly ridiculous in her Crusader gear, but Wright's heart leaped at the sight of her.

"Morgan's the same kind of alien as Merlin," she continued, "and if you're descended from Morgan, you must be part alien."

"Ugh, Taylan Ellis," said Orr. "You're the other one who can hurt me." Her gaze traveled from Taylan to Arthur. "There's something strange happening here."

"You're right." Merlin's expression was full of delight. "The patterns are converging. There will finally be an outcome, Morgan!"

"Hopefully not the one you think." She scowled at him.

"If these *two* can hurt me," Orr said to her, "and Merlin can hurt *you*, who else can hurt you?"

Morgan's scowl faded and began to turn into something like fear.

"It's obvious," said Taylan.

"Yes, it is!" Orr announced triumphantly.

"This isn't fair!" Morgan shouted at Merlin. "You broke the rules. You told her!"

"I did nothing of the kind," he replied.

Orr snatched Wright's beamer from its holster, aimed, and fired at Morgan.

The shot went wide.

Before Wright could stop her, she fired again.

This time, she scored a hit, but Morgan had already begun to dissolve into black mist. The pulse round passed through her, and though she grimaced in pain there was no blood or sign of damage.

"Merlin, you cheated," said Morgan, her voice growing

faint. "I'm taking this to the adjudicator, and I'm making a formal complaint."

The alien only smiled smugly.

What had been Morgan le Fay was now only a vapor, rapidly fading from sight.

"What...just...happened?" Jonte asked.

"It was a game," said Arthur grimly. "They were playing a game with us." He faced Merlin. "All the murdering I did, all the sin I committed, it was a diversion for you. We are an amusement."

"Now then, my old friend," Merlin replied, reaching out to touch the man's arm. "You had a good life. A charmed life, some might say. You were a great king, worshipped and adored by many. And you set a great example. Your name was remembered over millennia, an inspiration to those who love valor and honor."

"How many of us died and suffered to give you pleasure?" said Arthur.

Things about Merlin that had puzzled and annoyed Wright were suddenly making sense. "What happened to the *Fearless*?" he asked. "Was that you?"

"Not directly," Merlin replied. "That was my handicap at the beginning of this round."

"Imposed by who?" asked Taylan.

"I'm not going to explain the whole game to you. That would be tiresome. The round is over, and I must be going. I'll be back at some point." He smirked.

"No!" Arthur yelled. "You cannot go unpunished. If Kala Orr could hurt Morgan, that means..." He drew his sword from its scabbard.

Merlin backed away. The edges of him were beginning to dissolve. "Stop!"

Arthur whirled his blade in a wide arc.

"Someone stop him!" Merlin cried.

He screamed, but his scream was cut short when Excalibur sliced through his neck. A fountain of blood erupted from it and his head hit the floor with a dull thud. His unseeing eyes glazed over and his tongue lolled while his body gave a convulsive twitch.

But the vaporizing process continued. Within two or three seconds, every part of him had dissolved to nothingness, even his spilled blood.

47

Taylan watched the heli land in the plaza. The Crusaders had cleared out of the way pretty quickly when it began to descend. When it was down and its rotors began to slow, Marines poured out of it.

"For the last time, come with us," said Wright.

He looked so upset, she felt really bad. "I can't. I'm sorry. I just can't, even if Colbourn would let me, which she won't."

The brigadier was watching them from inside the building as Taylan and Wright stood in the doorway.

"I can bring her around," said Wright. "I have to explain to you what happened in Australia."

"You've already explained, and I understand."

He'd told her how he and Abacha had been forced to turn back because they had no water. She *did* understand. Kind of. She sighed. "It's like, I understand here..." she touched her head "...but not here." She pointed at her heart.

"I get it," he said. "I only thought if you heard the details..."

"Don't worry, I don't blame you."

He didn't look convinced.

"And now I know the country they were taken to," she went on, "I might be able to find them."

"I might see you there. I'm going to ask permission to join the search."

She looked at him sadly. He could have said he would resign and join her, but the military would always come first with Major Wright. "Do you honestly think you'll get it?"

"I don't see why not. I was the one who uncovered the trafficking. It would make sense for me to be involved."

"What about Merlin and Morgan and the rest of the aliens out there playing with our lives? None of the world powers will tolerate this situation we're in. Not the Antarctic Project, for sure. Ua Talman has to factor hostile extra-terrestrials into his plan now. And the Alliance and EAC will want to prevent us from becoming part of another game."

"I suppose so," said Wright, "but what does that have to do with me?"

"Time to move out, Major," said Colbourn, approaching them.

Marines were escorting Kala Orr and her son out of the hall.

"I'll be there in a moment," he replied.

Colbourn glared at them as she passed by.

Taylan felt like poking her tongue out at her.

When the brigadier was out of earshot she said, "They're going to ask you to be a part of the team who finds out who these aliens are. Arthur, too, as he's one of the few people who can hurt them."

He grimaced. "Yes, you could be right. But what about you? You've also been caught up in this thing from the beginning. The Alliance will ask you too."

"They can ask, but I'm not a Marine, remember? There's no way I'm going to stop looking for my kids."

"No, but you're part of the pattern, as Merlin would say, and so are others."

"Excuse me, please," said Hans Jonte.

They moved out of his way, but before he left he said, "It was good knowing you, Taylan Ellis. I don't think I ever thanked you for saving my life."

"You're welcome," she replied, "though, to be fair, I don't think your life would have been in danger if it hadn't been for my big mouth."

"There is that." Jonte smiled. "Nevertheless, thank you. Perhaps our paths will cross again one day."

"Maybe, Joseph Fry."

Jonte walked out.

"Joseph Fry?" Wright asked. "No, don't tell me. I have to go now."

Everyone who would travel on the heli had boarded.

"Major!" Colbourn bellowed.

"Yes, you'd better," Taylan said, "or you're going to get in trouble."

"I'm already in trouble. And you know what? I don't care."

She chuckled. "There's hope for you yet."

"Come here." He gently pulled her inside the building out of sight of the heli. "You're sure you don't blame me for turning back in the desert?"

"No, it just makes me sad."

He looked relieved.

"I don't want you to be sad."

"I know." She pulled him close.

They kissed.

"*Major!*" Colbourn's strained tones floated through the open door.

AUTHOR'S NOTES

Hello again, stalwart reader of Star Legend! I hope you enjoyed this latest episode in Taylan and Wright's story. Many thanks once more to my awesome shipmates, especially Liza Wood, Mike Phillips, Mike Paddick, ex-submariners Brady Shugart and Ken Whiting, and the Review Crew, whose help has been invaluable in the writing of this series. Here are a few notes on *The Resolute* you might find interesting.

Wright's Bagel

If you thought the story of Wright altering the *Resolute's* heading to get the sun out of his eyes seemed familiar, you might have read it before. The story first appeared on Reddit, and it was so good and perfect for Wright I shamelessly stole it. Did it really happen? Who knows? In the original, the bagel-eater was an Operations Officer on a US military ship.

Xiangqi

You probably remember this game appearing in earlier Star Legend books, and of course in *The Resolute* it plays a bigger role. It's a real game, and I've played it, though very badly. If you're wondering how to pronounce the name, the 'x' is a hard 'sh' as if you were saying sheet, and the 'q' is a hard 'ch'. So it's something like sheeangchee. It's one of the most popular games in China and, like chess, it's very old. The basic rules as described in *The Resolute* are correct, but there's a lot more to it, as Abacha would tell you.

Kala's Coping Strategy

The inspiration for how Kala stays sane while locked entirely within her mind was the story of Odette Hallowes, a French-British spy who worked for Special Operations Executive in France during World War II. Odette was taken prisoner by the Nazis and endured torture without giving away any secrets or betraying her comrades. One of her less painful tortures was a combination of solitary confinement, starvation, and extreme heat, all endured in darkness. To help pass the time, she imagined dresses to sew for her daughters in meticulous detail.

Speak Well of Your Friend

The code phrase Taylan and Seren use to safely connect is a Welsh proverb. Speak well of your friend. Of your enemy say nothing is the English translation of "Dywed yn dda am dy gyfaill, am dy elyn dywed ddim". The town where Taylan meets Hans Jonte, Abertawe, is the Welsh name for Swansea. I was tempted to set that part of the story in Cardiff, but I'm pretty sure that city's Welsh name, Caerdydd, would defeat my pronunciation abilities for the audiobook.

Arthur's Religiosity

If, like me, you were not raised in a religious household, it might be hard to imagine how strongly Arthur's beliefs figure in everything he thinks and does, but if he ever existed, they would have been everything to him. In the Netflix series *The Last Kingdom*, the character of Alfred the Great displays the same fervor. Be prepared to see sparks fly in the next book as he comes to grips with the fact he's committed terrible sins purely as part of Merlin's game.

If you'd like to read Star Legend book five, *The Dauntless*, a few weeks earlier than it will appear on Amazon, become a Patreon supporter.

To chat about the series or meet other readers, come along to the Starship JJ Green Shipmates Facebook group. I'd love to see you there.

Sign up to my reader group for exclusive free books, discounts on new releases, review crew invitations and other interesting stuff:

https://jjgreenauthor.com/free-books/

DOWNLOAD YOUR FREE READERS' GUIDE TO THE SCIENCE FICTION NOVELS OF J.J. GREEN

Copyright © 2021 by J.J. Green

All rights reserved.

No part of this book may be reproduced in any form or by any electronic or mechanical means, including information storage and retrieval systems, without written permission from the author, except for the use of brief quotations in a book review.

❦ Created with Vellum

Printed in Great Britain
by Amazon